THE SIX GRANDDAUGHTERS OF CECIL SLAUGHTER

A novel by

Susan Hahn

Published in 2012. First Edition.

Printed in the United States on acid-free paper.

Fifth Star Press
1333 West Devon Avenue, Suite 221
Chicago, Illinois 60660

Distributed by Small Press United.

20 19 18 17 16 15 14 13 12   1 2 3 4 5

ISBN: 978-0-9846510-0-9

For Fred and Rick
The two great gifts
of my life

and

For Jean and Jacob and Charlie
The three great gifts
of years more recent

THE BELLS XI

I tie a string of bells around my ankle.
I am told I make a jingle
of delight. Sometimes, when I dance
I think my feet might burst.
Yet, I toll of my own accord.
I am not the maiden who threw herself

into the melting pot so that the metals
would fuse—perfect the sound—
make the air notes sweet and strong.
I am not that sacrifice.
Still, when my toes toss off
the earth, I can frighten away

the browsing snake.
I know someday I might break
and close my eyes to that scare,
pretend I glow like ruby and sapphire,
am a choir of tinkle and chime—
dainty, joyful, charmed, and wayward.

c. slaughter

THE CROSSES V

Cross my fingers, cross my heart,
arms extended, legs together, not apart,
I make of myself a cross.
In my pockets bright blue beads,
small clay gods, scarabs,
four leaf clovers, bejeweled mezziahs.
In my hat cockleshells
to exorcize the demons,
to keep hidden the seventh chakra,
the tonsure, the bald compulsion.
Cross my fingers, cross my heart,
arms extended, legs together, not apart.
In my ears little bells of confusion,
to frighten away eyes of evil.
On my breast a foul sachet
to repel the lick of the Devil.
Cross my fingers, cross my heart.
In my window a glass witch ball
to guard against the shatter
from intruders.
Cross my fingers.

c. slaughter

CONTENTS

Cecil Slaughter Family Tree

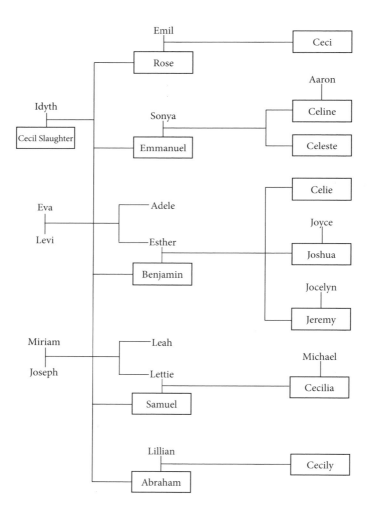

WIDDERSHINS I

Turn counter to the clock
tick, its annoying tic,
stir the pot
left to right, set
the table west to east,
steer the small boat
from the harbor
against the sun path.

Traveling the heavens
has not led to protection.

c. slaughter

WHEN I FINALLY FELT the full impact of the death of
Herr M and the awfulness that came after—that a
member of my family was involved—I fled to Lao Tzu for
advice. I *knew* there was nothing I could have done to stop
it, but I needed specific instructions as to what to do *now*.
"What should I do?" were my exact words as my mind
went running off. It was an impulsive action—this mind-
running—and even though I knew it was wrong-spirited
at the time, I did not think to stop myself.

Here, far below the earth's surface, I continue to discover mountains where the glory of all seasons converge and
burst into full bloom—the English oaks, German silver
firs, Burmese banyan figs, and African acacias, all in their

quiet dignity, existing together—and the lakes where still waters throw a perfect reflection and where the limestone resembles majestic waterfalls. A world I had now—with this news—temporarily abandoned, my mind and sight not focused on all the beauty I had come to find on this path to visit Lao Tzu.

I ran past the jubilant summer gardens filled with flowers crowded together without outline—boneless—existing with riotous exuberance and ease, past the venerable plum trees, gnarled and lichen covered, and the lotus flowers floating in the rivers, past the peach trees in the full glory of their blush and fragrance, past the flowering almond ones, their rosy blossoms dusting the ground beneath my feet as I ran faster and faster to Lao Tzu for advice.

Clearly, my alarmed reaction was an above-the-ground one, my emotional, panicky leap up there—my "trip up"—a backward step. But I had my reasons. I always felt, because I was the eldest of my cousins, that as the years passed and I grew wiser I would be able to fix things for them, and for that matter for others in my family. I wanted to polish the egos of those left so tarnished and dim the lights on those so focused upon the gloss of themselves and their possessions, much of the damage having been done by my father and my mother. But my life was cut off, shut down midcourse and therefore all my hopes for this—whether they were altruistic or egocentric or some combination of both—were thwarted.

When the long journey of my illness concluded with my forced detour to beneath the ground, intruding on all my good intentions, it was inevitable that I carried with me this over-responsibility, this overburdening of concern and resolve and however much I try not to, I continue, even at this distance, to assume the quiet, watchful role of the Slaughter family's night nurse.

Now, I excuse myself for many reasons, starting with the fact that my time spent in eternity has been short and therefore my behavior, especially when I am under extreme pressure, is still more blatantly alarmist-human than otherworldly calm. Also, there was the act itself— that Herr M had been murdered. And a murder was definitely on the far side of that which goes against the natural life flow. Yes, everything I did after the instant of my full knowledge of what had happened—of *all* that I had witnessed—seemed to be going in reverse.

FLOWERS

With her thumbs she'd press at the beginning
stems, try to push them back into her chest
as if that could arrest the budding.
Not wanting anyone to see,
so they couldn't point, make fun,
she'd stretch her sweaters
down around her knees,
the yarn slackened and blanketing
her body. She didn't know then that

a young man would come with flowers
which felt like the soft skin
of her own grown breasts, their areolas
knowing how to roughen into crinkled leaves,
nipples ruddy. She didn't realize how easily

they all could decay,
that someday they'd be taken from her,
the way she imagined her caller stole
each bloom from its stem, a risk
he took for the fantasy of touching her,
his fingers working carefully, anxious
that he'd get in trouble, have to stop—

all blossoms plucked from their hands.

c. slaughter

I AM SURE MY mother knew that her nieces hated her and that she understood it to a point. She knew her nickname—the one her brothers called her openly, and often to her face—"American Beauty Rose"—got to them, irritated and upset them. She understood why not only her nieces, but I too—her own daughter—would go through our lives always troubled by having such beauty in the family. She knew she was the standard-bearer of beauty not just for us, but for any female who encountered her, and that no matter what any of them did to copy her or rebel against such beauty, she believed no one could compete. Consequently, she, as burden or blessing depending on who you were, remained unfazed and moved forward with her life.

Since I was born homely, I gave up rather early on how I looked, refusing makeup, not watching my weight, barely combing my intentionally chopped-up hair, and most certainly giving no thought to what I wore. Eventually my parents accepted how I looked and set me on a different path. I was to become a famous philosopher—*a true scholar*. I would equal or surpass Grandfather Cecil.

All of the female offspring were named after him—me (Ceci), Cecilia, Cecily, Celine, Celie, and Celeste—a fact that Cecilia thought really dumb and voiced to me. She believed it ridiculous to pay such homage to a man when there was only anecdotal evidence—"glory stories," she called them—of his brilliance. "Frankly," she told me when she was ten and I was twelve, "it's Grandmother Idyth whom they should have honored—that woman locked away for all these years—her impressive stamina for a long life, however much the doctors drugged her." When she talked like this my eyes would grow so big they felt like they might burst. And Cecilia talked like this a lot. Especially to me, because of how well I listened and laughed at what she said, for deep inside me, there was a rebel—an iconoclast—but I just could not quite bring it forth. Only Cecilia allowed herself to be free enough to give such ideas voice, however quietly she whispered them. She felt with me a safe place, which made our relationship special, for she did not feel there were many safe places in this world for her.

My parents liked to compare things and people to flowers. They would brag unrelentingly about Cecil's genius—say my mind was so similar, compare it to a rare and gorgeous orchid. At the Passover Seder each year where my father presided with great authority, I was always given the role of the Wise Son, which made me flush terribly with discomfort and guilt. Cecilia was predictably and painfully designated the Wicked Son, and the Simple Son was alternately assigned to Celie, Celine, or Cecily. Joshua and Jeremy, Celie's brothers, were far younger than the rest of us—either had not yet been born or were too little to be called upon. My father always spoke with great pedantic pleasure on behalf of the Son Who Does Not Know How to Ask.

Once, they called Cecilia a dandelion—which, as everyone knows, is just a weed. It got back to Aunt Lettie—Cecilia's mother. So directly and quietly, with a sadness and dismay in her voice, she asked, "Ceci, is it *true* that your parents called Cecilia this?" Telling Aunt Lettie, "It is," made me sick.

Rather quickly the dandelion comparison made its convoluted path to Cecilia and she cried. She was six. It tangled her mind—bound her to awful bottom thoughts about herself—snarled through her body and knotted it. However, when she was old enough, she looked up "dandelion" in the dictionary and discovered the root was from the French, *dent de lion*—meaning "lion's tooth." From that moment, she felt a little stronger and happier. She found it, perhaps, a divine message. Cecilia thought like that. And she waited . . .

Cecilia really detested my mother—perhaps the most of my cousins. She thought her soul a muddy, bog-like place—a sewage pit—and I could not argue with any of this, although thinking about her soul in such a manner hurt. The subtle, subversive way my mother talked—always starting out so sweetly, then ending with a twist, an insult—punctured like a dart. For example, she would say, "Cecilia, you look so pretty—*today*—even though you're so thin. Doesn't your mother feed you?" Or, "That beauty mark on your cheek, Cecilia, looks so artificial. Did you place it there with a pencil?" In truth, it *was* real.

Aunt Lettie would tell Cecilia, "When one has such beauty, it can do two things to you—either cause you to have great trouble or to have great luck in life and in Rose's case, it's great luck. We just have to get used to the fact of it—that Rose can, because of how she looks, get away with how she speaks and what she does. Don't you see," she would continue with amazement in her voice, plus a pinch of bitter, "it never rains when Rose throws an outside party? The sun always shines on her. That's why everyone wants to get married, or celebrate their anniversaries or birthdays, in that huge and glorious backyard."

It was true—it never rained on my mother's plans, only on the other days, so that her flowers could grow as lovely as they were capable, while the dandelions ran amuck in the field beyond her elaborate, expensive wrought-iron fence. When very young, I would wonder if the clouds, the rain, the scary rock hail, too, were dazzled by her and also a little afraid of her powers—her wrath if they dared to intrude.

Eventually, Cecilia came to love the freedom of the dandelions—their unpredictable paths—the independence of their ways. And once, I even said in an almost angry voice to her, "You are lucky, you are special, you do exactly what you want." Then I paused, took a breath and said in a whisper, "I envy you." I said this at the point when I got really sick and began to completely disappear, disorienting Cecilia so much she felt herself becoming all dandelion puff—her mind a'scatter. Those were among the last words I ever said to her. Words which I now truly regret, thinking how wrong I was to envy her gifts, given that they were the direct cause of what happened to her with Herr M.

Cecilia's mother *had said* nothing bad would ever happen to my mother, *had said it always* and it was because of this Cecilia found what happened to me impossible and unacceptable. She could not fit it into her mind—it became a chunk of granite that she would never be able to push through any door, no matter how she tried to angle it.

She concluded God had made a mistake. That she, Cecilia Slaughter, was the daughter who should have gotten sick. She was the daughter who should have died. But it was, in fact, my mother who had lost a daughter. It was my parents who were forced to place a daughter in the earth.

On the day I was buried, Cecilia told her mother and father how she felt—about being the one who should have died. Her father, Samuel, said a too-loud, "Hush," so upset that his sister Rose was having to go through all of this. Aunt Lettie just remained stunned silent that the myth had a crack, that it had, in fact, split wide open and what oozed out was too grotesque.

The whole family was stupefied that Rose—the golden beauty of the family, of the neighborhood, of the community—had suffered such a loss. From that day, my mother looked at her nieces with an outrage so deep, yet carefully hidden behind her fixed blue eyes, I was pretty sure Cecilia, with her acute eye for detail and ability to pick up on what was too subtle for the others, was the only one who felt the direct hit of it.

That day at my grave Aunt Sonya's face was empty of emotion, for all feelings of loss had long ago been scoured out of her with the death of Celeste, her baby daughter. Uncle Emmanuel wept violently, his tears really for Celeste, too, and because he was prone to making a spectacle of himself.

Cecilia just stood there numb, staring at each of them—Celine, fussing with the flower pin on her too-tight suit, trying hard not to think of Celeste, her dead little sister; Celie, averting her eyes as she always did in any kind of tense situation; Cecily, tapping her foot as if all she really wanted to do was kick someone, which was not uncommon. Michael, Cecilia's husband, stood in back of her, his hands on her waist, helping to hold her up. Joshua and Jeremy were in their late teens and traveling through Europe.

My mother's other brothers and their wives cried hard, while my father stood immobile, stiffly clutching my mother, only the color in his huge face moving tumultuously—from boiling red to violent purple. After the service he turned his back to his nieces. From that moment they ceased to exist.

Cecilia was truly the only one who took on the long, mourning task, as if her whole life had been building to it. She could not get out of her mind how I had called the tumors growing inside me, my dying, rotting flowers. Cecilia, with her dandelion tenacity, could not stop digging into the ground pit of herself, forever looking for the *why* of it. The *why* of *any* of it . . .

"Survivor's guilt" was what the psychiatrist called it, and perhaps he was right, however crazy he was from his own polluted history, which eventually he told her because he had fallen in love—in love with her. A *bad luck* story because as Cecilia grew up she had become the other side of what can happen to beauty—a beauty which immediately drew Herr M to her, and, ultimately, led to violent acts and conclusions.

"The ugly duckling to the swan"—how Cecilia remembers that book, which her mother read to her over and over when she was little, as Aunt Lettie sighed and looked at her daughter, whispering to herself, "Well, maybe . . . "

Cecilia would stare at the psychiatrist, sitting there in his perfectly coiffed strawberry-blond toupee, for an hour three times a week puzzled, until she eventually figured out he had four different ones of varying lengths so by the fourth week he looked like he really needed a trim— which of course he got by returning the next week to toupee number one. It took her three months to figure out this cycle. That is what she focused on while he gawked at her, eventually convincing her that she had to come more often—that she *needed* him—and cut his price to a third of what it was originally. Finally, when he nervously said, "Perhaps I should no longer charge you," then hesitated, leaned too far forward, and continued, "maybe someday, and soon, we could go for a ride, and then have lunch," she fled his office.

She ran to an overweight, bald psychologist who constantly popped Jelly Bellys into the cupped hole of his mouth while he spoke. After about a month he said to her, "You've brought all of your troubles on yourself. Everything is your fault and the flirting with me will have to stop." Again, she ran—this time to an older, overpriced analyst with his *own* gray hair, who always wore khaki pants, a crisp white dress shirt with the cuffs flipped up like dove wings, which rose and fell through the air as he moved his animated arms, and brightly colored bow ties with lively paisley patterns on them. Here, she felt perhaps there would be some peace because of his upbeat style—that she would be able to talk about me and how she should have been the dead one. She hoped his hearty enthusiasm could help lift her out of the hole where she had dropped herself. Luckily, because she really could not afford him, at her fifth session he said, "You're gorgeous! I want to lick you. I want to taste your sour milk." She raced out of there quicker than ever.

Alone, she began hurting herself, again. Her tonsure became larger and she made small cuts on her thighs, her arms. Afterward she would dab the sores with Q-tips dipped in alcohol, her body becoming a mess of raw, red dots. No one could see any of this except Michael, who was still her husband. Michael, who tolerated a lot. Michael, who thought her fabulous. "Your hair, your eyes," he would say with such passion. He was full of so many compliments for her with which she could never quite connect—as if he were talking to a person who was standing a little past her left shoulder. Sometimes Cecilia would even look around to see if she could find her.

Michael did not understand all the fuss about my mother—for what he saw was an aging clichéd blonde—and he would say to Cecilia, "Perhaps you're too much of a threat to her, that all your intensity is too much of a challenge to her own shallow-surface self. Perhaps, that's why she always puts you down in her coyly angled ways." It was the "she puts you down" part that repeated in Cecilia's mind at my service.

Immediately after my funeral my parents left on a trip to the Alps. They wrote postcards about how "one must appreciate nature. Its great loveliness." They sent their words to everyone in the family, becoming even more, the family philosophers.

Eventually and predictably, they began to throw their large, lavish parties and, of course, it never rained. Cecilia thought it was because the gods had finally taken their revenge. Always their plan, to let the humans believe in their own perfection, then *show them*. Again, they gave my parents a garden to play in—gave them back their flowers with all the startling beauty that their gardeners could think to plant. "Very Gatsby, my dear Ceci," was what she told me as she began to write her poetry . . .

Poetry that eventually got published, though her father underplayed it and her measured mother knew best to only take pleasure in it within herself so as to not make any outside spirits jealous. My parents ignored it, as did the rest of the family, because such accomplishment from the dandelion challenged the family myth, almost as much as my death.

My mother's brothers needed their older sister to be the center—the centerpiece—of their lives. She had pulled them through the worst time of their childhood. When their father died and their mother went quickly mad afterward, it was she who made the plans for them. She found them each a place to stay with distant relatives in small towns with curious names like "Rock Island" and "*Normal.*" However bad their situation, when the latter name was told and retold to me and all my cousins, including Celie's little brothers, we had to cover our mouths to hide our smiles, because each of us in our own way—at our own level—felt the irony.

And when my mother met my father, the wealthy Emil, how he helped the brothers because he loved their Rose—the blond hair, the blue eyes, the curve of her calves. She was unlike any Jew he had ever seen. Short and squat with a large flat face, Emil could show the world what *he* could have—yes, what money could do. And my mother loved him for all of what he did, and her brothers did too.

He helped them go to school, start businesses, make smart investments, and even bought a cheap building in the city and fixed it up a bit so they would have a place with the lowest rent after they married. He welcomed their young wives into the family and then their children on the implied condition that he and my mother be the king and queen of their fairy tale, allowing them all to sit at their royal "shipped from England" table with the finest linen covering it, my mother presiding at one end, my father at the other and a huge glass bowl in the center with the heads of flowers piled high and floating in it.

Together they built an aristocracy that no outsider within the family could follow with the perfection demanded of them, each falling short—meaning the sisters-in-law. Each with a therapist—social worker, psychologist, psychiatrist, psychoanalyst, depending on their status, meaning what they could afford. But no matter what kind of help they got, that is exactly what they continued to try to do—follow. Even after my father's sudden death seven years after mine, the devastated brothers, their depressed wives, and their bewildered children followed.

"Just an overnight, minor surgery," he had laughed, holding Proust's *Remembrance of Things Past* in his lap as he waited his turn. He wanted everyone in the hospital to know they were in the presence of a scholar—emulating the man he had never met, his beloved Rose's father. That night an allergic reaction to pain medication detonated his heart and killed him. Again it had happened and the chorus cried and sadly sang, *impossible, impossible.*

To everyone this seemed even more unfathomable than my death—which left Cecilia totally baffled and crushed, as if I had become, maybe always had been, a nothing too—*a dandelion*—which, of course, was true.

Seven years it took Cecilia to get over the guilt, let go of most of her destructive rituals, and start to publish her poetry. Same as the timing between my death and my father's. Cecilia thought it all "very biblical—the land fallow, then not." She said this with a wry smile to Michael. Michael, who after all of this still loved her and loved that she was well—or as well as she would ever be, always thinking, "*The weed* forever hopelessly there, just dormant, not dead inside her."

After my father's death, my mother slowed down some in terms of entertaining and traveling and eventually when the air was warm and the sky too blue, she came to position herself on the large veranda that surrounded our house, at the head of a too-sticky, lemonade-stained glass table. There, she would await her guests who regularly and punctually arrived, a paid companion sometimes standing there brushing or braiding her long hair over the slowly growing thickness at the base of her neck. Celie, Cecily, and Celine often talked about "the hump" and her hair—how it did not look like she colored it, yet it was impossible that she did not.

Brushing and *braiding* were the words that stuck in Cecilia's mind from our cousins' reports. She was not there to directly discuss any of this or to view the flowers from the now less well-tended, patchy garden. She was busy saying "yes" to invitations for readings and symposiums—her words like dandelion spores, blowing every which way with the wind, scattering themselves to distant places. Her melancholy words, always embedded in the twists of memory—of family.

Though none of this was a cure—neither an ending nor a beginning for her. Only a middle. Like the bowl that was always placed in the center of my parent's highly polished table—mahogany, the same as my father's and my caskets.

That bowl. Her mind focused on the intricate pattern of it as she sat for hours in the various hotel rooms before her readings—twirling and knotting, then trying to unravel the long strands of her hair. "*Not* brushing and braiding," she would anxiously think, as she wrote about things too intricate, too fragile, too beautiful. "*That bowl,*" she would recall, "with its careful, intentional, deep carvings, how easily the dazzling, trapped, decapitated flowers and the elegant glass containing them could fall to the floor while attempting to place it in the perfect spot—the gods eternally looking down, deciding who should be so unexpectedly cut."

Cecilia was forever there, waiting for its crash, which eventually arrived some years later with the appearance of Herr M . . .

WIDDERSHINS II

Only a backward spin

my mangled body threaded
through spokes of the leaden wheel,
seated in the spiked metal
interrogation chair—the agony
from beneath. The crown of my head
shoved into the steel cap, the huge screw
tightened at the top, my pressured skull
drilling my teeth into my jaw, eyes out.
The tongue of confession,

then forgiveness, nowhere to be heard—
screaming, I am

running through the blade
grass. Away from the sun,
his unleashed, slash, god advance,
his rage all ways
disassembling me—

this time, to plant. Now, made
to look up, forever face his gaze

if I am to survive.

c. slaughter

When I finally reached Lao Tzu he smiled a gentle smile and I very much felt his warmth. He opened his arms wide and his answer embraced me. "Nothing," he calmly replied to my question. After what seemed like a forever pause, because of how agitated I was, he continued by quoting Hui Hai:

> When things happen make no response:
> Keep your mind from dwelling on anything whatsoever.

Then, he added, "There is nothing to do with that which *has been* done or for that matter with what is *about* to be done, if you are not the doer. That which has happened, has happened. That which is about to happen, is about to happen." Again he paused that feeling forever pause, finally saying, "Stay still," and he shut his eyes. At that moment, I tried not to show my embarrassment—the sudden, acute humiliation I felt—yet I knew he had seen it and could still see it through his quietly closed, translucent lids.

A frantic energy would not stop emanating from me—would not leave me—and I looked away from him so as to shield myself—I hoped—from his sense of me and thought, "If I had just taken some time—a long pause—I could have absorbed it better, and most certainly would not have fled to him in this bone-panic and presented my alarm in a way which revealed that I had learned absolutely nothing."

I then turned toward him, bowed slowly, and quietly left his presence, yet I continued to feel stupid and terribly unsettled. I *knew* if I had just stopped and considered the news—considered it with the deep, large world breaths in this place where I *now* exist—I could have been more centered and remembered how those above the ground so often go against a nature that can positively move them forward, if they are not so quick to act. It takes great negative energy to turn behavior against its natural forward flow, snarl it into troubles which then become, at best, bad habits and, at worst, self-mutilations—physical or psychological—or when turned outward, into a catastrophe such as murder.

Once again, the beating on myself began with the self-defeating language, "If I had been a better student all the time of his lessons, I would not be feeling such a discombobulation. By now, I should have achieved a much more balanced composure, no matter *what* had happened above the ground." I was judging myself harshly by the parental standards of my childhood and early adult years and falling short. The building disdain I had for myself, the rush and escalation of these musty, old, sick feelings disoriented me as to where *exactly* I was—*what world was I really inhabiting?*—and caused a vertigo I had not experienced since the minutes before I died.

I had thought my soul in better condition—more shaped by now—and perhaps it was this vanity, this earthly thought-indulgence, this arrogance that inflated and deluded me into thinking too well of myself—of what a *wonderful* student I had been during the time of my tutelage under Lao Tzu—that had done me in. I was clearly too proud. Too proud of myself in death like my father had been of himself in life. My father who lies near to me in blown-up ego pieces, which I fear will never be put together well enough for him to understand the possibilities of the journeys to be taken here—all the dazzling depths and peaks just waiting to be plumbed, climbed, viewed, and considered.

I presented myself to Lao Tzu in such disarray, I can only imagine his surprise and disappointment. Although another part of me peeks through my more refurbished crevices, knowing he fully accepts whatever behavior I exhibit. Still, I cannot stop obsessing on this misstep. I know all this inane self-measuring, the degrading feelings I have about losing control, are ancient material and, especially now, self-imposed—old baggage I still lug with me that gets in the way of the peace I long for and which so obviously is still out of reach. Here, I remain very much the immigrant. Yes, I think, "Miles to go . . . " as Frost put it, but not for sleep, rather for the wisdom found in the serenity of self-acceptance.

Suddenly, I longed for Wyatt—the man who made of me an ecstasy of the flesh. I wanted to forget my deadness—how my father and uncles had ripped my happiness from me and how much I hated them at the time for this and, yes, now *here* in this present moment. I once again became *all flesh need* with its rough, erotic seeds and seediness so as to try to forget everything that had just happened and only inhabit that place of the physical orgasmic surge.

I continued to make excuses for myself upon leaving Lao Tzu—I excused myself for my sudden backward turn to human want and concern, my defense in part being that I am greatly exhausted by *this waiting*. This waiting for my mother. For her arrival. For she who does not arrive. Like the characters and audience in the play *Waiting for Godot*, this waiting seems endless. I have begun to think that she never will, if for no other reason than she refuses to do so, that she will not let go of the prize that is her life. She will not let go of the physical shell of who she was—Rose, the woman who always won the beauty competition, always took home the crown; Rose, who still believes she *is* that young empress of loveliness in complete control of her domain. In truth, she has become like an old tree—its wood weaker because it is harder and more brittle, no longer able to bend with the wind, its branches no longer exquisite, looking more like clawed tentacles.

She was thirty-three when I was born—an age considered old in those days to have a first child, but she was reluctant to give up her figure, however temporarily. So far, she has lived almost fifty years longer than I. I died at thirty-two—one year short of her age at my birth.

Yet, even now as she lies half paralyzed, she grabs hard with her one good hand to that old life. With her one still strong fist she holds it firmly and thinks, "Why? Why should I leave here—this place that has held me so dear? To go where?" She intuits right. Never again will she reign over such a space.

Here, if she does not enlarge herself, she will inhabit a tight corner in a tiny room of withered spirits who think minute thoughts and whine and wonder to themselves and to each other why no one pays attention to them with all their once earthly gifts of perfect symmetry of face and body, money, fame, or sometimes, earned accomplishments—but only for the low motive of trying to gather more power and attention. They reminisce a lot and moan, "Why is no one interested?" Though I wish I did not, sometimes I, too, still hear their voices.

I know my mother will most likely live in such an enclosure here—a small apartment of the heart—but I still long for her. I have been without her for what sometimes feels forever and I have missed her, and I admit with what I hope is just a crumb of hubris that perhaps, when she does arrive, I can designate myself to be her guide. Maybe the loft of such a thought is part of the reason she keeps from me. I think Lao Tzu might agree.

Yet, there is another part of me that *is* pleased she is not dead. Losing a mother is quite sad, even for the child who has great ambivalence about her mother, *even* for the child already dead. Among the living I can so easily find her, predict her behavior, even the clothes she chooses to wear, see her in the familiar places she inhabits. I can both decide to find her and to lose her whenever I want to— death is not like that. Choices are not as fluid, the paths we cut for ourselves, whether with hacksaws or pen knives, are filled with innumerable bramble bushes. The Mother Goose lines easily apply—

> He jumped into a bramble bush
> And scratched out both his eyes.

One must move slowly here for the ways are clogged with thousands of possible thorny directions and thunderous, innumerable voices. It truly is hard to search out and find the delicate bell music. It is as confounding a place as *Wonderland*, with all its ramifications. And, yes, sometimes I still do feel as bewildered as Alice repeatedly begging the Cheshire Cat (Lao Tzu?) for directions.

Also, I fear when she does arrive, she might turn away from me. She could. She is capable of such an act. Turn away for eternity, like Great Aunt Eva did from her daughter Adele. A spirit can harden into a forever disregard—an indifference—or non-forgiveness, no matter the blood relation and in life, I was not entirely agreeable to my mother.

Clearly, absorbing the fact of Herr M's death and its horrific aftermath shook me from my mother-watch trance and I wanted an easy fix for all my upset. I know I could not have stopped the act, even as I saw it arriving—arriving from so many possible people with overdetermined motives. Too many negative fantasies about him were floating in that atmosphere, threatening his earth-existence. Reasons, however skewed, were piling too high like the snow and ice of this too bitter winter in the lives of my cousins and over the graves of those who loved them. I could feel Aunt Esther, Aunt Lillian, and Aunt Lettie—even in her stiffened, frightened silence—egging their daughters on for their own strange and diverse reasons—for their own unfinished earthly business.

While some are stunned to stillness with true grief or just shocked surprise, others are planning to temporarily flee the country from the family's humiliation, as I rest in my disintegrated silk cloth, which now covers just a few patches of bone. Finally, I have quieted my mind and contemplate Herr M's death and its terrible repercussions—why it became so necessary for others to consider it and consequently make such a fantasy a reality. And I consider his own brutal acts. How the velocity of them led to this violent conclusion. It is true he was not a good person, but I cannot help but wonder if there could have been a better closure. I think of Lao Tzu's words:

> That every victory is a funeral:
> When you win a war,
> You celebrate by mourning.

So I mourn this troubled man, while I try not to be too upset by all that has happened above—try not to be too upset by what has happened to those whom I love. But it is hard. *Very hard.*

QUEEN BEE

Queen of me
Queen of my father's family . . .

c. slaughter

THERE IS NOTHING SPECIAL about the dead weaving the story—their voices being the loom that pulls together what the living can tell only in bits and pieces. In life sometimes I saw myself as the weaver Ariadne who possessed the spun thread that lead Theseus to the center of the labyrinth of her half-brother the Minotaur to slay him and then safely out again. As I have said, I would have liked to have done such things for my family—kill, however metaphorically, "the monster" in some of my relatives. In death, I know all I can offer is our stories. As object lessons? Hardly. But to give them some amount of clarity, yes. Souls still living cannot help but slant, exaggerate, or embellish the facts of their lives. They do not necessarily mean to do this—to sew bias into their words—but they are still too busy, busy living life with all its manifold distractions and misdirected emphases and they do not have access to the full and ongoing adventure. They also depend so much on rumor—on gossip— and that troubles me too, especially when it is about the Slaughter family, both past and present.

Here, no one and no disease can interrupt—stop me short from what I have to say—and that is a good thing for

I can tell you some facts not only about the family above, but about the family beneath.

There are many relatives already where I am now. Aunt Lettie, Cecilia's mother, who mostly prefers to sleep— all sounds to her still have no music, just the march of German soldiers with their black boots slamming onto concrete—and Aunt Esther, Celie's mother, who is shocked by her troubled sister Adele's recent arrival and Adele's—now forever—proximity to her. I felt Esther's agitation even though she is graves away from mine and I understand her concern, for in life Adele was the cause of great misery to both herself and to others. I could hear the twist of their mother, Eva's, bones as she turned away from Adele's, as Eva ultimately turned herself away from this daughter in life.

Great Aunt Eva never wanted her daughter Esther to date, let alone marry, Uncle Benjamin—one of my mother's brothers. She did not want her to be part of the Slaughter family or anywhere near them. She remembered Cecil and Idyth from down the hall of her first apartment in this country, when both she and Idyth were young wives and mothers. Even before Grandfather Cecil suddenly died, Eva found Idyth too strange—too unable to adjust to America and Eva wanted so much—too much—to fit in, to appear comfortable, and to be successful in her new sur-roundings. She certainly did not want to add the Slaugh-ters to her list of burdens.

Eva had watched from her door as the men in white coats forcibly took the kicking, shrieking Idyth out of her apartment. She watched from her window as they put her in the white car to be hauled off to the asylum and she car-ried this whole scenario with her always, forever afraid that if she did not adhere to her rigid concerns—the carefully planned paths she took—it could be she who would be carted away. So it was understandable that when her gifted Esther became infatuated with Benjamin Slaughter it just added to her many fears.

The two women's separate journeys across the ocean had saved their lives, unlike the families they left behind, but once they arrived both women's misery proved large. Though Eva, however much she was unhappy, would concede Idyth's fate was far worse than hers. And Eva rarely felt her own grief could be surpassed.

Grandfather Cecil left many debts since he was not good with his accounts. There was no money to pay anyone after he was lowered into the earth, and the people he owed arrived at Idyth and her frightened children's small apartment to collect something—anything. They took the precious books Cecil carried in his satchel from Europe— his beloved Tolstoy, Zhukovsky, and Pushkin. They carried away the cheap furniture he and Idyth had bought in this country—their used, discolored pots and pans, even his worn, tweed winter coat and his one black hat that Idyth had carefully patched from the inside.

Idyth screamed hysterically and could not be quieted. Even years later in the mental hospital this was so, though by then she had given up almost all talk— her voice a sporadic, guttural howl, her mind a siege of paranoia with unending images rising up of people arriving, constantly arriving, to take something from her. No pills they ever found could stop the tumult— you could see the terror in her searing stare, see it in how she backed away when anyone approached, even my mother. I actually experienced this directly once and heard my mother speak of it a lot, but only to my father and her brothers, when she thought I was not near.

My mother had wanted to bring her mother closer to where the rest of the family lived—to have her in a small, private house where they took individual care of a few *sick* people. My father, however, preferred his mother-in-law a three-hour drive away. They would spend hours circling the close-by, innocent looking white brick house with half-drawn, fringe-tipped shades that made the windows look like sleepy eyes, and an arched, white wooden entrance with vines of healthy green leaves laced through it, which was attached to a white picket fence with flowers painted on it, perhaps by the people who lived inside.

I was in the back seat, listening to their too-loud voices with my father repeatedly saying, "It's safer, much safer the way it is, Rose." Which really meant safer for him, for his style of living—the pomp of it. Having a crazy relative nearby—that threat—could turn out to be bad for the image he had slowly, conscientiously created and continued to nurture until his death.

"What if she caused a commotion, Rose, or perhaps even ran away?" he would continue. Eventually my mother's pleas and all high-pitched, tense conversations on this subject stopped, my mother finally saying, with a large sigh, "Okay, Emil. Okay." So my grandmother stayed put—held in by large, thick, brick walls of a public institution with its dank smells and cold, unending, paint-chipped halls, a heavy, eight foot iron fence locking in the square block it haunted.

When I was six, my mother took me to visit her mother. I do not know what my mother was thinking by doing this—maybe she thought my presence would have a calming effect on my grandmother. I would like to believe this. She dressed me in a polished-cotton flowered dress with large pockets—my summer best. She said the three of us would go out for ice cream. I was excited. It seemed a great adventure—that long ride alone with my mother to see her mother.

I remember leaping out of the car, thinking that my grandmother's enthusiasm would match mine—to see me, her neatly dressed and properly behaved little granddaughter. Then, I saw her standing there outside the building's huge steel door. A man dressed in white had a grip on her shoulder. She wore a dark blue smock and her hair was short and gray with a too-blunt cut. To me it almost looked like it had been hacked off with an axe. At the time, reading Grimm's Fairy Tales to children was the fashion and Grandmother Idyth looked like someone who belonged in that scary book.

Yet, however strange and strained she looked, I could not but help run toward her and say "Hi, Grandma, I'm Ceci!" When I did this, she looked at me with great alarm and backed away. Then suddenly she lurched at me, focusing on the pockets of my dress, and stuck a hand into each, grabbing at their insides as if searching for something and upon finding nothing, screamed. She had half-torn the left one from its seams—I remember its droop.

Of course, after this there was no outing for ice cream. My mother and I followed her back to her room. Now, there were two men dressed in white flanking her, each with an even tighter grip on her shoulders. The inside of the building had the odor of a kennel I had been to twice with my father to look at dogs. It made me hold my breath as long as I possibly could, until I had to either breathe in the air or choke. The men stopped us at the door to her room. I never saw where she lived—whether she had books to read, a television, a radio, or even a window from which she could look out.

When my mother kissed her mother goodbye, she did not seem outwardly bothered that my grandmother stood there stiffly with no reaction. I guess she was used to this. I, however, was left quite agitated and on the way home asked my mother too many questions—too many whys. I did not understand *why* my grandmother pulled at the pockets of my dress, *why* she did not want to look at me, *why* she had to live in such a "smelly" place. My mother just kept driving, looking straight forward, and finally said, "That's the way it is. That's *just* the way it *is*." And when my questions would not stop, she yelled at me just one word—"Enough!" At that moment I thought of my grandmother tearing at my empty pockets and her wail when she found nothing. That was the feeling I was left with that day too, only I stayed silent, my scream internal. It was my first powerful memory of how little I would receive from my mother and, of course, I was never taken to see my grandmother again.

After Grandmother Idyth was taken away, my mother and her four brothers, Emmanuel (Manny), Samuel, Benjamin, and Abraham were parceled out to distant relatives across the Midwest, each considered the "poor thing" in the family who took them in.

When they reunited as adults, they publicly deified their father and spoke only among themselves about their mother, all the while binding themselves to each other with a unified, enormous dream of possessing all things material—property that they clearly owned and that no one would dare to steal. My father had a staff of lawyers to make sure.

My mother, the oldest, was thirteen, her brothers twelve, ten, nine, and seven, when they witnessed all that had been grabbed from them and my father learned how to use what he knew of their history to be in charge of them. He used this *always* to be in control of everyone.

Although Grandfather Cecil and Grandmother Idyth are buried miles away, their sons and my father are here and soon my mother will be. Right now she is in a private health care facility with around-the-clock staff taking care of her every need, plus two private nurses she has had at her house for well over a year. My mother's money saves her—prolongs her unbearably long days on the earth's thin, broken crust. Perhaps being poorer at this point in the life cycle would be better.

She *is* oblivious to the horrific news that frequently breaks through the television set, yet no one would want to live as she does now, not able to move without help or get nourishment without a feeding tube. Not that she ever cared that much about the larger world, although she spent much time raising money for good causes at charity events. Everyone wanted to have her and my father at their table. My mother definitely knew how to make an entrance. It is her exit with which she is having trouble.

In her present state she can still recognize people when she chooses to open her eyes—the gift of sight is a faculty she has not yet lost. She can still glance at the anxious faces of her extended family. She has become their entire focus. The mandala of their lives. She smiles at them as they file by and tell her about their daily lives. Everyone arrives at specifically assigned times—her nieces and nephews, Celine, Cecily, Celie, Joshua, and Jeremy, and the twins they married, Joyce and Jocelyn. Everyone, that is, except Cecilia. She sends my mother flowers every two weeks. The flowers are gorgeous and arrive in a glass vase. Her cards are kind and she signs them "with love"—always in the lowercase.

Right before I died, I went blind. I could not recognize faces, just voices. My mother and I had a code. She would ask me a question and I would blink once for yes and twice for no. Mostly I blinked once, for convenience. Then, after years of being sick, then well, then sick again, this cycle stopped and I left suddenly, in the blink of an eye.

Cecilia told me as I lay beneath the ground that the sicker her mother became the more clearly and more vividly she saw things. Unlike myself, the cancer never reached Aunt Lettie's brain, and her eyes became her most powerful guide through the final months of her life, as if they could see in each finite thing the detailing of the infinite. In late autumn—the last season she went outside for a little enjoyment—she and Cecilia ended up at a local beach. There, Aunt Lettie pointed out the yellow leaves on an oak tree and said with a dazzling smile, "Look, Cecilia, I have found the Golden Fleece. Perhaps Aeetes placed it there for me."

Aunt Lettie liked the Greek myths because they were far away from real time, real history. When Cecilia as a child would beg her mother to tell her about her own mother and father—"Grandma Miriam" and "Grandpa Joseph"—and what *exactly* had happened to them, Aunt Lettie would divert her by opening *Bulfinch's Mythology*.

I do believe that day at the beach—where the water

meets the sky—Aunt Lettie saw the subtle astral colors, which are usually hidden from humans—except perhaps from the greatest painters, who can pick up such vibrations. After I died my own sight returned in such a way.

Here, if I choose, I am able to take in so much from many spheres. It can, if I am not careful, become a buzz a million times worse than the noise of all the cicadas that rise from the ground every seventeen years. When the dialects and the clamor become too much, I travel to a place where the music is choral—the *Nada Brahma,* the *Anahata Nadam,* the *Saute Surmad*—the original tones of the world, all voices in universal hum. Or I go to the single, pure sound of one delicate bell softly tinkling in a faraway background. Being dead can be quite lovely if one can just let go of body and ego.

I think my mother will have a hard time with this, because of the beauty she was born with and that stayed with her well into her late seventies. She wanted to believe she had no rivals, that she was mythic, and the Slaughter family continuously reinforced this. Now, she has become the extreme image of beauty's always sad-end story.

Cecilia would snuggle against me when she was almost eight and I was ten and softly—and with much glee— chant "Queen Bee, Queen of Me, Queen of My Father's Family." How we would giggle. Even then Cecilia seemed so privileged with the permissions she gave herself for sacrilege—at least on the surface.

After I died, she began limiting herself, becoming strange—in a quiet way, not at all like Grandmother Idyth. She would wash her hair repeatedly, never able in her mind to get it clean enough, while Michael was forever washing towels, then handing her the newly cleaned ones. However, if one touched anything—the handle of a door or just the wood of its frame—Cecilia considered it soiled. She could not wash away the fact of my death, no matter how hard she scrubbed at it. (Similar issues flared up inside her after her horrific encounter with Herr M.)

Michael would visit my grave often and pray to me to help Cecilia. I stayed silent—letting his own good soul speak for itself. It was the beginning of my learning that it is impossible for the dead to instruct the living. It is what we leave them with—their memories of us (yes, I know this is cliché) that can possibly help. With Cecilia I know I was her first audience. How hard I would laugh at her comments on all the folly that surrounded us, and I do believe her memories of this were a part of what protected her from falling into complete darkness.

"Not quite crazy, but definitely mind sick," is what Michael would say to me. He was right. It took many months for her to pick up a pen and some paper and find an outlet for her grief that eventually would become her above-the-ground bell music. Then the washings, all the tiny tearings at herself, began to slowly disappear—except for the small tonsure she created long ago on the top of her head, which she still carefully maintains, actually prunes, and someday will die with. I am sure the undertaker will find it quite curious.

It is a legacy from her mother, Lettie—an outlet for Lettie, those hair tearings, from her own grief story. Cecilia began to wound herself in such way, too, at the age of eight, as she strained to hear what her mother was saying to the adults. She would open her bedroom door just an inch and try hard to string together the words that were being said, her long hair loosened and swirled around her like a coat of fur, with her fingers pulling at a single strand.

When Lettie would whisper to the relatives in the living room about the soldiers, the train, the camp, only her husband, Samuel, would leave the room. He wanted to forget about all of it. How he hated his wife's repeated returns to her story. It is a small mystery as to why he chose Lettie to marry, for no one brought with her a sadder or more complex history. Perhaps it was because he suddenly found himself to be the last unmarried Slaughter brother, so when Aunt Esther introduced him to Lettie— her young, docile, pretty neighbor—she seemed so right. The terror-stricken, gouged-out pieces of Lettie's soul were not obvious. She had not yet allowed them to rise up to her surface.

When I began my large journey beneath the ground and my parents again began their own grand trips, Cecilia was the only one who entirely stopped—sitting in her chair for well over a year with her strange thoughts about loss and death and cleanliness and then getting up and going through her carefully created rituals to keep her fragile center together.

Initially, I tried to communicate with her that I was doing okay—actually better than she—and not to worry, that there was another side, that the Reform Judaism we were taught in Sunday school had left out a lot, which I have to admit still leaves me a bit angry. The dead are not necessarily serene. (I guess that is already obvious, given my earlier mentions of Aunt Lettie, Great Aunt Eva and, of course, myself.) We bring with us our unfinished business—our angers about being treated badly, our unfulfilled ambitions, our unrequited longings about love—the innumerable hungers and unresolved issues of the flesh. Of course, some do this more than others. I am on the side of the ones who do this more than less.

Some things definitely are not yet finished for me— maybe never will be—like the impulses to fix, explain, and protect my family. Surprisingly, unconcluded business is okay here—it is the norm. You can imagine when the psychiatrists arrive here how appalled they are, actually stunned, by this fact and it makes the more thoughtful ones doubt doubly what real use they were in life, and rush to seek out Freud and Jung to talk about it and find out what they think.

Here, I have started traveling to Lao Tzu—the Chinese philosopher born five hundred years before Christ, because I need some lessons in the letting go of ego—that which Freud thought to strengthen, as he did with his construct of superego and, of course, there was also his mission to weaken the id. Lao Tzu believes the opposite, that our true nature when left unfettered—untethered by society's aggressive competitions and demands—is quite lovely, gentle, and kind and should be nurtured. (I know this way of thinking is problematic when considering the behavior of a man such as Herr M, so I am left somewhat confused. Probably because I am only at the beginning of an authentic understanding of this new way of thinking.)

Recently a specialist has been hired to carefully move my mother's arms and legs. While he is doing this, he sings Hungarian lullabies to her. This knowledge especially touches me, because I imagine it is reminding my mother of her mother singing to her when she was an infant—a time when Grandmother Idyth was at her calmest, when she had only one child to care for and Grandfather Cecil was very much alive. I picture him reading his books, his head bent over, his frameless spectacles on, with a smile on his face, as Grandmother Idyth sings to their baby Rose in their native language. A rare, almost singular, above-the-ground moment where everything peacefully and naturally connected for the Slaughter family, when it was at its smallest and, perhaps, at its best.

Because my mother cannot move the right side of her body at all, her private caregivers prop up her in a chair and comb her waist-length hair. There, she watches herself in the mirror, wasting away. Cecilia's hair, too, is almost waist-length. And *yes*, I did—still do—envy Cecilia a bit—her longer life, her distinctive beauty, her high-spiritedness, her explosions of talent. But for all of it this, I am forever aware she pays a large price.

With her auburn hair, deep violet eyes, and pale skin Cecilia is almost a rainbow of contrasts. My mother's eyes have no depth, almost look like cheap blue glass, but coupled with her long blond hair, the result had a striking effect—that is, for a Jew. "The Golden Calf Effect" was what Cecilia called it, and my father made sure his "jewel" was bejeweled with emeralds, diamonds, sapphires, couture clothes—her favorite, Dior—and a white Mercedes—a car which Aunt Lettie always made excuses not to ride in, would not go near, as she would not anything German.

I was the plainest plain—not quite ugly, just rather poorly defined. I looked like my father, with imprecise jelly features, a nose with too much cartilage at the tip, so that when I would smile it would bump into my upper lip and make my face look almost cartoonish. When I wore lipstick, which was not often, there would always be a smudge of it on my nose stem between my nostrils. I was forever scrubbing it off. Early on I gave up on makeup. The most I ever had on was when I was embalmed.

I was, however, highly accomplished with a PhD in English from Princeton "no less." My father would tag on the "no less" every time he said Princeton. When my sickness reappeared the final time, I had been the associate editor of a journal entitled *Contemporary Philology* for well over six years. My parents would brag about this, too, and it always made me queasy. My face would grow hot and I would start to sweat. I had no grace.

My most distinctive feature was enormous breasts with huge areolas and long nipples—everything about them felt and looked cowish to me. Only one man obsessed on them. I was, however, quite taken by the whole of him. He was a mechanic—all hands that moved with quick precision. I found his rough, scabby skin and his dirty nails quite sensual—quite reptilian. When he touched me I always felt I was experimenting with the forbidden. I became Eve *after* the knowledge of all the trouble this could cause, and I did not care.

I loved the soiling stimulation. Our house was kept so antiseptic spotless and intact, filled with furniture made in England and France, rugs flown in from the Orient, and crystal from Waterford and Baccarat. If the smallest figurine collected a bit of dust, it was quickly wiped off by a housekeeper, or if an object were for some reason moved from its place, it was upon my parents' notice, immediately set right according to their rules and taste.

I met Wyatt—a high school dropout—when I was sixteen and he eighteen. My mother's car was in the shop a lot and one day, after I got my driver's license, she asked me to pick it up. I bicycled over there and it was Wyatt who lifted my bike with one arm, as if it weighed nothing, and put it in the trunk for me. I saw the curves of his muscles—their flex—and the strength in his huge hands. I thought, "If it had been a motorcycle he could have done it with equal ease." Soon after, he started putting those powerful, greasy hands on my breasts and eventually on the rest of me.

He nicknamed me "CT," a play on "Ceci." It was for what he called my "cow teats," which he would milk forcibly with great prowess. The pain I would feel from this was at once excruciating and exhilarating, like continuously being annihilated and then brought back to life. Afterward I would look in the mirror and study how my areolas flamed to a blood red and my nipples further elongated and were cracked from small cuts made by his teeth. Of course, at the time I would have never used such descriptiveness. The seasoning of being here *has* made me freer.

It is true, sometimes in the physical life there is a convergence between over-excitement and humiliation. Even early on I felt this. Had I lived longer I would have written an in-depth essay or, perhaps, a book on it, connecting it to the classical myths with their own seductions, strange conversions, abuses, and exaltations—Zeus as the swan and Leda opening up wider and wider to him, needing to swallow him inside her as much as He needed to enter her, no matter the pain. I had many incidents with Wyatt to draw on.

One winter Sunday afternoon when we thought my house was empty, we curled into each other in the library on the wine color leather couch, naked, covering ourselves with the thickly braided, ecru cashmere afghan that my mother had knitted. All the family agreed it was so absolutely plush and gorgeous, which, in fact, it was. Under its beauty, Wyatt and I made a tent of baseness—quite the opposite of the dignified decor of the room.

The library's walls were lined with photographs of my parents with the newly rich and, sometimes, truly famous. Over the couch there was a large photograph of my father shaking hands with Eleanor Roosevelt and next to it my mother solicitously bending over Carl Sandburg—her décolletage revealing more than a hint of breasts—offering him another helping of beef as he sat at our dining room table for dinner. He had a polite, but quizzical expression on his face as if saying to himself, "Who are these people and what in the world am I doing here?" When the day of that dinner arrived, Cecilia, at ten, told me almost prophetically, "I'm *never* cooking for Carl Sandburg. I'll just be him and then your mother can cook for *me*."

Wyatt had abruptly spread my knees apart with his muscular thighs—as he always did—and was about to jam himself into me, when my father and my uncles stormed into the room. I still remember how the air smelled with that unexpected burst of old, winter soot. They yanked at Wyatt—pulled us apart—and threw him out of the house. I do not think anyone except Uncle Emmanuel saw my naked body. He focused on my breasts. I saw his long pause and he knew I saw it.

Everyone knew Emmanuel Slaughter to be a smutty man, knew he caused his brother Abraham, Abraham's daughter Cecily, and his own wife Sonya, great unhappiness. After his death Aunt Sonya bleached her gray hair blond again, bought stylish clothes, and put an ad in the personals and, of course, cut her age by fifteen years. Obviously, this did not sit well with the family, but it did give them a lot to talk about. Celine, her daughter, never acknowledged this. In her mind her mother will always remain "that dowdy, beaten-down, long-suffering broken woman"—something Celine has vowed never to become. After Celine put Aunt Sonya into the ground, she turned away, never looking back, never returning to her mother's grave. And although Cecily promised Celine never to write about her, she is putting Aunt Sonya's "man-packed" grave scene into one of her plays—the men being part of Celine's ever-increasing collection.

Cecily loves to write about our family. The only person she never writes about is her father, Uncle Abraham. While fighting in World War II, he was captured for well over a year, returning to this country a prisoner of his own mind. He was the only person who could brighten Grandmother Idyth's eyes, give them a little life. She would even take his hand. Maybe because he was her youngest—her baby—or maybe because she could tell he understood what it meant to have, if not a broken mind, at least one badly cut into—something Cecily believes she, too, understands well.

When Uncle Abraham returned after the war, as an outpatient in the rehabilitation hospital, he made a brace-let for Cecily. It was a strip of pliable tin with her name carved into it with open delicate spaces around each let-ter and small, carefully hammered pinpoint indentations in the shapes of two flowers at both ends. She was just a baby then, but as she grew up and grew into it, she has never taken the bracelet off. Because it is so tarnished now and oddly bent, it goes well with the stained look she has costumed for herself—"the stain" first put there by Uncle Emmanuel.

When Uncle Abraham died he left Cecily his Purple Heart. She feels it is the color of her own heart gone bloodless and when the anger and isolation she experiences grows too large, it is then she takes out her pen to fill the festering emptiness. I do understand this—to a point.

Unlike Aunt Lettie, Uncle Abraham never spoke about the war. About what it was like being held by the Japanese for so long. About what exactly had been done to him; what he saw being done to others. Yet he always listened intently to Aunt Lettie's stories, his face crimson, while everyone waited and hoped that he, too, would say something. That never happened. He took all those experiences into the ground with him.

If you go deep enough into most family histories in this cemetery you will find a gulag, a stalag, a pogrom, a concentration camp, and the souls who stayed so silent in their lives about what happened to them in such places talk freely to each other here. Sometimes the dead historians are allowed to listen. They then find out that their writings, their books, are so incomplete because the many voices who knew so much chose silence and it is also then that the dead historians worry that is why these horrors keep happening over and over again, which indicates an overthinking of the power of themselves and their writings.

In the weeks and months after Wyatt left, I would pull hard at my nipples, not just for the excitement it would bring, but for how much I needed to remember that he had once been there—in my life, in me. That he truly had existed and how he had the power to make me feel—feel wonderfully wild. When I would tell Cecilia, "He Was My Greek God, My Satyr, My Myth," she would laugh with such joy, and when she quieted, she would take both my hands in hers and whisper the most melancholy, "*yes, yes,*

Ceci, oh yes." She never tired of how many times I needed to say this and needed to hear her response. I can still hear her sweet girlish voice.

I often wondered if money were involved—if my father gave Wyatt money to leave me alone—for he never called again, and eventually I learned he had left town. I know it was then that the cells in my body began their slow mutations into an unrelenting grief that would chew at me piece by piece and eventually swallow my life. Of course, there were other factors that conspired with this. I had put myself on birth control pills when they were filled with mega-doses of hormones, which I continued taking for over seven years, always hoping for Wyatt's return. Celine knew a doctor to whom I quite eagerly, boldly, and naively went and came away with a large prescription. Having such a beautiful mother also did not help my anguish, especially as I grew older. I would see the alarm in people's eyes when they first met me, as if I were an alien, a mutation, a mutt, not just a physically unattractive person.

Alan Gross did not help either. He was the editor of *Contemporary Philology.* At first we got along quite well, but when I started getting published in places where his work had been rejected, he became quite cruel—verbally abusive—called me awkward, ugly, fat, and stupid. One day I taped a bulky recorder to my chest and put on a loose-fitting sweater to cover it. When I saw him, I ran into the ladies' room and in a stall, I clicked it on. It was perfect. I caught all his meanness on that tape. However, when I went to Human Resources at the university, the woman there said my evidence was not good enough. I did see her eyes tear up as she listened to his words—she *did* feel how they burned, how they branded. But, she then composed herself and said, "There is nothing I can do with this, no matter how terrible it truly is. There has to be proof of physical abuse or that he has stolen something personal from your office or your purse for you to file a complaint." I remember her voice. The tremble of it.

I found out that day that legally you could say such things to women in the early 1980s and easily get away with them. Alan Gross's *just* verbal assaults, however, did have a terrible effect on my still living body and soul. He did, in fact, steal something from me. I cannot blame him for my illness, but I will forever believe he helped put a halt to its remission.

I remember the day he told me, "Look it, if there's to be one star in this office, it's going to be me." He always used too many words when he spoke. Throwaway ones like *look it, you know*, and *like maybe*. He loved himself much more than any affection he had for language. However, I thought it so odd when he claimed one-star status. His perception was so off, his vision so narrowed, as if he were trying to shine a lit matchstick on himself. Philologists are never famous in the larger world of fast food, wide Technicolor movie screens, television sitcoms, easily accessible pornography, and missiles that can take out cities far away.

Everything about him I found repulsive and ridiculous, although I loved his last name because of how well it fit him. He had a bulbous nose, with at least a double layer of cartilage—far worse than mine. Sometimes when I looked at him I thought this might be why he was always so angry. I obviously had my own longstanding issues with unattractive excess, so I could almost understand his problems with *Gross* homeliness. Though he did not lack for sexual favors from women—mostly his students. In the eighties you could also easily get away with this. They bought into his cachet because they were so young and thought that they, too, could become *famous* philologists.

In Greek *philos* means "love" and *logos* means "word." I loved the ancient texts, the myths—the study of grammar, the classical traditions associated with a given language. For this I had a passion even larger than when Wyatt long ago had so deftly—and ferally—manipulated my breasts. Of course, looking at all the Greek god statues, especially in their nakedness, did remind me of him and the glory of his body, which always resulted in reigniting my despondency.

I would take out Frank Sinatra's "Only the Lonely" record album and play the music over and over, while staring at its cover—Sinatra with that one tear running down his cheek, looking like a sad clown—looking like Perriot.

Secret references to my obsession with Wyatt and my memories of his sculpted image can be found in the papers I wrote, and writing these did give me some amount of pleasure—as does the fact that they are still being discussed in tiny circles along with the one book I published. I do admit to still liking a small amount of polish on my own ego—something I continue to work on.

Alan Gross is never talked about except by he, himself to his most naive students, although having sex with them is far more problematic because of recent university rules and the fact that he is now old. Soon he will die and the stars will stare down on him in all his anonymity. He will never have even a moment of the twinkle and shine he still hungers after, unlike my mother, who has enjoyed a long stay in the spotlight of a small space—center stage.

I am readying myself for her arrival. She will lie between

my father and me. My father exhausted himself in life from all his bloat about himself, causing not only his ego but also his soul to fragment from the fatigue of needing to work so hard to keep itself whole, and he remains quite scattered and quiet. I, however, have spoiled well—that awful, thick makeup they smothered me with is long gone and I am left with just sleek bones and a few fibers of the white silk chemise that was slipped onto whatever the doctors did not cut from me—and I have also been quite spoiled by the richness I have found in all the worlds I can now enter and the freedom they bring to my words.

Here, no one cares to—or can—yank from me my story.

TRICHOTILLOMANIA

Mother twisted every action
to suit my father's mood,
which ran from sour to bittersweet.
Mother only had one motion of her own—
she picked
her scalp as if searching for the right
hair would lessen
all the tension. I'd watch

her hand curlicue into a question
mark, tear out the nervous
answer, examine what
she plucked, toss her head,
then pat it
as she would to soothe
my cousin's in the crib.
Once I brought a tweezers
to help her

grab what I thought
she wanted. She let me explore
the ruins underneath her beauty
shop creation. I touched
the sores and stubble, tried to
yank out all the trouble
until she yelled

to stop. From then I never could.
I keep looking for the spot
on my own head, ask anyone
who will to rub.
When I'm alone,
I use two mirrors, struggle
to see if I can get hold
of the anxiety. Deep within
my skull a stem is snarling
and will split the bone.

c. slaughter

I WAS TO BE *the One,* the one great success of the Slaughter family offspring—my parents *had said it* and their word on all matters was considered biblical—so when I was dropped from their world to the one beneath, my cousins and their parents, each with his or her individual agenda embedded in the larger family one, were disoriented as to who would be the flag bearer of the family's legacy.

Years later, Celie would come to say, "Cecilia and Cecily have all the talent in the family, because they were given the *extra* syllable." She meant they had an extra syllable in their names. She considered that maybe because my name, "Ceci," had just two syllables it had not been powerful enough to hold me to that promise. (Celie is more prone than any of us—even Cecilia—to magical and convoluted thinking, her thoughts often arriving through a side door or the even stranger back door in her mind. But there are reasons for this.)

By then Cecilia had published five poetry books and Cecily had two plays produced in non-equity, storefront theaters where the plumbing in the bathrooms was fairly non-existent. Cecilia told me this with some amount of humor when she visited my grave one day, adding, "Ceci, I think there were peepholes in both places with someone snapping pictures or videotaping us. I heard little clicks or a tiny buzz and I saw little ragged openings in the walls and the ceilings. Or maybe they were just made by the rodents living there." Then she laughed, "Same thing I guess." Some things deeply bothered Cecilia; some things she could easily joke about, when others could not—peepholes in the bathrooms both intrigued and amused her, at least before Herr M entered her life. Then, her reaction to *any* possible intrusion ignited her to full-blown alarm.

Cecily's two plays received not-great reviews, but now she has written a third one which she believes is a huge improvement. So far, however, no theater seems that interested and she has become wise enough not to call too often for updates on it. Alone, in her large, half-furnished apartment, she thinks, "Perhaps they feel if they ignore you enough—not return your phone calls—you'll go away." The emptiness of the place in which she lives has become a metaphor for both who she is and how she feels.

She thinks about going away a lot, but not in the way you first might think. Going away, not as in stopping calling about the play or as in going on a trip, rather she thinks about disappearing. She is tired. Tired of being Cecily Slaughter, granddaughter of the mythically brilliant Cecil Slaughter, cousin of the highly praised poet Cecilia Slaughter, daughter of the sad and broken late Abraham Slaughter, victim of the dead monster Emmanuel Slaughter, daughter of the also deceased Lillian—who, she believes, really did love her in her own weak way.

As for my other female Slaughter cousins, Celine (unlike

her baby sister, Celeste, who was gone before she could speak an understandable word) survives rather well in the world she has constructed for herself with flashy colors—most of them variations of shocking pink—her whole being a shock of pink. Celine, is known for such statements as, "Well, *I can't help it* if there's *at least* two men in love with me." And, then there is Celie—the one most prone to dissociative thinking—shy, modest Celie, who works in a high-end suburban dress shop. Celie, who *seems* of little threat to anyone except herself. Celie, who needs love so much and receives so little, except from Cecilia.

In Cecily's third play the dying mother, *Tanya,* is all light and grace. Cecily, *of course*, is *not* the daughter in the play. She is a poet and although she has borrowed "a bit" from Cecilia's life, she justifies it in the name of art. The fact that Cecilia is disturbingly beautiful with five applauded books, makes it difficult for Cecily not to hate her, though Cecily, at least consciously, believes she does not. She feels she can fairly assess the adventures that all Cecilia's beauty and so-called talent have taken her on—borrow from them and create art.

Some people would call them less adventures than misfortunes. (And then, of course, there was one person for sure—Herr M—who believed Cecilia Slaughter deserved all the bad things that happened to her—had ever so directly caused them herself.) Cecily believes she is neutral—so she can present a somewhat disguised story of Cecilia's travails on stage with a clear, clean eye. Although she is beginning to worry that maybe the reason no one has called her back about the play is that they all think she has burgled Cecilia's life and that "isn't right or nice or whatever." She continues to further excuse her feelings about Cecilia, thinking, "Celine believes whatever's happened to Cecilia is no big deal. That Cecilia clearly just doesn't know how to handle men." Then Cecily thinks about Cecilia's "not so secret habit."

Cecilia's mother's head was a mess of tiny sores from tearing at her hair. One by one Aunt Lettie would pull each out and examine it when she thought no one was watching, but all of the cousins at one time or another saw her doing this. Sometimes, I would hide behind a chair and stare. She would sit on her worn beige couch, almost hypnotizing herself with this motion. If she did not comb her hair just right you could see those irritated moth holes all over her head.

Cecilia only has one moth hole—right at the top of her head. The crown. She calls it her Seventh Chakra. Believes the light of God is able to pour right into that spot, allowing her to be filled with all the magic that the universe has to offer. Yes, Cecilia does have a way of turning a gross neurotic habit into something poetic, odd, lovely, and disturbing all at the same time.

Most unfortunately, Cecilia showed her newly created spot to Cecily when Cecily was seven. Under the bushes next to their three-flat apartment, the one my father bought for the Slaughter brothers when they began to marry, the eight year old Cecilia spread her hair and bowed her head to Cecily and asked her if she'd like to kiss it. "*Kiss it?*" Years later, Cecily would tell anyone who would listen, "Thank goodness she has an outlet with her poetry, otherwise she'd end up quite crazy, be institutionalized like Grandmother Slaughter."

My father would boast to his friends that the building where Uncles Emmanuel, Abraham, and Samuel lived cost him "next to nothing," adding, "Of course, I fixed it up better than the other properties I own." Then he would laugh. After marrying Esther, Uncle Benjamin moved into his mother-in-law's apartment, which was a half a block away. The two buildings were almost identical—each with dark, chipped bricks, a patch of grass in front, and a dirt alley in the back that ran the length of a half mile. I would always feel guilty when I visited, given our mansion in the suburbs, situated on an acre of well cared for lawn.

Even now I can easily bring forth the smells that permeated the narrow, poorly lit hallways of those two buildings, the scents coming from those small, clean kitchens—cabbage soup, a chicken, tongue boiling in a large old pot. And, unfortunately, the sounds, most especially the shouts—Uncle Emmanuel and Aunt Sonya yelling at each other and, down the street, Great Aunt Eva screaming at her daughter Adele, or *about* her, to anyone who would listen.

Of course, each brother's goal was to move to the suburb where we lived, and each eventually did achieve this. By the time I was fourteen, Cecilia, Celine, Cecily, and Celie all lived within several miles of me. But this did not lessen my shame, for within our mansion my father would mock what he called their "matchbox houses."

Growing up we would hear her story over and over—how Idyth Slaughter could not adjust to America and left Cecil to go back to Hungary because she missed her country too much, only to return to him because she missed him more and all of this before she turned seventeen. She finally lost him when she was twenty-nine.

Cecily tells her therapists that Cecil, being much older, must have been both a *great lover* and a father figure to her. "Can you imagine the to-do they make when I say such a thing?" she says to Celine, who takes such delight in this as she does all things sexual.

Through the years her therapists have appeared, sequentially, in their dull, cramped, stuffy offices, scribbling with their pencils—not that they have helped her. However, Cecily's internist insists that she talk with someone because when he asks her "How are you?" she always says the truth, "terrible," and it is not about the physical. Cecily, like each of us, has many issues. It was unavoidable given the atmosphere created by the too many adults that hung over us—their thick breath as heavy as the smoke that covered us from their cigarettes—their weighted, buckled histories and agendas continuously smothering us.

Listening to how handsome Cecil was, of his great charisma and, of course, his brilliance—how there was no one like him, and that is why Idyth got sick after she lost him—we all agreed, was tiresome. Anyway, it has almost become a silent story. Cecil and Idyth now lie side by side at Waldheim Jewish Cemetery. Quietly, or at least that is what those above the ground would like to believe. They do not yet know of the turmoil we bring with us wherever we go.

Last night Cecily could hear a banging in her head like cymbals crashing together. The sound was spaced at about fifteen-second intervals. She was dreaming. Dreaming that she *was* dead. And death was impossibly loud and nerveracking. When she awoke she wondered, "Is that where the playwrights go—to some designated circle I don't know of—especially the ones who borrow on the lives of their poet relatives? Dante did find a not-too-terrible place for the poets in Limbo." And yes, she can see Cecilia there someday, wandering with her long, silky hair spread wide exposing the moth hole, asking the other desperate souls there to *Please, just kiss it.*

In Cecily's play, *Lissa*, the poet, is always tearing at her hair—just one spot that she shows to the audience three times. Sometimes, she has her suck on the follicle bulb tip. In its own way it is quite sexual. Quite intimate. Cecily does know not to overuse the moment. The lights are directed to shine right into that slick, wet baldness. And then to pause on it. She wants the audience to care about *Lissa*. Cecily feels she really cares about her, too. Certainly more than she actually does about Cecilia. She *knows* it is hard not to be at least a little jealous of her cousin—among other things, for her pale perfect skin. In adolescence Cecily spent a lot of time at the dermatologist. From the back, she is sometimes mistaken for Cecilia. People run after her, calling "Cecilia, Cecilia." Then, when they get close enough, they pause, disappointed, and say "Sorry, Cecily, I thought you were . . ."

However, Cecily does believe her play portrays the poet in a most fair way. And although it focuses on how crazy she is—she does kill herself in the end—the audience, she is sure, will be moved to tears. "That is, if there ever *is* an audience," she obsesses.

Celie has asked her if she worries about Cecilia finding out about the play. That perhaps this will hurt or embarrass Cecilia in a very serious way. And she does not even know the many details of it. Cecily thinks, "Celie's so sweet. A little simple, but sweet. Maybe it's her simpleness that makes her this way." Celine, however, has said that Celie is far more complicated than she imagines. Cecily knows Celie *was* hospitalized for what was labeled "exhaustion," but to Cecily that seemed something of an indulgence. When Celine talks about Celie this way—as if she knows a secret—Cecily believes, "That's just Celine again, trying to stand out, trying to make herself feel special."

In the dress shop where Celie works all her customers love her. Many of them are educated, rich, bored, frustrated, freaky-thin women—who are dismayed that they have wound up being such clichés. The dressing rooms, however elaborate, have cardboard walls. And even I can listen, though I try not to, for I have learned there are far, far better places to spend eternity's time.

They talk about their latest diets and their psychiatrists, who are probably equally dismayed that they went to medical school and beyond only to end up listening hour after hour to their patients' self-indulgent complaints. Although I imagine these paid listeners have large paneled offices with many exotic artifacts from their travels, which they carefully display.

Celie makes her customers feel hopeful—that the *next* item she brings them to try on will, most certainly, reinvent them. That suddenly they will see themselves in the mirror as they want to be seen—both by others and by themselves. Some tell her she is better than any therapist. "Better, but not cheaper." Celie just smiles.

Celine is always at the shop, buying up all the pinks, while Cecily and Cecilia occasionally come by for the blacks. Once Cecilia said to her, "Cecily, did you know that just because you wear all black, doesn't mean you exactly match? There are so many shades of black. And of course, there is also the issue of the fabric and how the black is absorbed in it." Even though it was all too much irrelevant concern for Cecily, she had to admit that after she concentrated on it, Cecilia was right. Since, like Cecilia, she wears mostly black, after Cecilia said this, she noticed, especially in the sunlight, that sometimes she did not match. In Cecily's play, *Lissa,* of course, always dresses in black. She now believes she will have to keep her eye on the costume designer to make sure he or she knows to keep them matched.

If, however, you are thinking Cecily is some poor man's Cecilia, do not even give a hint of this to her, for she will attack you with unforgettable rage, screaming, "There's no bald spot atop my head—*and even if there were, I certainly wouldn't tell anyone*—and no man—artist or otherwise—has actually raped me or even attempted. It's true, Cecilia brings out the fire in men, which—trust me—*isn't* always a good thing. So, big deal." What Cecily does not yet know is that this *will* become a big deal—not just for Cecilia, but for her, and the others, too.

Then only to herself Cecily says, "*In the play Lissa brings out that fire, too.* And yes, there is a rape. But it's quite inventive—more like a dance. It shows the complexities, the contradictions. *Exactly who is provoking whom?* Not that I'm saying in real life Cecilia was or wasn't raped. I don't know. But, what if the critic asked? . . . Yes, at the dinner in his apartment, where she went alone though she barely knew him. (*Here, the stage is so stark, the audience as tense in the moment as the characters. I can just see it!*) What if he asked? Asked about the spot, asked if it truly did exist, asked to see it. It *is* all over her poetry. And she showed it to him—allowed it. I imagine how she unclipped the golden barrettes she wore that night and let her hair run wild over her deep V-necked, soft, black sweater, over her thin black tank top—her shoulders, her breasts—as she parted the shimmering strands (*highlighted in the candlelight*) with her delicate fingertips (*like Lissa does in the play*), bowed her head to him and said that the most sacred thing one can do is to kiss it. And he did . . ."

NO SAD SONGS
SUNG HERE

How quiet the stretched skin over
the singular body—its coo and hum
and minute beat on the planet
crust. The mattress
is so bumpy and sunk,
squeaking on—sad song

sing-along to a distant memory
of a ram's horn trumpet inside
the temple's walls. *Sing to me*

asked the woman of the man
and just a hollow column of air appeared,
begged the man to his god
and just one plucked string was heard,
cried the child in her crib. *So I did*

something spontaneous, I then forgot.
Afterward, we slept all
coo and hum, only the child
firm on the words she dreamed on.

c. slaughter

CELINE SHOPS A LOT. She likes pretty things. Pretty things on herself. They make her feel prettier, as in *prettier than* my mother, which we were all taught to believe was the most difficult "pretty" to conquer—that, quite frankly, unreachable goal, especially in my father's and my four uncles' eyes.

Celine's father, Uncle Emmanuel, would say to her, and often, "Celine, you *are* the prettiest of your first cousins." He would hug her tightly and call her the sweetest, the prettiest of all the little raisins. *Raisins?* It would make her feel so small, so shrunken, although I am sure he meant it as a compliment in his own distorted way. However, he also believed my mother—all sunflower, all golden, in full bloom—glowed above Celine, no matter what the season of Celine's life, and she felt it.

When Celine wears the best and brightest clothes she can find, she feels she, too, glows. It is a warmth that starts outside her body when she touches the silk, the velvet, the cashmere. Then it travels deep within her, the luxurious threads weaving her insides—holding her together—making her feel rich and valuable and worthy. She thinks, "Clothes have a permanence. That is, if you take good care of them. They can last forever. People, no matter how much care you give them—take care with them, *care* for them, love them—can disappear from you, sometimes slowly, sometimes in an instant."

Her father, although he did seem to care some for Aunt Sonya, had many women. They, too, were never enough for him. In her adolescence it became quite clear to Celine that he was always searching for someone, someone like his sister—as were all the Slaughter brothers. He never found her. Aunt Sonya knew. Everyone did. Except Celeste. She would have, if she had grown old enough.

After her second child was born, Aunt Sonya could not stand the coercion from the family to name *yet* another child after Cecil Slaughter, but Manny put so much pressure on her to do so that she felt she had no choice. However, when alone with her baby "Celeste," Sonya would call her "Sonyi," thereby naming her precious new daughter after herself. She loved being alone with her baby and calling her this. She loved the secret power it gave her. Celine and Uncle Emmanuel never knew of this and, for the few short months she was a Slaughter, to them she was always Celeste.

When Celeste died before she turned six months, Aunt Sonya shrieked and shrieked, sobbing to everyone, "It was from hell fever—*his* behavior cursed this family and caused it." She believed the curse Manny Slaughter put on their house was so strong no voodoo magic could wash it out. No Star of David hung around their necks, no mezuzah nailed to the door, nothing could help. The three of them watched Celeste so suddenly grow hotter than the hottest summer and disappear. Hell fever. It was August when they put her in that little box.

Of course, along with her other sisters-in-law, Aunt Sonya could not stand how my mother always looked so young, so perfect, no matter that she was at least a decade older than any of them. Her long, thick blond hair pulled back and twisted into a neat figure-eight bun. "Eight" as in eternity's number, for she never seemed to age in anyone's eyes. Her own included. Nor could they stand their husbands' deep and obvious attraction to their sister.

People would stop Aunt Sonya and Celine on the street, or anyone for that matter whose last name was known to be Slaughter, just to talk and talk about how lucky they were to be related to my mother. "Her honey beauty—that natural blond hair," they would marvel. "That Ginger Rogers look." "American Beauty *Rose*," is what they called her, too—something everyone heard from her brothers. An "Aryan Jew" is what Celine thought as she got older and learned more about the war—meaning World War II. "Couldn't the others see it? Instead of craving such a look, why didn't it make them sick?" she questioned. Although, now Celine does admit she loves her beauty-shop-blond hair and repeatedly explains, "My goal is certainly *not* to look like Aunt Rose. Anyway, times *have* changed."

How Grandfather Cecil and Grandmother Idyth adored my mother—their firstborn, so beautiful. Idyth, already pregnant with Uncle Emmanuel, would stroll her down Devon Avenue past Manzelman the grocer and Savitsky the butcher, and each would come out of his shop along with his customers and linger over baby Rose, just eight months old. It is all part of the family lore and allure and *lure*—at least if you are female and a Slaughter.

Everyone standing there, staring at Idyth's angel fallen to earth, would spit over his or her left shoulder and say a *kine-ahora* to keep the *evil eye* away from her. Demonic spirits, diabolic ghouls, and evil sprites can become jealous too, at least that was what many at the time thought—and many now still do.

"God's gift—a haloed girl," everyone would say. Some of the women would even drop a little salt or a crumb of bread into her pink knitted booties for further protection. Celine, like the rest of us, had heard all the stories. "As if not just *any* healthy baby were exactly that," Celine would angrily think, after Celeste so sadly and abruptly left.

When first married to Uncle Emmanuel, right after the war, Aunt Sonya expanded to Celine, "I dyed my hair blond and grew it long. But the ends split and it looked too frizzy. So I cut it short and went for the Betty Grable look. That didn't quite work either." After Celeste died, Aunt Sonya went all gray and almost silent, except for her frequent, frenzied bursts of rage toward Manny.

She found him once—actually found him—with another woman. Straight out found them in their house. Flesh on flesh seesawing together. When Celine got older, Aunt Sonya told her, "That's what the devils in hell look like—all swelled up, putrid, and naked in their fat, locked together so tight they can never unlatch from each other." According to Aunt Sonya, "Hell was just one unending fuck. And that's where Manny Slaughter went." In his last months, even with all the morphine being dripped into him, he would scream and swear from the pain, as if he were already well on his way to that place of relentless fire.

She made Celine promise that when she died she would be buried far away—a completely different cemetery from Manny, somewhere far across the city. She would tell Celine this over and over. Now they sleep forever separate as they did so much in life—but hopefully with less fury. I have made a point of *not* checking this out.

Many men *are* attracted to Celine. She believes it is something she cannot help—that she does nothing to make this so, thinking, "Although I know I don't look anything like Rose, I am my own flower. Perhaps a pink hibiscus. I know Celie, Cecilia, and Cecily think I'm vain and superficial and, although Cecilia is a poet and Cecily a playwright,

I'm as smart as either of them and most certainly have had more success with men. And unlike either, I am no gloom cloud. Aaron adores me and hasn't a clue about Morris or Lew—or for that matter, any of the others."

It is true, Aaron just expects her home for dinner—to make the meal and occasionally sit with him while he watches his TV programs. His favorite is *Wheel of Fortune*. She turns her cell phone off and lets all messages go to voice mail. Early the next day, she picks them up and chooses what she will do from whatever plans are offered to her.

Mostly, she spends mornings with Lew. They travel to the different sites where he owns property. They turn the radio on high to the oldies station. They neck, they pet, and sometimes do it in one of his half-filled condominiums, when an owner is on vacation. Evenings are mostly saved for Morris, but only when Aaron is out of town, or working, or just going to bed early. Again the radio's on the oldies station. She is always listening to Bobby Vinton, Nat King Cole, the Lettermen—songs filled with longing and love, but nothing too sad, too operatic. Someday she plans to needlepoint a canvas that reads "No Sad Songs Sung Here," frame it, and hang it on the door of her closet.

Afternoons she tries to stop at the lavish dress shop where Celie works. Often Celie lets her have her discount because—in truth—Celie has no use for such clothes. Celine feels Celie is her best *cousin* friend however much she gets frustrated with her passivity, her dowdiness. She thinks, "At least I take the time to listen to her and go with her to places, when she asks." Celine believes Cecilia is usually too sadly sunk into herself to bring much to anyone else and is perplexed and a bit jealous by how much Celie adores her.

Although Celine, too, cares for Cecilia, she cannot stand how mixed up she is. Celine tells a miscellaneous friend, "You only have to read her poems to know this, and *now,* with whatever is going on with this 'creature'—real or imagined—she refers to as 'Herr M' in more than one of her poems. *Well,* what's a person to think? However, Cecily is *the one* who is just downright crazy. Totally obsessed with trying, always trying, to top Cecilia's demitasse spoonful of success."

Though Celine does find Cecily easy to talk to—an awfully good listener—so she tells her things she does not tell the others. Things that she probably should not tell her. Celine knows this, but cannot resist sharing them with someone, and she sees how much Cecily enjoys hearing what she says. She does believe they make Cecily's life a little richer, distract her from her Cecilia fixation.

On the surface, at least, telling Cecily private things does make some sense for Celine used to be really close with her—both thirteen, they would sit in her Uncle Emmanuel's gold Chrysler Imperial in the driveway of Celine's house and talk and talk. Mostly about boys—Celine's boys. Cecily was shy and not dating, yet. They would laugh a lot, while Uncle Emmanuel would often peer out the window. One day when Celine went inside, he told her he thought Cecily might be a homosexual. He talked about homosexuals a lot, especially after his business trips to Las Vegas. He would tell Celine and Aunt Sonya about the shows he had seen and who *was* and was *not* a "homo." At first when he used the word Celine did not know what it meant and paid little attention to it. But after he said it about Cecily, she asked her mother. When Aunt Sonya told her, Celine just could not agree with her father. It seemed silly, and at the same time startling. It made her feel upset—confused—but she kept it to herself.

However, soon after Uncle Emmanuel said this, Aunt Lillian got a phone call from another mother saying she did not want her daughter to have any more contact with Cecily. When he heard this from Sonya, Manny just laughed. He and his brother Abraham, Cecily's father, were in business together. Carpets. They had had a terrible fight, which led him to create the rumor. Manny Slaughter could become very scary when he got angry.

Sometimes when I would see Cecily, I could not help but worry that this gossip had completely overwhelmed her. It was soon after that she began to wear thick eye shadow on her eyelids to give herself a deliberately tormented look. What was said clearly got permanently lodged in her mind all of the time. Celine's too—but not all of the time, just some of the time. *All* of the time for Celine was reserved for Celeste. Sometimes she would even wonder if Celeste had been accidentally dropped into the wrong house and got a second chance at life with a more peaceful family. She also thought at lot about how nice it would have been to have her little sister back—have someone with whom she could have shared her thoughts, someone she could truly trust, someone who could have made her feel less alone—help her deal with all the chaos between her mother and father. Whenever she meets a person who has a sister with the name Celeste, she glues a smile onto her too bright lipstick. She knows how to cover the tormented look with cheery color.

Celine was six when Celeste died. Manny Slaughter wept for hours at the funeral parlor over her stilled body, where he had taken Celine, Sonya too broken apart to go. Then, suddenly, he picked Celeste up and shook her. Screamed at her to wake up. "Wake up, wake up." Celine sat frozen in the corner, watching this. She cannot forget the image of her father shaking that baby—her small sister—and that shout. She hears it when she feels too alone in the dark.

The doctor had to come there and give him a shot. Then he drove both him and Celine home. For a while after, Manny Slaughter went to temple every morning. Gave up the women. For a while. Even after he went back to his old ways, Sonya stayed. Hell fire.

When Sonya and he moved to Key Biscayne, they dug up Celeste and took her with them. Buried her under the hot, rotting sun. Celine stayed here in the Midwest, where the seasons change often enough so that she would never be locked in one forever. Celine has an issue about being closed in—stuck. Stuck in one dress, one place, one thought. She needs diversity and change. She needs light—the sheen on satin, jokes, and cocktail talk.

On her birthdays she would get double the presents from her father. Two bracelets, two rings—whatever. As if he believed he still had two daughters. Her mother sent hers separately. Something for a little girl. Something a little girl would wear. It sort of made Celine sick. But she stayed sweet. "Surface perfect," is what she called it, toward both of them until each of their ends.

At her father's funeral she wore a sophisticated black St. John's knit suit with a Versace silk blouse, the pattern a splash of shocking pink flowers. You could not see it at the service. The jacket covered it, except for the edges of the cuffs. During the service, to distract herself, she stared at them a lot.

At her mother's funeral she wore a white cotton piqué Dior dress with a cinched waist and full skirt. It was midsummer, but not too hot—at dusk, when they finally lowered the casket into the ground, there was even a chill in the air so Aaron wrapped a light pink Donna Karan cashmere sweater over her shoulders. Then he hugged her and called her "my sweet girl." From beneath the ground I saw Celie, Cecilia, and Cecily smirking a bit when he did this, while trying hard to stay posed-solemn. They stood across from Celine, all dressed in black Carolina Herrera, which Celine had rejected at the shop. Morris and Lew stood at opposite ends of the roped-in portion of the grave, staring at each other. Several other well-dressed men were there whom nobody seemed to recognize. As she looked around Celine was so pleased when she realized all her men had worn Armani.

THE INTERIOR
OF THE SUN

It is the dream of reentering
Eden—innocent and running
up three flights of stairs
through the back door
into the kitchen.
They are there: mother, father.
No death here—not yet—no

lymph glands have swelled, buckled
the skin, lungs easily inhale
the fragrance from the thick brisket
steaming in the pot.
No one yet coughs. The blood

clot in father's heart is
only a metaphor for
a child's loss. Later, she'll beg
her most violent lover to hit her
down there. Up

here dinner's almost ready. The flowered
oilcloth sweats on the Formica
while she can't wait to watch the fire-
flies attach and electrify against
the scorched window screen.
How she loves to singe

her fingertips with its prison pattern.
Her mother will insist
that now she must again go wash.
Will she ever get clean of the burnt-
out center of others' lives? *Hit me,*

she whispered last night
to her lover—Herr M. *There,*
pointing to the wiry pit. How it fascinates—
the way the two of them mix

up love with hate. When he bites
her nipples to blood,
she can almost hear him cry
to his dead mama.
Hers just sits quiet and bald,
a million miles away. Chemotherapy
is doing its trick.
The trick is hope

that when she opens
the next door, they'll be standing there—
waiting for her. She's come in
from play. It's summer again
and someone loves her.

c. slaughter

Zipping up the peach chiffon dress that Deidre Fox
bought for her daughter's early July wedding, she was clear
in her mind, once again. She was more interested in getting information from Celie about our family and most
especially about Cecilia than in having the dress properly

fitted. It is obvious Deidre is obsessed with Cecilia and it is also obvious she thinks Celie is too blanked out to notice. But however delicate, however breakable Celie is, she is hawk-like aware of every move Deidre makes. What Deidre does not know is how protective Celie is of Cecilia, as Cecilia is of her. And, with Cecilia's growing popularity, Celie sees some of the negative consequences of her success and this makes her all the more concerned for her.

It is evident that Cecilia has become the sun in Deidre's solar system and that she is desperate to know everything about her interior core—which, quite frankly, is impossible. I do, however, understand Deidre's need to a point, for she is an unsuccessful poet and most clearly Cecilia is not. And one thing that stands out among our many flaws as humans is how badly we want to be perceived as successful. As if success were an inanimate outer, loud adornment—like a flashy broach or a medal—not an inner, silent bloom to be watered and nourished.

Being that she is one of Celie's best customers—comes to the shop almost three times a week, mostly looking to see if Cecilia is there—Celie tells her the most superficial things that come to mind. Facts that everyone knows. For Celie, too, in her own small way wants success—though she is satisfied with what many consider a ridiculously tiny portion of it.

Celie goes along with the family myth and tells her that Cecil Slaughter was reportedly a brilliant Jew and she provides some family facts that have been passed down through the years. That he was an émigré from Hungary who, when asked his name upon reaching Ellis Island, thought he was being questioned as to who he *was*—meaning what he did. He paused, then made an inadvertent hissing sound through the gaps in his teeth—whistle-like, and answered in his best English, *"scholar."* (He *did* have a position as an adjunct lecturer in philosophy at a small institute of advanced learning before he left his country.)

The tired, impatient man behind the desk recorded *Cecil* from the whistle and from the broken-English *scholar*, he recorded "Slaughter"; rather prophetic, because the newly invented Cecil Slaughter ended up working in a kosher butcher shop, hacking meat. In the back room he did, however, teach himself to speak perfect English and to read books on literature and history in his new language. When he died of pneumonia at forty-eight his young wife, also from Hungary, went mad. Had to be institutionalized.

Celie tells this to Deidre because, as I said, some things about us are not secrets, *are* public knowledge. She can see how big-eyed Deidre becomes when she speaks of this—as if Deidre has heard all this for the first time, which Celie believes is not true, given how unendingly inquisitive she is about our family and how she is known to make attempts to find out things about us from others.

What Celie does not tell her is that my mother and her four brothers chose to ennoble Cecil to genius status so as to make up for the shame they felt about their mother's madness. It was this feeling about her, coupled with the blatant, totally public poverty of their early years—their sweeping self-consciousness about all of this—that made them more determined to create a *brilliant* Cecil—he who had no equal.

One day when Deidre spotted Cecilia at the shop buying an expensive black lamb's wool sweater laced with seed pearls around the neck, she bought one, too. Celie does reinforce her. While she wrapped it, she explained to her how when Cecil died and left a daughter and four young sons for Idyth to raise, it became too much for her and the children were separated and shuffled off to distant relatives. Eventually each married, each had a firstborn daughter and named her after their father—all variations of his name, as if to make up for the fact that the child was female. "To watch a daughter blossom was like watching a peony in June, watch it dry up as July closed in, into a nothing to be blown away. That's how they saw it. No blessing in a daughter." That is how Cecilia had described it to Celie and how Celie repeated it to Deidre, who truly looked at that moment as if she had been handed a million dollars, because she had been given a *Cecilia Quote.*

"Some men still believe that," Celie continued. Deidre replied, "Celie, I know this all *too* well." Celie already had heard this, because Deidre had said it to Celine. Celine had taken Deidre to lunch at Cecilia's request. Cecilia thought this would appease Deidre. Be enough. Celine was also assigned to help figure out if Deidre was dangerous. The best scenario, of course, was that with this connection to Celine, Deidre would stop trying so hard to bump into Cecilia at the shop and quit going to every local poetry event where Cecilia was reading and buying far too many of her poetry books, which gave her extra time with Cecilia as she stood there asking her to sign each book with specific inscriptions to people Cecilia felt she was just inventing so she could hang around her longer. "Sort of stalker-scary," was how Cecilia put it—reminding her of Herr M and how he was now tracking her every published word.

At the lunch with Celine, Deidre spoke about how disappointed her husband, Harrold, was with her because they had only produced a daughter, although intellectually he knew it was his sperm that made that determination. "I, too, know something about masculine narcissism, domination, and coldness," she confided to Celine, adding, "I fled a first husband reckless with testosterone. We honeymooned in Las Vegas. I can still picture him ogling the showgirls, their tight thighs, their bare breasts, their painted nipples, and doll faces. I began to feel dizzy and, after a day there, did get physically sick with a high fever, which he paid no attention to—just kept having sex with me, taking me to places the cartographers had yet to map!"

Celine said, "Celie, she acted as if she were *proud* of this. Then, she segued into the questions—the rumors that were circulating about some critic and Cecilia. Had he really threatened Cecilia? Tried to ruin her career? *Attacked* her? Asking who is this Herr M—the one mentioned in her most recently published poem—'The Interior of the Sun?'"

Frankly, the thing that impressed Celie most about what Celine reported was that Celine could actually *remember* so many details of what Deidre had said. As if she had memorized them. But, then again, they did have to do with sex—Celine's favorite topic. Although, she did continue her reportage with the same specificity, making Celie wonder if she had taken notes right afterward or perhaps had placed a small recording device inside her bra. Everyone knows how much she forever wants to impress upon Cecilia and Cecily that she is as sharp as they are—or sharper.

Celine confirmed to Celie that she stayed quiet as she was instructed to do, while Deidre continued with a relish she could not quite cover up, "The gossip is everywhere," she said in as compassionate a voice as she could muster, and went on. "*All* her recently published poems are imbued with an eerie beauty, yet filled with unseemly acts of violence. Very Edgar Allen Poe-like." After a pause, she continued, "Did she really let the critic hit her for his own delight or, worse, for hers? Did she deep down hate herself that much? Or was she just making it all up to add to the effectiveness of her writing?" Again, she paused, then said with great authority, "You know, some writers *do* this."

Celine thought the questions impertinent and beyond this, could not envision any of it, given her own conquests. Failure with men was just *not* in Celine's repertoire. Nor was she as intrigued as everyone else seemed to be by "whoever or whatever this Herr M was." It was clear to Celine that Deidre led a fairly barren life, yet if Cecilia would just give her some attention she would feel immediately filled up—which Celine did feel "*was* a little bent."

All of this Celine told Celie and Celie, in turn, told Cecilia. That Deidre even said to Celine, "I wish Cecilia and I could share our pain, our poetry—become sisters in the art. Maybe even *save* each other. I do see Cecilia in me, if only she'd see me in her." It was then that Deidre's talk made Celine feel "really creeped out" so she changed the subject to clothes and asked what Deidre had bought recently at the shop.

Deidre told her about the lamb's wool sweater and how Cecilia had bought the same one. Celine just could not get her off the subject of Cecilia, and once again Celine tried to change the topic—this time to men. She talked about how some man in the far corner could not stop looking at her. How difficult it was to avoid his stare. She talked about how cute the waiter was, how he could not stop smiling at her. Did Deidre notice? Which again turned the conversation back to Cecilia and the critic with Deidre asking, "Is he obsessed with her? Do you *know* what happened between them? *Do you?*" Then she quoted lines from Cecilia's poem "The Interior of the Sun":

> . . . *Hit me,*
> she whispered . . .
> . . . It's summer again
> and someone loves her.

This made Celine almost totally crazy, quickly asking for the check so as to get away from this "Cecilia-crazed woman."

Celine was so enraged that Celie and Cecilia had sent her on this mission that to calm her Celie immediately gave her another of her shop discounts—forty percent off. Satisfied, Celine went off to buy a short-sleeved pink angora sweater, which greatly pleased her.

Sometimes Celie feels truly sad for Deidre, especially when she watches her looking at herself in the shop's triple mirrors. She thinks, "Yes, she does look 'like a peony drying up.'" Celine had added that Deidre all too casually mentioned, "My second husband never comes near me. We never have sex. Harrold is the opposite of my first, and I chose him in large part because of this." Then, Deidre had snorted out a laugh and continued, "I guess, when you make your bed, you do have to *sleep* in it."

When reporting this to Celie, Celine shook her head from side to side as if she were trying to get rid of such a thought, and said, "I couldn't tell if she was kidding or not, but I couldn't take any more of such talk. Anyway, why would anyone share that? Just nuts!"

It is true, a life of such celibacy would be like death to Celine. However, Celie believes what Deidre said is true, as she watches her in the mirror. She does look like she has been pickled in a jar—well preserved, but with a blood-lessness to her flesh as if she has not been touched. Sadly, Celie's own skin has a similar look.

After Celie filled Cecilia in on all of this, they concluded that however pathetic Deidre was, she seemed fairly harmless and maybe if Cecilia blanked out anytime she encountered Deidre and Celie stopped *all* "Slaughter talk," Deidre would grow tired and eventually get the message and keep her distance. Though Celie hates to lose such a customer—she buys so much, especially if she knows Cecilia has bought it first.

Today, however, while Celie was wrapping the Hermès scarf Deidre had just bought, Deidre told her that she heard that Cecily had written a play about a poet and a critic and she asked, "Did you know of this?" Celie was astonished that she had such information, but stayed calm on the surface and said, "I did not." Which, of course, was not true. Deidre then asked, "Are you worried?" Celie replied, "No," which seemed like a joke inside herself, for Celie worries about everything. She just cannot show it, especially after certain things that have happened to her and seem to be known by everybody.

Celie diverted her attention to a black Calvin Klein coat, telling her that Cecilia had just purchased one, which she knew was not nice. Of course, Deidre immediately tried it on in her size and there Celie was, ringing up another large sale.

While she did this, Deidre said, cautiously and softly, "I've heard that Cecilia is having thoughts of suicide because of this man she calls Herr M—you know, the one in the poem." She then paused to see if Celie would react and when she did not, Deidre continued, "Isn't that why Idyth Slaughter was sedated and locked away, because she attempted to kill herself?" It was *then* that Celie became completely shaken by Deidre's not so subtle, manipulative intrusions. She felt her old vertigo returning, but carefully and rather coldly answered—avoiding the mention of a Herr M or Grandmother Idyth—"Oh, no. It's true she's thinking about the subject of suicide for a book, but that's it. Something she's going to do all in verse." "How interesting!" Deidre replied, with a certain amount of doubt and disingenuous enthusiasm in her voice, as Celie felt the floor begin to move even more.

After she left, Celie took her pills and called Cecilia, telling her, "I've concluded she really won't be that easy to get rid of. Her curiosity is becoming more meddlesome, more aggressive." Then she added, "Cecilia, who is Herr M?" Cecilia quickly answered in a weakening voice, "No one, Celie. No one. Just a fiction." She then said, "Thank you, Celie, for all you've already done, but I might have to ask you to do one additional small thing." After a sigh, she continued, "Did you know that Deidre told Celine that she's thinking of changing her name to *Ceil*, so that she can feel she's more a part of our family? Celine just told me this." Astonished, Celie said, "No!" and wondered why Celine had failed to report this. Then she figured that Celine had been too distracted choosing a purchase with the discount—or maybe, on second thought, she had saved the best tidbit of information to tell to Cecilia directly, so as to prove, once again, her high value.

Cecilia continued, "Maybe we'll have to take care of

this with a poem." Celie did not know exactly what she meant, except that the floor had straightened and she accepted that Cecilia knew what she was doing, unlike myself who understood more and more, as the years passed and my disappearance to beneath the ground lengthened, that this was not always true and became most especially obvious to me with Cecilia's encounters with a very real Herr M. All of which coincided with her mother's long, final journey toward what humans call *death*—the place where I now live and more than exist.

THE DEVIL'S LEGS

His pants unzip fast
and he stands in his pure white
underwear, which he pulls down
and kicks off.
His hard curvy
calves, a perfect pair,
kiss each other
like well-matched lovers,
while his thighs rise and rise
to the heaven above, to the
promise of his mountainous

voice calling to her from her
cold place down
on the floor.
Touch Me Up
Here. I'll Take You
In. Be Your Heat.
And with her palms stretched
to their widest,
she pushes herself over
the silent flat world—her thin

legs soon to encircle
all that is round, all that is
pumped, all that is hyped, all that
is hot, all
that is brash, all that is his
full unending
laugh.

c. slaughter

DURING THE TIME Cecilia's mother was dying, Cecilia was trying to tell her something about herself that she knew her mother would rather not know—something Aunt Lettie would not want to carry with her to the next world. Yet Cecilia continued, even though it was clear Aunt Lettie chose to skip over Cecilia's small but consistent mentions of Herr M. Maybe it was the nickname Cecilia had given him that bothered Aunt Lettie so much, proving to be a trigger—a reminder—for her. The *Herr*, of course, too German. However, the more Cecilia used it, the more his real name faded, until finally, the latter did not have the acute impact within herself as to what he—Herr M— had done to her. The metaphoric distance she created with this pseudonym did help. Every time she heard his real name mentioned Cecilia would grow nauseous and her body would quiver. At those moments she would feel like a small, trapped animal.

Aunt Lettie would never live to know Herr M's real name, and for this I knew she was grateful. It was not that she did not feel enormous concern for Cecilia. It was, I believe, quite the opposite. Given her own history, even if she had been healthy she probably would have thought that she was the last person who could help her daughter. Yet, it was so clear how much Cecilia wanted to tell her mother. Cecilia thought, "After all, she *is* still here. She *is* still my mother. And I need her."

Because Aunt Lettie could not seem to stand to hear even an edge of her talk about Herr M, she would abruptly change the subject and say, "Cecilia, could you adjust my pillow?" or "Could you bring me another blanket?" Cecilia was more than happy to do this for she knew her mother was close to death and she would have done anything she felt might extend her life by a day, an hour—even minutes. During those days, hours, and minutes, they were standing in separate earth—separate dirt—as Aunt Lettie was about to leave this world, leave Cecilia in what Aunt Lettie was known to call "this fallen place." The only thing Cecilia could not seem to do for her mother was to stop bringing up Herr M.

Cecilia watched her mother's whole being become translucent and she envied her—her thinning journey out of this life almost over. There Aunt Lettie sat with that permanent shunt—just the right place for a beautiful pin, except this was under layers of her skin—for the transfusions that gave her back a little life for a week or two. They allowed her to go home and even go out to lunch and for a drive next to the lake right after new blood was infused into her. However, as her sickness progressed, the more quickly the healthy cells became polluted with her disease, and ultimately all a transfusion did was to give her enough energy to leave her bedroom and go downstairs for some sunlight for an hour or two. Then, Cecilia's father would carry her back to her upstairs room, which she kept dark—the shades always drawn.

Her bully-critic was not literary, but all too literal— Adonai, solemn in the temple, about to inscribe her in the *Book of Death*, Lucifer grinning in hell hoping to greet her or, going the furthest back Cecilia could remember, the god Thoth waiting patiently to weigh her soul. "Who knows?" she thought.

Flashes of Karl would arrive more quickly to Lettie the sicker she became. Sometimes she would see him in his uniform standing over her and then, just as quickly, his image would evaporate into the stale hospital room air as if he were never there. Had never existed. He would always show up

*unexpectedly in the corners of her room, frightening her. So
nothing had really changed from when she was at the camp,
except that after she got out and came to America, married
Samuel, and had Cecilia, he did show up less and less. She
had almost begun to believe it was possible that someday he
would disappear forever. It was only when she got sick for the
final time that he started appearing more frequently.*

*Sometimes, too, her own mother and father would appear
in the hospital room, waving "goodbye"—or was it "hello"?
Each had one arm in the air, so together they formed the wings
of a single bird. And sometimes a gorgeous bird would quietly
materialize next to her bed and carefully fan her, try to cool
her. Lettie would reach out to it when it appeared and attempt
to touch its feathered tips, as if by doing so she would be trans-
formed into a healthy being by the bird's majesty. But she could
never quite get to it—touch it—before it, too, disappeared.*

*She would tell Cecilia about the bird—that she thought
it was an ibis. "A scarlet ibis!" she would exclaim, and then
she would remind Cecilia to make sure to bury her in her red
suit. She told her many times where to find it in her closet.*

*Lettie knew Cecilia would try hard to appear calm as
she went along with her ibis image. Cecilia would tell her
about how in ancient Egypt the ibis was always buried in the
deceased Pharaoh's tomb so as to ensure the Pharaoh safe passage to the next world and Lettie, not quite listening, would
smile and return to the story of her parents' last wave to her—
how its arc had formed the wings of a single bird. She did
let Cecilia in on a bit of the less awful details of her past as
Cecilia got older—and that wave seemed safe enough. They
would have this conversation, over and over. Almost all talk
near the end became a repetition. Lettie made sure of this.*

*In fact, the last time she had seen her parents and they
waved goodbye was many years ago. A Tuesday at 9:20 A.M.*

She still had her watch on—no one had yet taken it from her—and for some reason it felt important to make a record of that moment in her mind. Tuesday, February 1—a day filled with a heavy, awful smell that she would learn to live with, a smell she would never entirely forget, from which she would never get clean enough.

Her parents' wave had been so casual, as if nothing too terrible was happening—as if they were trying to assure her and her sister, Leah, that they, "of course," would see them both tomorrow. That is how Lettie would always remember it—and all the moments that came before and after . . .

Lettie's mother, Miriam, had gently pushed Leah and her out of their line when the officer shouted for "Doctors" and "Twins," whispering to them in Yiddish, "Geyn, Geyn" in her most gentle mother voice. Joseph, their father, nodded with a forced smile as if saying, "Do as your mother says," as he often told them out loud in better times. And, as always, Lettie and Leah did what they were told to do, because Miriam and Joseph were good parents and had always given them the best advice.

Often when Lettie focused on her own daughter—her daughter with the auburn hair and violet eyes—it was easy to forget about the past. "Beauty does that," she would tell Samuel, who never wanted to hear her mention any of it—meaning the camp and Karl. She did understand this, though there were times she wished he would allow her to talk about it. All of it. She wanted to think at least she was able to do that with her husband if she had chosen to, but it was not true.

Now, in the hospital, she has become more like Samuel when Cecilia tries to talk to her about this man, Herr M, whom she knows has hurt her daughter. She sometimes even wonders if Cecilia calls him this because of the stories she has heard from relatives about the German. *She had forbidden herself to share too much of her sad history with Cecilia. She wanted so much to protect her, always fearing others cared about this less.*

She does, however, have moments when she thinks if she were given just one more remission, if she could become a little stronger, maybe she could help Cecilia—talk with her. That is what she ambivalently prays for to her "so-called God"— the one she can never quite believe in again or forgive. But she also feels that whatever has happened to her daughter is already done and that she is most probably not the right person to ease Cecilia's pain—and so this prayer only rises to a weak flutter inside her.

Another way Aunt Lettie would change the subject was to ask Cecilia to read to her, to take out the books filled with the "good pictures" on the nightstand shelf next to her railed hospital bed. The ones on Nijinsky, Pavlova, and Stravinsky. It was the old Europe—before both wars—that she loved to drift back to, a time before she was born— Paris, 1912. The performance of *Afternoon of a Faun*. Her mother, Miriam, had gone there with her own mother to see the great Nijinsky dance. Miriam was twelve. The same age Lettie was when Miriam let go of her hand and uttered the words, *"Geyn, Geyn."*

After a little while had passed she would tire of looking at the books and she would ask Cecilia to place the tape of Debussy's music from the ballet in the small CD player kept on a shelf in the medicine cabinet in the hospital bathroom. Cecilia would put the player on the sink's thick rim and the music would flow into the room where she lay in bed. She would then ask Cecilia to dance. "Dance Cecilia. *Dance to the music*," she would say with such passion and joy—her words sewn together with just a touch of desperateness.

Cecilia would always try to resist—it made her too upset to do this. Aunt Lettie had not become the ballet dancer her mother Miriam had wished. Both she and Leah had been well on their way to giving this to their mother before the train came for all of them. "I could have granted my mother that wish, if the war hadn't ruined everything," she would whisper to her American relatives. "I was *that* good." Then she would pause and say, "No one had seen anything like it." Cecilia could always hear what she imagined to be her Grandmother Miriam's voice fluttering into her mother's when she talked about the description of the ballet. "Nijinsky as the Faun! On stage he became half-animal, half-human! The difference between his flesh and costume indecipherable. He wore coffee-colored tights with brown spots. They were also painted on his bare arms and legs." Her voice was filled with an uncharacteristic exuberance and authority, especially when she added, "A tight, gold cord wig with two small, flat, curled horns cupped his head." Cecilia imagined when her mother said this that her arms rose up as if she were placing a crown atop her own head. She would strain to listen to all of this as she lay curled on the floor of her bedroom, behind her carefully opened door.

Cecilia knew she lacked the talent to become a ballerina even though her mother would never admit to this and had her take unending lessons. When she became a poet, Aunt Lettie accepted it, and Cecilia could tell that eventually it did make her proud—prouder than she could ever express, for Aunt Lettie had trouble showing strong emotions, both positive and negative. After the war, she was only capable of giving herself teaspoons of pleasure— if that.

She never told Cecilia that she found her poems too unhappy and that she feared that her own heavy grief had seeped into her. But Cecilia knew it. Nor did she tell Cecilia how she loved the applause at the end of her readings, but Cecilia could see it as her mother looked around and watched the others' enthusiasm and then nodded a *yes* to her. Sometimes when Aunt Lettie heard the applause, she would close her eyes and smile wistfully and Cecilia would think, "She's imagining her own self curtsying in her toe shoes before a huge audience with *her mother* glowing in the front row, watching her on a large stage in an elegant theater. Perhaps Paris."

When the soldier shouted, "Women to the left," "Men to the right," they all stood stunned. Then quickly, the same soldier, not seeing that they had not moved, yelled for "Doctors" and "Twins." It was only then that Miriam awoke from the shock of everything that was happening and told Leah and Lettie to go to that line. Afterward, she went to the line for women and Joseph to the one for men. And there ended the least of it—Miriam's dream of a Pavlova or even an Isadora in the family. For even then, everyone knew that however innovative Isadora was, she was a far lesser talent.

Lettie wanted so much that her only child, her only daughter, become a dancer. But Cecilia eluded the gift, almost refused to nurture it. She supposed it was possible, too, the gift eluded her. Somehow that was more difficult to accept. But after talking with her sister-in-law Esther and learning how Esther's mother, Eva, had pushed and pushed at Adele and Esther to be famous, and seeing the terrible effect this had on Adele, Lettie let go a little more easily of her dream for Cecilia.

She finally concluded that Cecilia's becoming a poet was nice. Seeing her standing up there with her words did please her. She just imagined with this daughter she would be able to leave a different kind of legacy. In this country she got greedy. Once, even having a lovely daughter was more than she could have ever envisioned, could have believed would ever happen . . .

While searching for a special nightgown her mother had requested during her last hospital stay—in her last days— Cecilia happened on her mother's diary hidden deep beneath her soft nightwear. She did not feel guilty when she broke its lock. She had been pushed out of too many rooms too many times, while her mother had talked with the others. And now, especially, she needed to know everything her mother refused to speak about with her. She needed to know all she could about the mother she was losing. She grabbed at anything, as if that would allow her to hold on to her mother a little longer.

And there it was, there in the diary, that she found more complete answers. Answers to many of the questions that had barbed her mind since she was a child. She took it home and went into a small walk-in closet and sat for hours reading it. Of course, she had overheard some things about a soldier, a bad man, a German, but when her mother spoke of him with the others, she would hesitate and either never quite finish her sentences or grow too quiet for Cecilia to hear.

A few of the sections she copied over in her own hand on long, yellow sheets of paper, as if in rewriting this, she were allowing herself to become her mother, which began to scare her. Consequently, she decided to break her mother's lines differently than in the diary, shaping them to look more like poems. It was familiar and created a little distance as to what she was doing, what she was taking in, sort of like when she created the pseudonym Herr M.

Feb. 1
When they grabbed my satchel away
from me, I was left
holding just the string that had helped
to keep it shut.
I tied the string around my hair
making of it a small bow
at the top. This kept my hair out of my face,
for the wind was impossibly harsh.

That day

Mother had made Leah and me go to the line for "Twins."
I could tell she thought this a good thing—I could tell
she thought we'd be given special attention. I knew
my mother's face so well.

Karl saw us in that line—saw me. He ignored Leah.
He came toward me. He came very close
and touched the string, the bow, my hair.
He chose me. Suddenly,

I turned around and found Leah
had disappeared.
I kept looking for her
until he told me she was
sent elsewhere and
not to worry.

He touched my bow, again.
Called me his
"pretty little maiden." Then
he asked, "How old?" I remember
saying, "I'm twelve.
I'm Lettie. I'm twelve."

Feb. 2
A woman shaved all the hair off
my body. Her hands were quick
and rough. She said
it was to prevent lice. I looked almost
brand new. Then I saw

the others

who also had been shaved—older people
now looking like withered children.

They told us how the shavings were "good for us."
That everything they were doing to us
was "good for us."

Soon the older people disappeared.

Feb. 3
Karl came back. He touched my scalp
and smiled.
My baldness didn't seem to bother him.
Then, he took my hand
and led me to another room.

Feb. 20
Because I had no choice—this was the life
that was given me—and Karl
kept telling me I was
safe,
I had to believe him—
too fear-frozen
not to.

And I was twelve.

And the red brick building with the small windows
brightened by white frilled curtains
and the picket fence around it "looked safe."

That's what I told my small, bald, broken self.

Mar. 14
Everything became so familiar, the uniforms,
all of them, the bodies that inhabited them—
the strong, healthy ones, the bird-thin sick ones—
all the smells that were created when they commingled.
This place where life and death

collided and the earth opened herself up like the whore
that she was and swallowed
us into her putrid womb, this womb
became my home.
And because it was my home
and I was twelve and had no choice,
I tried to make my mind think everything would be alright,
but I never truly believed it.

Inside

I was violently heartsick.

June 4
After mama and papa and Leah disappeared,
for the longest time I thought they would come back
and right before the last time the cancer returned,
I had this dream—that they did. They
all came through the door of that red brick building
with the sweet ruffled curtains on the small
windows and found me standing there.
Mama took my right hand, papa took my left—
and we all walked away
together into the clean
warm summer air.

It was only as she got deeper into the diary that Cecilia began to fully understand why her mother kept asking not just for the books about Nijinsky, Pavlova, and Stravinsky, but also for the history books with those awful pictures inside—the books that she dutifully brought her from the library and had to be hidden from her father, buried under an extra blanket in the hospital closet. Her mother was still looking for them—looking for her mother and father and Leah.

She never found anything in the diary that spoke explicitly of what Karl had done to her mother. The closest she came to writing anything sexual or sensual about him was a mention of *his bare, long, perfect legs, his sculpted calves—like a dancer might have.* After reading this, Cecilia thought she might faint—she felt herself grow dizzy, her face becoming too hot, as she remembered Herr M standing above her, naked, with his godlike legs.

Cecilia read the diary many times, each time becoming more and more sensitive to the details—and to the things left out. She had no idea when her mother had written any of this. Clearly, parts of it were quite recent. And since no years were recorded, she knew some of it came from her mother's still quick memory. And with this she remembered how, in all her notes and letters, her mother never put a year on anything, as if she were trying to protect herself from an exact record of *all* things and when they had happened.

After each reading Cecilia threw up and in the last couple of days of her mother's life the guilt of having read the diary—the secrets her mother kept, the secrets of her mother's frightening, small girl life—grew larger and the habit of pulling at her hair from the top of her head became wilder.

On the last day of her mother's life, Cecilia found her mother tearing out the many petals on a small flower from an arrangement her father had brought her. With each pluck she repeated the words, "The man who loves me hates me." Cecilia truly did not know if her mother meant her father or Karl.

She did this until the flower was completely bald. As Cecilia watched from the doorway—a witness to the flower losing its beauty—her eyes filled with tears so much so that it became impossible for them not to flood her face.

When Lettie saw her standing there, she wanted so much to hold her. Hold on to her daughter forever. Cecilia's breathing seemed so heavy these past few weeks and Lettie worried what had happened with this man she called Herr M had also made her daughter physically sick. It was then she tried to talk to her about him. She asked her to tell her. Tell her everything. Tell her exactly what he had done to her—her rage against this man who had hurt her daughter in some awful way expanding in her brain, in her heart, pushing at her waning body. But when Cecilia embraced her—held her close—Lettie knew Cecilia could feel how fragile she had become—her bird bones—how she truly was about to break, and she could sense Cecilia's decision that the time for telling had passed as she released her. So they sat there together, wiping each other's faces with soft tissue, taking pleasure in doing this and quietly laughing like small girls—the stripped stem of the flower between them. At that moment Lettie could only hope that someday Herr M would get his retribution from someone—someone would hurt him in the large way he had hurt her daughter.

On that last night, as Cecilia was leaving her mother's room, she carefully wrapped the naked flower in one of the tissues they had used to wipe each other's tears and placed it in the pocket of her coat. On the long ride home she kept touching it in its moist blanket. She could not stop. At home the first thing she did was to take what was left of it and press it between two pages of her mother's broken book. Then, she took the book and buried it deep in a drawer—next to her own most painful, secret thing— never to look at it again.

Aunt Lettie died twice in her life; both times it was February 1.

YOM KIPPUR
NIGHT DANCE

At the end of each prayer, she'd add her own—
to find someone to marry.
In shul, where the men and women were separated
by an aisle, she'd lament and vow
to change the ways she wasn't good, then

break the fast with family and rush
to dress for the Yom Kippur Night Dance.
There, she'd wait with the girls in taffeta and years
later with the women in rayon knit.
Often she took a man

for the night, let him slide into her
because she felt she could hold him
there, pretend her life was like some
romantic song. Beyond the long somber chants,
the half wails of the chorus,

in the dark she'd start to sing
at the high pitch of happiness,
her appetite as huge as Eve's
before she knew she'd have to leave

the bliss, bow her head
and ask again for forgiveness.

c. slaughter

WEEKS AFTER AUNT LETTIE'S DEATH, Celie began to experience an acute anxiety that her mother's sister, Adele, had just died—more and more she was fearing this. If Adele were alive, Celie definitely felt Adele would have told anyone who would listen, "Celie is helping to kill me." And the fact that I knew that Adele was not yet buried here—was still alive at the time of Celie's heightened worry about Adele's existence—is immaterial. (Adele arrived way over a year later—just a few weeks before the conclusion of the Herr M horror.) It is only what Celie chooses to find out or not find out which is important. Some stories we would rather avoid, not know their endings; we would rather have someone pull them from our minds—if such a thing were possible.

In Celie's case not knowing—not wanting to find out—*was* a form of protection, actually a good defense, from the too heavy responsibility she felt as a child—as if five pound weights had been placed in each of her vulnerable, toddler hands. Her mind and body have ached ever since.

If Celie knew Adele to be dead, she would have thought that she *did* in some way participate in killing her. The truth is Celie knows Adele has had a terrible life—whether she is alive or dead. Not the kind, of course, that you see on the television these days—the unending, awful stories that make the news. No, Adele had an ethnic American immigrant-influenced twentieth-century kind of terrible life.

Adele and Celie's mother, Esther, were separated in birth by two years, Adele being the older sister. Celie's Grandmother Eva wanted two perfect daughters who were better than any of her cousins' American-born children. Eva had never become a citizen of this country, and she never learned to read. Both were secrets. But it was okay to laugh about the citizen part, especially when their family took driving trips and crossed the border into Windsor, Canada. Celie's little brothers would chuckle about how their grandmother would have to be left there and that would make more room for them in the back seat on the return trip. Eva did not seem to mind such talk—they were her "little men." That is what she called them. Celie took the threat more seriously, believing they could all end up imprisoned.

Her brothers did not know about the other secret—that their grandmother could not read. When they moved out of her crowded apartment, Celie was nine, Joshua was two, and Jeremy one. They do not have the same memories of that place that Celie does—they pay no important price, have no psychiatric expense. Everything in life adds up fairly easily for them. Both are now accountants, following in their father Benjamin's footsteps. Their tally books are neat and precise, their life ledgers always balanced.

Celie can never wipe her mind clean of her grandmother's screams—her screams at Adele. They are forever background noise—a tinnitus in her ears. Eva would scare Celie so much that sometimes she would hide in the closet and whisper to the disembodied coats how much she could not stand it. "Adele, stop eating! Adele, you're too fat! Adele, no man will ever marry you!" Over and over—those words, "Adele. Adele. Adele. Stop. Too fat. No man will . . ."

Actually, someone did ask Adele to marry, but when Eva saw the ring she screamed, "You call this a diamond?" Needless to say, the would-be fiancé took himself and his minuscule gem somewhere else and last Celie heard he had married and had two children. "That was many years ago, so perhaps he, too, was dead," Celie considered, "but then again, maybe not."

Celie would quietly come up to her grandmother with a book and ask her to read it to her. Eva would take a quick break from her focus on Adele and say nicely, "No, Celie, not today." Celie would say, "Tomorrow?" with her nicest little girl smile—similar to the one she perfected as an adult and now always wears at the shop. She did it again and again and often. It was a way of helping her small self release some of the tension she felt from living in that apartment. Knowing Eva's secret made her feel in control—however momentarily. This secret was Celie's bullet and she used it—however metaphorically. Celie believed this made her an evil child, so if she tells you that perhaps she did aid and abet in the killing of Adele, she means it should be taken seriously. She thinks, "I *can* carry a rage as big as the hump I most certainly will grow someday on my all-too-brittle spine—if I live long enough—and this makes me quite capable of hurting a man like Herr M—*of hurting Herr M, if necessary.*"

If the rumors as to what he has done to Cecilia are true (which she tries hard to believe are not) she feels she would have to lunge at him in some way and directly destroy him. Not like when she followed her grandmother around with her book with Eva saying, "No, Celie, not today," and Celie's too sweet response, "Tomorrow, Grandma Eva, tomorrow?" It was their circle in hell—albeit a shallow one. With Herr M, if the gossip proved to be true—that he had attacked Cecilia, Celie believes Herr M's and her circle would reach into the depths of hell. Of course, she keeps this all to herself, just listening to what the others are saying—trying to sift through all the stuff being flung at her—and also continuously observing Cecilia's increasingly jittery behavior and reading her poems for more mentions of Herr M.

Adele threw up a lot when she was little. Celie's mother told her this. Eva had bought a baby grand piano that sat front and center in the apartment's living room. It was the only piece of furniture not sealed in plastic, although Celie was forbidden to touch it. Eva had wanted Adele to be a great pianist. Adele tried—tried to be what her mother had dreamed for her. But she would vomit too much before each recital. So much so that the doctors said she would have to quit because she could die. According to Esther, her whole digestive tract would become inflamed. Between performances she would eat and eat and look like she might burst. No one in that 1930s neighborhood analyzed it much—just concluded the recitals would have to stop. After that, the piano stayed quiet. The lid on the keyboard slammed shut. No music.

Esther was to be a famous actress. She *was* written up in several newspapers and called a child prodigy. Starting when she was five, she gave recitations all over the city. At sixteen she auditioned at the Goodman Theatre for the part of Juliet. She got it. Except when the director asked her to meet him later at the Palmer House and she said, "Yes," adding, "I'll have to bring my mother." He replied, "Don't bother."

Soon after, Esther met Benjamin and never went on stage again. She was relieved. All those memorized lines in her small child's mind became a cage of gnarled rope that imprisoned her brain. She believed Benjamin Slaughter would help cut her free, but that was not to be and she grew into an all-too-silent woman.

Adele hated her sister—her suburban home, her three children who actually loved her. She thought Esther had it so easy—which she did not. But she did have it easier than Adele. Adele was left in the apartment of her mother with her screams—"You're so _____," "You'll never _____." And throughout her life, at least the part I witnessed, Adele was "so _____" and she "never _____."

Celie once heard Adele had stolen a bicycle. When Celie was seven, she told Cecilia and me, with such a flourish, "I hope it's true and that she rode it really fast before she got caught!" Both of us hoped so, too.

However, something Celie does know to be absolutely true is the memory, when she was four, five, six, seven, eight, and nine, of watching Adele get ready—ready for the Yom Kippur Night Dance. After our most solemn day—made up of fasting and silence and prayer for what bad people we had been in the past year, Celie would watch Adele put on thick makeup, pink rouge, and red lipstick. How she gussied herself up with flaming colors— silky dresses that clung to her. What a night of promise it was as Adele prepared to find her beau. Celie's grand- father, Levi, and her father would come out of the back room where they would sit and smoke and say how nice she looked. Even Eva was chatty.

Year after year Adele would leave and return late into the night—her purse probably already stuffed with things she would have to repent for next year. Celie thought about that a lot as she got older. She would wait for her key to open the lock of the apartment door, then she would fall asleep so happy because she knew the next day Adele would tell her stories about the *dance*—the music, the food, the clothes, and the best part, about the *beau* she had found. Adele always had one to talk and talk about. Then Celie would watch her wait by the telephone in the weeks after for him to reappear. Celie would grow sadder and sadder as she sat next to her.

On Mother's Day Celie always made sure to give Adele a present. Those were the days when she thought she could save her. She even thought she could save her grandmother, and, of course, her too quiet mother. She was always very busy with wrapping paper and ribbons trying to tie everything together into a big, bright, perfect bow. Now, Eva's gone, as is Esther—wrapped in some eternal package Celie cannot unknot no matter how much she thinks about ways to do it, all the time wondering if Adele's in there, too— and if her grandmother is still screaming at Adele.

As Adele grew older, it was easier to deal with her when she got depressed. I know it is terrible to say this—but it is true. Everyone in our extended family experienced this—never knowing which Adele would show up. She would become timid and sweet, weepy-sweet to be sure, but that was better than her open-blister rage or her all-knowing PhD, Nobel-Prize-winning arrogance when she was manic. In that state, she would go into stores and buy up everything as if she were an heiress. Eva was called frequently by the local owners, and when she eventually refused to deal with it and then passed away, all the burden went to Esther.

When Esther got so finally sick, Adele became one hundred percent manic—a horrible happy manic. Refused to take her pills, called every day to tell Esther of all her activities—how busy she was, all the places she had gone from morning to night. What fun she was having. Esther listened with good patience. Every day Celie would hear her mother on the phone positioned next to her bed saying, "Oh Adele, how wonderful!" Until one day, coming up the stairs to visit her completely bedridden, bald mother, she heard its crash into its cradle. Celie stood in the doorway and saw her mother smiling a huge smile.

Esther told Celie with such gusto—not at all like a sick person—"Your Aunt Adele just reported on her *busy, busy* day and after forty-five minutes of babbling, she finally asked what I'd been *doing*. I replied, 'Well, Adele, if you haven't noticed, I'm very busy, too. I'm very busy *dying.*'" It was then Esther bashed the phone into Adele's ear and smiled that stunning smile. When Celie remembers this, it still makes *her* smile. Esther never talked to Adele again. Refused her calls. Had a few weeks of peace from her sister before she left.

That time was also the beginning of Celie losing Adele, of not knowing or wanting to know where her mother's sister was. She visited her only once in the hospital after she had a surgery. Adele seemed overjoyed with her newfound illness. Her affect so impossibly off, it made Celie want to run back into the coat closet. Adele believed being sick would get her more attention. She wanted the love Celie and her brothers had for their mother. She demanded it. She said, "It was their duty." When she left the hospital, Celie just sent her flowers. Joshua and Jeremy distanced themselves further, as did Celie's father—just disappeared from her. She did not figure into any of the equations that made up their lives.

The next and last time Celie saw Adele she seemed physically fine, yet furious. She called from across the room, "Celia." Not "Celie," and from just this Celie knew trouble was heading toward her. She wanted to turn away, but Adele was quick—approached and kissed her. Then, she dug her long, red-painted nails into Celie's arm and thanked her for the flowers. Then, digging deeper, she screamed, "Was that the best you could do?" Before Celie could answer, she added, "Well it just isn't good enough, Celia. Celia, do you hear me?" Celie stared at her, then ripped her arm from Adele's grip and ran out of the house where they both were guests. She ran and ran until she threw up. Her heart was pounding outside her chest. She thought she was going to break. In fact she did.

Even with therapy and pills, sometimes when Celie closes her eyes and the room is completely dark—the TV off— Eva's screams roar through her head and she does not know if *she is* dead or alive. No man has ever asked to marry her and she is overweight. She just goes from the upscale dress shop, selling party clothes to the suburban women on the North Shore to her apartment to eat carryout and watch old movies. She particularly likes the silent ones.

However, she does know she is very good at her job. She can always find her customers the perfect outfit. When they say, "Celie, I need your help," she likes that. She knows a lot about their lives. She finds them outfits for their children's bar or bat mitzvahs, confirmations, graduations, weddings, and for the Opera Ball—all the charity benefits. Their festivities are endless. She likes to hear about each event—the food, the music, how they danced and danced through the night.

Yet sometimes, when a client accepts her offer of hot coffee or a cold drink while waiting for a fitting, Celie has the urge to throw the drink into her client's face. This impulse frightens her. It makes her feel she *could* do anything to anyone. She has worked on this in her therapy sessions and now realizes that this is similar to what Adele felt toward Esther.

Unlike Adele, however, Celie is a terrible dancer. Adele was really great. She would even show Celie steps and tell her she needed to relax. Celie thinks about her often—I guess this is obvious. And sometimes Celie dreams of both of them at the Yom Kippur Night Dance. They are twirling with their beaus, so bright and flushed they are with life—forever freed from all sin, all guilt, all of the past. The only rage they know of is in the flamboyant colors of their clothes.

THE SIN-EATER
OF THE FAMILY

Ointment rubbed over the skin—
3 drops Frankincense,
2 drops Peppermint,
1 drop Clove, 1 drop Pine—
could not bring on the exorcism.
All hands blunt clumsy.
Too much food had been eaten.
Egg and chop and leg of duck

were placed on the breast
of the dead one,
then passed to my lone figure
in the corner—*the sin-eater*
of the family *chewing, chewing*
so the beloved's soul could be free,
made light to have
an easy journey.

c. slaughter

IN THE YEAR BEFORE Great Aunt Eva died she cared less and
less to understand, fix, or tell anything to anyone about her
own troubles—and if she got angry she no longer yelled,
just suffered silently. She also did not care to hold anyone
close or captive. This is one way some people prepare for
their above-the-ground exit—quite the opposite of Uncle

Manny's fury to grab anyone near and try to take them with him into his wretchedness.

Eva believed she had been a kind, generous person and to people who did not get too near to her, there was no one finer. She gave Mario the handyman large tips—even though money was terribly short—and on his holiday, Christmas, a present and she still, "at her age," made a hot lunch for Odette and served it to her, when Odette came twice a month to help Eva clean her apartment and move the heavy furniture. And when the young, handsome, Catholic president was shot, how Eva grieved, and lit a *Yarzheit* candle for him on the first Yom Kippur after his death—the rabbi at the temple telling her this was a *mitzvah*. True, she had not voted for him, since she never realized her good intention to learn to read English and consequently never became a citizen of her "new country"—but she was dazzled by his Hollywood image, his star-like family, and was stunned for a long time by what had happened to him, similar to when her son-in-law Benjamin's sister, the "perfect Rose," as Eva called her in a sour way, had lost a daughter—meaning *me*.

Mostly alone, she took long walks on her avenue no matter what the weather. Always with her huge, worn, black leatherette purse and orange nylon net bag to carry a few groceries—an apple, a pear, whatever—both hooked on to her left arm. The net bag matched the color of her hair. Once she was a true redhead.

Often her daughter Esther came down from the suburbs to walk with her. Celie sometimes came too, but then Celie began to visit less and less and that was okay with Eva. So different from years past, when she would clutch Celie so tightly, Celie thought she might break.

In truth, it sort of made Celie sick to be with her grandmother, because she felt her grandmother was walking with Death and Celie is petrified of Death—goes to a psychiatrist because of this and other terrors. He gives her pills that open her up to the day and others that close her down at night. The pills help too with the rituals—obsessions, compulsions are what the doctor calls them—the repetitive checkings and numbered spinnings that she does for safekeeping before she leaves her apartment. She has tailor-made them for herself to keep Death away.

Celie remembered when her grandmother, at seventy-five, whispered to her, while riding past a cemetery, that she no longer feared Death. That she was *tired—just so tired.* In her earlier years Eva feared it with such ferociousness that she would squeeze Celie so hard with her large hands that they would leave red marks on Celie's body—sometimes a discoloration that could last for a couple of weeks. From the age of one onward, Eva made Celie stand next to her at the living room window and, whenever anyone was more than five minutes late, Eva would start to shake and hold on to Celie muttering, "Celie, your father (mother—whoever it was) is late, yes, late—*too late.*" Then, Eva would slip into Yiddish and chant the word. *Niftorim. Niftorim.* Way before Celie was three, she clearly understood that meant *dead person.*

Eva did not mean to scare her granddaughter; she just needed to share her anxiety and it was the small Celie who was the most available. Anyone would have done as well—her daughters Esther or Adele, her husband Levi, or her son-in-law, the most unavailable of all. Benjamin left Esther and Celie, and some years later Joshua and Jeremy, in that tiny apartment a lot. He was busy working in the shipping department of a downtown department store during the day and going to school at night, studying to become a CPA and then a lawyer. He was saving his money so that someday "they"—meaning his own family—could move away, out of that crowded apartment to the suburb where we lived and where his other brothers had already migrated—something that caused him no small irritation.

Benjamin was determined to follow my mother's and his brothers' paths as soon as he had saved enough. Then, he and Esther and their children would escape. Not just because of how physically closed in it was in the apartment, but because of the crowd of words that crashed into each other every night—the fights, which he could not tolerate.

Esther's begging him to just move to another apartment was not enough, nor was how she eventually developed patches of eczema on her arms and legs from the stress of that place. He needed to be in *that* suburb, in a house, and he wanted a better house than what his brothers had settled for, something resembling his sister's, even if it were in miniature. It took twelve years for that to happen and it was then, in the weeks before the move, that Eva completely lost control—alternating between screams of betrayal and tears of grief that her beloved Esther was leaving, leaving her. Moving away—twenty miles *dead* north of her. How would *she* survive? Celie wasn't sure if her grandmother meant herself, her mother—or maybe even Celie. Then, in the final week before the move Eva went mute—spoke absolutely no words. *Niftorim*.

On the last day, in mid-February—as bleak and cold and dead a day as she could remember—Celie cried uncontrollably, not wanting to leave the apartment, not wanting her own room. She needed the familiarity of the cot laid out each night in the dining room, which her father carried her to when the grown-ups were done with their after-dinner fights. In the earlier evening she would sleep in Adele's bed in the back room. Under Adele's scratchy sheets, permeated by a strange fish smell and human sweat, Celie would curl herself into as tight a fetal ball as she could and pretend she was Cinderella waiting for the prince. No matter how distasteful, she was used to this. To this day Celie fears change, even if it is for the better.

Mostly the adults fought over Adele—what to do with her, her rebellious ways. She often came home late at night, or sometimes not at all. The fights were about putting her in the hospital. They would lower their voices when they said *hospital*, but Celie could still hear them. It was a secret place that eventually she figured out was for people sick in the mind, not the body. "A place like where Grandmother Idyth was," she would think, "maybe the *same* place."

If Adele happened to come in, they still fought about her. *The problem. The failure.* Eva wanted to put her away and Esther and Levi wanted to give her another chance—even after the police brought her home one night, showed them the pin and the ring that they found on her that were reported stolen by the neighborhood jeweler. Benjamin avoided all discussions about Adele, just as he refused to discuss his mother, Idyth, with any of them.

When Celie would hear the loud adult talk, she would twist further into her small self and in a strange way be glad—glad none of this shouting was about her. But there

was a sadness, too, for sometimes she really liked Adele—
the freedoms she gave herself. She especially liked her on
the Saturdays when Adele would sneak home a paper bag
with two non-kosher hot dogs, one for herself and one
for Celie, and they would escape down the paint-chipped,
creaky, wooden back stairs of the apartment, sit in the outside air on the first floor landing and eat the "forbidden
fruit," as Adele called it. Celie loved this.

Later in life, when Celie saw the title of one of
Cecilia's poems, "The Sin-Eater of the Family"—although
Celie was pretty sure Cecilia did not have Adele in mind
when she wrote it, more her own self—Celie thought of
Adele in that old apartment, forced to wear a jagged,
tilted, tarnished crown—all the precious jewels fallen
out of it, leaving just rusted, empty holes. I also know
Celie, Cecily, and even Celine—had she chosen to focus
on it, which she did not—would think the title more than
applied to themselves. Here beneath the ground, I, too,
identified with it, which surprised me for I thought I had
worked far past the victim concept.

Overweight, out of control, unable to keep a job, unen-
gaged with no man in sight, Adele grew into her mother's
worst nightmare. Adele was not filled with beautiful music,
only mood swings—out-of-sync, out-of-pitch, high-to-low,
low-to-high—never to become the concert pianist Eva had
dreamed for this daughter. The baby grand piano in the living room was never to be touched again, after "Adele failed
it"—that is how Eva phrased it. "It" became the monument—the Monument to Failure.

Once, Celie bolted from her chair in the kitchen during dinner and ran into the living room, lifted the highly-
polished, wooden cover over the keys and banged on them

wildly. She was five. It was a loud, manic moment, similar
to one when she was seven and she leapt from the dining
room table when Aunt Bertha, Eva's cousin, came for her
monthly Saturday night dinner, her crutches always positioned in the same place against the doorway that led to the
coat closet. Celie fixated on them when Bertha was there—
could hardly look elsewhere. Polio had crippled Bertha's
legs, but with braces and the crutches she could get around
if adults were always on either side of her. Celie thought it
a sad parade, but it did not stop her from focusing on how
much she wanted to swing from them. She imagined herself an acrobat, flying away from the table—the room, the
people. On the day it became too much to restrain herself,
she caused an even larger chaos than the piano incident—
almost equal to any of Adele's. And it was not fun. Their
curved tops, even with their heavy padding, dug into her
armpits and caused a sharp pain. As for flying—she fell.

After Eva realized Adele would never be a joy, a pride, she
focused her complete attention on her younger daughter
and for a while Celie's mother made Eva quite proud. But
when she met Benjamin—"wild, tanned, handsome Ben,"
as Esther rhapsodized to anyone who would listen—Ben,
who told her stories about how he and his brothers would
run naked through the woods in Michigan, howling like
wolves, Esther imagined such a freedom. She thought
Ben, with his movie star looks, would be her savior, would
free her from the stage, from her mother, from her trapped
life—the too many words, the too many directions to be
remembered, to be memorized. So when he proposed, she
said a quick, ecstatic, "Yes!"

When Esther would speak of him this way and her
cheeks would flame with life, all Eva felt was her own

world shifting again and growing cold—almost to frozen. With Eva's awful memories of her first neighbor, Idyth Slaughter, still very much alive, she could not help but believe a dybbuk inhabited *that family* and one day it would again spring to life and cause great damage to someone— anyone—named Slaughter. So when her treasured Esther fell in love with one of Idyth's sons, this became an addition to Eva's list of nightmares.

However, when Ben showed up the first time for dinner, dressed in a white linen suit and straw hat, and handed Eva—not Esther—violets, it was the beginning of Ben winning—winning over Eva—especially after he talked so politely with Eva and Levi about all his plans for the future—all his great ambitions. And a few months later, when Eva tested the water by suggesting perhaps they live with them after the marriage—that it would cost them "almost nothing"—and Ben, without even looking at Esther, eagerly agreed (thinking about all the money he could save and knowing this was even a better deal than what his brothers Emmanuel and Abraham had made with my father—Samuel eventually moving into their building once he married Lettie) Eva was even more reassured, thinking, "Even though he is a Slaughter, I'll be able to keep an eye on him and make this work."

She and Levi threw them the *best* wedding—one they really could not afford—and, regularly and often, she would pull out the pictures from the top drawer of her bureau, spread them carefully across the oilcloth on the kitchen table like a deck of cards and make everyone sit down, so she could talk about how it all was "so perfect."

Celie often wondered where that other Benjamin went. The Ben who ran naked through the summer nights, making wild and wonderful animal sounds—the one her mother had told her about, described to her with such delight. To Celie, because her grandmother approved of her father so much, he must have died. And she missed him, although she never knew him. *Niftorim.*

When he finally took his family twenty miles away, something died in Eva—again. And in Celie, too. She did not like the suburbs. They were filled with preadolescent girls who looked like the carefully manicured shrubs that lined the streets. Plus, they talked so much about their clothes. About their *cashmeres.* Celie had never heard the word cashmere before the move. When they asked her almost in unison, "How many do *you* own?" she did not know what to say and ran home to ask her mother. Esther laughed and answered, "None. Your sweaters are made of Orlon," which Celie felt she should keep to herself.

Now, Celie is legendary. She knows her fabrics better than the ultrathin women who wrap themselves in them and give no care to what anything costs. However, while covering the living with the expensive silks and satins and sequins that make their lives a'glitter, she spends her time waiting for Death, shrouding this fear with too much food, a fixed smile, and a too-jolly laugh. It is only in her dark eyes that her panic is etched, but her clients are too busy—busy looking at themselves in the gilded triple mirrors—to give it much, if any, notice. For this Celie is grateful.

Someday she hopes to open her own shop, not for clothes, but for linens. Linens with the highest thread count—the softest, finest bedding one can dream on. This is her one, perfect fantasy. This is her one great wish.

Eva did not understand how her granddaughter could settle on just selling clothes. It made her sad and uncomfortable. Actually, embarrassed. Benjamin's brother, Samuel, had a daughter who was a published poet. To her this was *so much* better. But she loved her granddaughter and on the surface accepted Celie's choice. Told her friends, "Celie is the best saleswoman in the Midwest—actually famous."

Eva had left her family at fourteen. Left them in Russia—five thousand miles away. She waved good-bye for the promise—the promise of the promised land. Her family had chosen her to be their messenger, their memory, their legacy. She carried that luggage with her always— their troubled waves goodbye and her own escape from the pogroms and the looming threat of the camps. And with this grew the need to be ambitious for her children—have a daughter who would be a great pianist or a celebrated actress and maybe someday even a granddaughter who would become a famous poet. Like Anna Akhmatova or Marina Tsvetayeva—well, maybe not exactly like Tsvetayeva, who she later learned had in the end hanged herself. "But, still, how wonderful," she thought, "it would be to bring such an inheritance across the ocean and be able to report on these accomplishments to my family back in Europe."

She would sit next to Esther by the radio, and listen to the news about the war—about the men named Roosevelt, Churchill, Stalin, Hitler—while Esther wrote letter after letter to the American Red Cross asking for their help. "Could they find her mother's family—her parents, her brothers, her sister?" Finally, in 1950 the answer arrived. A stamp over their names, DISAPPEARED. *Niftorim.*

So six years later, when Eva took the small Celie's hand and they stood at the living room window—the sounds from the baby grand piano long silenced, a heavily fringed, thick black wool shawl smothering the top of it—she needed, even more, everyone close by, on one street, in one place and never late. And it all became *Niftorim.*

Same as when Esther disappeared into the suburbs, even though she and Levi visited there every weekend. Benjamin would drive down to the city, pick them up and bring them back. Two hours in the car on Sundays. And when Levi was gone, he came just for Eva, although on the ride to take her back into the city he would bribe either Joshua or Jeremy to come along and sit in the front seat. Alone in the back, the only noise coming from Eva was that of an old woman checking and rechecking for her apartment keys in her huge, worn, leatherette purse.

As she walked her avenue, sometimes three times a day, snow or wind or rain never stopping her, she watched Manzelman the grocer, Satvitsky the butcher, and Ruben the tailor slowly disappear, and other stores rise up with owners whose names she could not pronounce, nor did she try.

And when Esther started to wear scarves—the most beautiful Celie could find to cover her mother's baldness, a side effect from the treatments—Eva never asked "Why?" Nor did she ever speak of Adele when she and Esther walked together.

Though one day, over the phone, she did talk of Adele to Esther. Said she saw her coming toward her—"a ghost in the night" was how she put it. But, before Adele saw her, Eva said, "I crossed over. Over to the other side."

She told that to Esther and then they were cut off— it sounded as if the receiver just dropped into its cradle. Eva took a too-difficult breath, pushed a chair as close as she could to the window that overlooked the avenue. Sat down and stared.

Esther called and called her mother back, but she did not answer. With Ben elsewhere and herself too weak to drive, Esther called Celie, begged her to *please* run down there, which she quickly agreed to do.

It was when Esther hung up the phone that she felt a deep pang of upset about her daughter and wished Celie would be more aggressive—more assertive in life—instead of always absorbing the pain of everyone else, never lashing out—so like Esther herself.

Unbeknownst to Esther, through the years Celie picked up on her mother's seething and the few times it burst open. One instance being Esther's thrilling smile when she so finally crashed the phone into her sister's ear. Another, when pregnant again, she hollered full strength at Benjamin, "If this child is a boy he will *not* be named after Cecil Slaughter! No son of mine will *ever* be named after him. *Enough!* If it's a boy he will be named after my dear Lettie's deceased father, Joseph. *I've had enough of all this! Do you hear me?*"

Frightened by the force of her wrath—the insanity he heard in her voice, reminding him, however momentarily, of the piercing screams which emanated from his mother Idyth—he acquiesced, thereby appalling my mother and father and for which he begged and begged huge forgiveness. Which, ultimately and nobly, they gave him.

Celie carried those sharp moments of her mother's ire

into her future, believing someday it would come quickly to her as to how to use her own ever-burgeoning anger.

Celie found her grandmother in the chair next to the window. She stood next to her. They were in position.

Niftorim.

CONFESSION

Admission

In the cabinet with the lattice
opening, I confess to all
the calls and hang ups—obsessions
with the glands and muscles
of the hair: follicle, papilla, blood vessel—
the soft bulb at root's bottom that I love
to pull out and suck. I knew
Krishna, Lucifer, and Zeus,
phoned them late at night
but would not speak.
When we'd meet at all the seedy strips
of airport motels, my heart
would swell and beat my body
wild until I'd heat into high
fever I thought would last forever.
I stalked their wives and lovers, had license
numbers, kept records of their busy
tones—who was talking
to whom. Adonai in the temple
said a silent prayer over
my bald spot and wept.

Interrogation

Do you swear to tell the whole truth . . . ?
No Sir, the truth hemorrhages in my pen,
but lies clotted on my tongue.

Do you want a lawyer?
No Sir, I like the unprotected exposure.

Are you a Confessional Poet?
No Sir, they all committed suicide
in the 60s and 70s.

How many lovers?
Once I thought there was one, Sir,
but in fact I have to answer "none."

Any rapes?
Including you, Sir, four—
no five, I forgot Herr M—
but no one got firmly in.
The last served me
a quarter of a chicken
and while I was delicately
trying to separate the meat
from the bone, yanked me
from my chair to his futon
on the soiled, hardwood floor.
His child had napped there
earlier. I could smell
the urine. I know it's sick
to say it, but his
desire made me feel young.

Have you considered plastic surgery?
Yes Sir, but just in places no one can see.
I keep looking for the soul—that pure egg
inside the body. How I long to hatch it.
I'd let my doctor-lover keep sucking

out the fat and grow so light—
translucent in the sun—
I'd find the perfect shape,
intercept it with my pen-
knife. Then, I'd sit on it like a hen.

Did you make all those calls?
Yes Sir, but just in June
when the hot pink peonies exploded
inside my head—thromboses of love.
My blood gushed like a bride's
bouquet, then dried and left me empty.

Do you really have a bald spot?
O Yes Sir, a perfect circle
of "Yesses." I look at it with awe.
It is my flawless flaw.

ARE YOU A CONFESSIONAL POET?
NO SIR, I ALREADY SAID THEY ARE ALL DEAD.

When do you die?
Sir, every morning when the world wakes
new I go to sleep naked and wrapped
in a simple white sheet.
Unembalmed as an Orthodox Jew,
I watch my body disintegrate.

Punishment

All agreed to leave her
disconnected—cut any pulse
of light that might travel

from her. Jailed, without
a mouthpiece—diaphragm
and carbon chamber—
it was believed
she could not call, never answer.

Truth

I love this claustrophobic box,
the formality of its walls,
the hidden arrangement,
the simple judgment chair.
I do not need another's ear,
just a pen and some paper.

c. slaughter

CECILIA GAVE CELIE the message to tell Deidre that if
she would like, she would be happy to read either a long
poem or several short ones. Her thinking was that by
spending a little time with Deidre in person, responding
to a poem or two of hers, Deidre would leave her and
Celie alone—or at least give them a respite. Celie did
not agree at all, saying, "It won't work, Cecilia. You don't
realize how overdetermined she is. This will only create a
further desire in her to get closer to you."

Cecilia told her that she had seen how easily pleased
the people were by her comments in the workshops she
occasionally taught and that no one bothered her for more
after that. Celie's voice deepened and dropped as she said,
"Okay. I'll do it, but it's a bad idea both for her and for
you." Her warning was prophetic.

In truth, Celie was sick of being the messenger, the middleman, stuck between other people's craziness. So when she hung up the phone she thought she might start screaming so much she would never be able to stop. But she calmed herself with extra pills and the thought, "I'm doing this for Cecilia. I'd *only* do such a thing for Cecilia." And this made her feel better.

Within two days, Celie called Cecilia and said, "I've got it. Deidre just left the shop, but not before handing me an envelope addressed to you." Celie then added, "She bought a beautiful black cashmere sweater set. The cardigan has large crystals for buttons which change every which way the light hits them, inside a dimly lit room or outside under the sun or moon, and she was particularly attracted to this, declaring, 'Oh Celie, they are like my moods!'"

Celie, startled by this admission, said to Cecilia, "I just stood there with my best shop-girl grin as she continued to jabber. 'Of course, I can never take off the cardigan—my upper arms are too unshaped. That's what Harrold said to me two weeks ago in bed. Not that I didn't already *know* this. *What woman doesn't*, when this is the case?'"

Celie continued, "She then laughed a chaotic laugh, almost a cackle, and confirmed to me what she had told Celine about the state of her sex life, saying, 'Oh, well, he *is* a clumsy man. We never touch in our parallel lives. The way we lie in bed together has become the essence of our marriage. Someday we'll lie forever like this—parallel and separate—in our caskets.'"

Celie and Cecilia did agree that Deidre seemed to have a borderline personality disorder and the last thing either of them needed at this point in their lives was someone so clearly uninhibited and peculiarly subversive. Celie then told Cecilia, again, that she felt her approach was all wrong. That she had had much more contact with Deidre than Cecilia and that Deidre was becoming unrelenting in her pursuit of her. She then reported, "I meticulously took her envelope, went to my desk, opened the locked drawer where I keep my purse and placed the envelope inside the drawer as she carefully watched. After I did this, she kissed me on the cheek and said, 'I'm off! I'm off!'"

"Clearly, Cecilia, she really *is* off," trying to emphasize further that her plan was a big mistake. Ignoring her warnings, Cecilia responded, "I'll get the envelope later today and do something about this in as simple a way as possible—maybe all that's needed is a new approach. Everyone needs a little focus, a little attention." However, when Cecilia hung up the phone she thought, "Am I capable of even solving anything in a simple way? Perhaps I just complicate every awfulness. Maybe Celie is right. My judgment of late has been as *off* as anything Deidre has ever done or said. Actually, more so."

After Cecilia picked up the envelope, she opened it and found a long poem. Celie asked her to read it out loud and Cecilia replied, "Are you sure? It's pretty bad. Do you need a long, bad poem in your head?" Celie laughed and said, "I already have that—my life—so thank you and no." This quick, decisive assertion made Celie feel good and she thought, "I'll have to remember to tell this to my therapist."

Cecilia told Celie, "Wait a week and then call Deidre. Give her my phone number. Celine and I will take her to lunch."

"Celine?" Celie said quite startled, "Why Celine?"

"Because she can keep the most inane conversations going and drive everything off topic, thereby making for a brief discussion on poetry. I thought you'd be pleased that I'll have protection." She said this facetiously and they both smiled. Cecilia then continued, "I know, I know, I'll have to buy Celine something big for this favor—a gift certificate from the shop. It's worth it."

At home in her room, Cecilia reread Deidre's poem "Confession." It had the same title as one of hers that had recently been published. In some way she found this less stalky-frightening than sad. She imagined this nutty, anxious woman waiting by the phone for a week, for some reply—all hope in her heart that something good was about to happen in her writing life. Every writer she knew had been there. But Cecilia also knew she could not really help this Deidre person, especially after reading the poem. Now, she just prayed Deidre would be appeased enough by the lunch and that her intrusions on Celie, herself, and even Celine would stall and then stop—that maybe she could take control of at least one small thing.

She could not be Deidre's lifeline to any particular heaven, but she could try to be nice. These past months she had felt her own lifeline was leading her toward a particular hell where Herr M was always present or, at best, an oblivion fraught with an unending, generalized agitation. However, she pushed these thoughts into a deep fold in her brain and continued on with her plan, which she convinced herself would work. That doing this would help give her some time to straighten out her own life without being distracted by Deidre's antics, and it also would give Celie some relief.

Exactly a week after Deidre dropped off the poem, Celie called her. Deidre picked up the phone immediately. Celie reported to Cecilia, "I told her I'd gotten in some long skirts for the fall—chiffon—with hand-painted flowers at the bottom and I immediately thought of her. I said she would love them and asked if I should hold a few."

Celie continued that Deidre seemed surprised by the talk of skirts, but, after a breath and a pause, replied, "Great. I'll be in tomorrow."

"I could hear her voice tumble down on the *tomorrow*. I felt guilty about prefacing the call about the poem with trying to sell her some skirts, but, then again, she has taken up so much of my time. However, it did make me feel badly."

"Yes," Cecilia said, "but don't worry about trying to sell her something. She's trying to sell something, too—herself." Cecilia then sighed, "Maybe that's what we all do."

Celie added, "It was only then I said, 'Oh, by the way, Cecilia has read your poem. She would like to talk with you about it. She wants to make a date.' I gave her your number. When I did this, I felt somewhat better."

Cecilia just replied, "Thanks, Celie, I owe you."

"Owe me?" she answered. "After everything you've done for me? Never, Cecilia. Never."

It is true Cecilia has done important things for Celie, but they were easy to do because she loves her and beyond this, all of the Slaughter cousins are bound together, be they in positive or negative ways. We are cut from the same cloth, our dyes a bit different—the patterns of our lives unique shapes—but we are part of the same design, the same picture, the same story and therefore—in life or in death—remain very much connected. We inhabit the same frame.

Sadly, sometimes the threads that make up who we are do snarl and snap and no crochet hook or sewing needle can repair the tear to make it appear even superficially right. However, with the murder of Herr M came the complete unraveling of some lives—a permanent, unfixable, rip in the canvas of who we were.

Cecilia thought of Deidre and what she probably was experiencing now—the natural high that comes when someone you believe to be of consequence is actually interested in your work. Again, she hoped Deidre would be satisfied with just the lunch and a few comments, but she was beginning to have real doubts. Also, she worried about herself—if she had enough composure left in her to carry this to a satisfactory conclusion.

Celine had already agreed to accompany her, the gift certificate the perfect payment. Cecilia told her, "As soon as Deidre calls we'll set a date. I'll let you know."

Buoyantly, Celine replied, "I'm ready! I've informed my boys that I'll be away for part of a day sometime soon on an important mission." She then quoted Yeats, "Only that which does not explain itself is irresistible."

Cecilia, perpetually shocked by Celine's knowledge and how she covers it up with cloaks upon cloaks of ditziness, on hearing this, thought, "Maybe she *is* the smartest of all of us. However loose the boundaries of her life, she does seem to keep everyone in their place, which is something I'll never achieve—forever unable to erase, correct, or learn from all that's happened in mine. Or maybe it's that she learned all too well the art of manipulation and deviousness from her father?" She carefully contemplated this. But thinking about Manny Slaughter began to make her sick as she vividly recalled all the far-reaching soul damage he had caused.

Celie told Cecilia, "She showed up at the shop and bought two skirts. When I asked if she'd called you, with a false casualness she replied, 'No, not yet.'" Celie excitedly added, "It's the first time she didn't try, even subtlety, to interrogate me about you, about the family. So I didn't have to shut down on her. Maybe this plan *will* really work. She seems so filled with hope."

"The thing with feathers," Cecilia replied, her voice cracking and sounding like it was falling down a well. And, however many pills she had taken to get through the day, the still quick-minded Celie answered, "Emily Dickinson." Then they laughed, both remembering the joke—between the three of us—that if you were born a Slaughter, hope was pretty much killed off. Cecilia adding, "Oh, Celie, how both of us and 'our now forever lost Ceci,' would laugh about hope being something of an oxy-*moron* in this family."

Later that afternoon when the phone rings and Cecilia sees from her caller ID it says "unavailable," she worries that it could be Herr M trying to get at her in *some* way— again. But his calls have never come up like this—usually "anonymous" or his actual number, so she picks it up. It is Deidre—she must have gone through information. Cecilia's guessing she knows all the phone tricks. Probably if she had not answered, Deidre would have hung up and she would never have known she called, thereby giving Deidre another chance at anonymity.

Cecilia's pleasant; she speaks softly but in an upbeat way and tells Deidre she has read the poem and looks forward to discussing it with her and, "No," she does not mind at all that Deidre's written a poem with the same title as one of her recently published ones. "It happens," she replies with nonchalance, continuing, "Anyway, they are *quite* different." Then surprising herself she continues, "I like the poem's complexity, the risks it takes, the isolation of the narrator, how it ends." She compares it to one of Tennyson's, all the while appalled by the words that are falling out of her mouth and she worries that she has completely lost control of her intentions, her language, her honesty. And she does not at the moment understand the *why* of this.

Then, getting some small command of herself, she says, "Let's meet next week at the Arts Club. My treat. Next Tuesday at 1:00 P.M. Does that work for you?" Deidre speaks carefully in a way that intends poise but just comes off as mannered nervousness, and answers, "Next Tuesday at 1:00 P.M. is perfect. Thank you so much." Actually, she sounds medicated, a bit robotic. They hang up.

Cecilia imagines Deidre's joy at all of this and the beginnings of her plans of what she will wear. She had been there—laying an outfit on her bed to study and then rejecting it, and the day before the big event, getting her hair done and a professional manicure at some upscale beauty shop—the choosing of a color for her nails becoming a too-large issue. She remembers once landing on Soft Shell Pink and how the next day she met her first publisher. For years she never deviated from that color.

Her fingertips were dipped in that shade of tender innocence the night of Herr M's attack. Now, she just paints them herself with the non-color "clear" as if that will help give her life more clarity—all of this she knows far beyond silly, somersaulting down into a pit of stupidity. "These days," she thinks, "I have no need to shrivel from Herr M's reproaches of me—I do this very well to myself."

On the day of Cecilia's truly lucky lunch to meet the person who would publish her first book, she took too many tranquilizers and Mylanta Extra-Strength tablets. Her insides were in total distress. She popped them into her mouth the way she now pops Life Savers when she gets too nervous, as if they can really save her life.

She arrived at the Arts Club far too early, getting sick twice in its large, beautiful, well-appointed bathroom filled with tissues of all kinds and sweetly scented sachets that kept the air smelling like a garden, clean of all bad odors.

She then sat down on the deep-green, velvet settee framed by a rich, dark—almost black—wood, trying to collect herself, and attempted to focus on the wallpaper which looked like silk, with thick stripes in various hues of green, eventually moving to the green velvet bench in front of the dressing table with a satin ecru skirt on it.

The large square mirror that hung above it, bordered in the same dark wood, allowed her to look at herself and realize she had worn too much makeup—that she was wearing the "clown look"—too much blusher to try to make her blanched skin look healthier. All her blood seemed to be draining out of her body as she grew cold, then colder, as a panic was about to overtake her.

Because her meeting also had been at 1:00 P.M., at 12:59 she climbed the austere staircase that had been designed by the architect Mies van der Rohe and brought over from the club's old building to this new space. She had a compulsive need to be precise. Still does.

As she did this, she thought about all the artists and the

wannabes who had climbed these stairs and she wondered how many of them had reached their destination—and how hard her own heart hurt for something *good* to happen. *Which it did,* that day.

Today, as she climbs these stairs, she thinks of the mess—the awful mess—that her life has become and the irony of it. "That some woman seems to be living only to spend time with me—to *be* me." Also, she feels a rage expanding inside her toward Deidre, as she tells herself, "I need to get this unwelcomed woman out of my life. There have been *enough intruders.* Maybe Celie was right. This *was* a bad idea."

Cecilia and Celine meet early, according to plan, so that they will be seated when Deidre appears. Celine has really outdone herself in terms of what she is wearing—she is impossible to miss in a tight, shocking pink sweater with large, red beads attached to it. Actually, she looks like a whore; an old whore; an old, high-priced whore. Especially when she carefully places her state-of-the-art cell phone next to her as if it were another piece of silverware.

When Cecilia sees the maitre d' escorting Deidre into the dining room, she also sees that Deidre's face is ashen with large spots of color standing out on her cheeks and thinks, "She is wearing the clown look." It is now clear Deidre has seen both Cecilia *and Celine* and she looks as if she has become dizzy, because she is holding on to the backs of some of the chairs at other tables as she approaches. Both Cecilia and Celine greet her with large smiles. Neither stands up, but they both hold out their hands for her to shake, which she does. Deidre's is wet and thick and all Cecilia wants to do is wash her hand of Deidre's sweat.

She pulls out a Wash'n Dri from her left pants pocket

and opens it beneath her napkin and wipes her palm. She does not think Deidre has noticed this and wonders why she even cares if she has. Maybe it is because of all the talk that has been swirling about her, Deidre being a substantial participant in this. These days it seems she does not know how to get clean of anything and *now* she is becoming even more locked into her anger toward Deidre—which she is realizing is in large part a displacement over what she is feeling toward Herr M.

Celine, however, is doing an outstanding job of distracting Deidre, as she sits there like a boil—a body about to burst—too forced into her clothes. With her cosmetically thickened lips, she gushes to Cecilia that she and Deidre are "old friends." "We've been to lunch—such fun!" she goes on. Celine clearly is earning her gift certificate.

Deidre carefully places herself in the empty chair next to Cecilia. She looks bewildered and definitely off balance and Cecilia is getting a little worried that she might faint, so she quickly says, "I told Celine I was having lunch with you, and she really wanted to come, too." But it is clear Deidre is beginning to feel this is a setup, for a hardness is starting to form at the corners of her mouth.

Cecilia wants to be nice to her, to give her something she can take away from this encounter that is positive so she will be satisfied for at least a while, but she is beginning to feel stuck, almost frozen, and her ability to talk is shrinking to mute.

Celine, true to form, is now showing them her new gold bracelet. "From Morris," she says with a wink to Cecilia, which even *I* feel is a little much, while Cecilia pretends to enjoy our cousin's jester-antics. Deidre says, "Your husband has terrific taste," which is met with a pause from both of them. Celine, even more aglow and pleased with herself, replies, "Well, actually Morris—" when Cecilia interrupts with, "Perhaps we should look at the menu. It's getting late." With this Cecilia sees a fury begin to swell Deidre's face. When it is her turn to order Deidre stammers out, "The salmon."

Cecilia thinks of the salmon forever swimming upstream to spawn and die and then being delivered to Deidre's plate and feels a triple misery—for herself, the salmon, and Deidre—which she knows Deidre would never believe. However, she also wants to scream at her, "Whatever gossip you've heard about me and repeated, you've idealized my life to the point, it seems, of *wanting* my life, which, if you believe *anything* of what you've heard, makes you *truly crazy.*"

Celine is now telling them about the rings and necklace she is wearing. She really *does* talk too much about herself and it is even getting on *my* nerves, no matter that I have been physically removed from Celine's presence for some amount of time and thought I had built up a far larger reserve of patience. The way she keeps her eye on her cell phone, checking and rechecking if it lights up is completely annoying. "The club's rule is you have to turn the ringer off," she chortles to them.

Then, suddenly, Celine asks Cecilia about Michael and Deidre's posture quickly straightens. "This *wasn't* in the script," Cecilia, rather startled, thinks, and wonders if Cecily put Celine up to this, but she stays as composed as she can, given all she is feeling, and replies in the fewest words that make any sense, "He came over last night. We watched the movie *Madame X.* We both agreed it was Lana Turner at her finest."

"It's so nice that the two of you can still be friends," Deidre says with a hint of sarcasm. Cecilia answers wistfully, "Yes, very nice." She can see from Deidre's eyes that Deidre has begun to hate her.

With dessert being served—a rainbow of tiny scoops of sorbet—and any pot of gold Deidre had hoped for from this day about to disappear, she jumps in and asks about her poem: the one Cecilia so enthusiastically had spoken about to her over the phone, the one Deidre so obviously was trying *not* to bring up, but has now found impossible not to, the one that had *supposedly* led to this lunch. *At this moment I feel heartsick for both of them.* And inside Cecilia's head—her clogged mind—she starts to retrace *why* she thought she could do this. *Why* she thought she could pull this off, given all that has happened. She thinks about her mother and how much she wants to talk to her—*right now*—and how she cannot, given that she is deep in a hole beneath the ground. Then the image of her taking a shovel filled with dirt and dropping it onto her mother's casket in that hole at the rabbi's request flashes across her mind. How she *obeyed* him, even though she absolutely did not want to do it. She now adds this to her mushrooming list of disgusts with herself.

Suddenly, Celine bursts in, "A poem? *You* write poems? Oh, yes, *now* I remember. Well, so do *I!*" Shaken out of her morbidity and completely surprised, Cecilia wonders if Celie had rehearsed this with her, because it is all so perfectly absurd. Then Celine's cell phone lights up and looking at the number she says, "Sorry girls, I *have* to take this. I'll be in the lobby."

Cecilia turns to Deidre and says, "Yes, the poem. I liked it." She then stops. She is unable to take this any further, thinking, "I have nothing to give. I just want you to *go away.*" Deidre's face is now so red, she puts both hands on her cheeks to cover her flush. It is clear she wants to kill Cecilia, or at least hurt her badly. Cecilia feels this and thinks, "And why not?" As they stare at each other, Cecilia feels they are two women about to break apart right in front of each other and she internally rages, "You could never understand what's going on with me, so blinded you are by your lust for success, with me your crumbling goddess of it sitting right next to you!"

Then Deidre, in her own despair, fury, and turmoil, starts praising Cecilia. With this, Cecilia knows that inside, Deidre is becoming appalling to herself. She speaks too fast and uses too much hyperbole, going over the top with too many empty adjectives. Her speed-dial talk will not quit—like how Cecilia was with Deidre over the phone about her poem. In their individual, almost out-of-control desperateness, Cecilia thinks, "How ridiculously similar we are."

By this time Celine returns, beaming, and says, "Cecilia, let's finish up. I've got to go." They get up and Deidre thanks Cecilia for the lovely time—neither of them extends her hand. Cecilia resists the feeling to do so. She does feel the impulse to say something to ease Deidre's pain, but she also feels completely depleted and immobile. Deidre then tells Celine how nice it was to see her again. Cecilia and Celine take the elevator. Deidre chooses the stairs.

Celine flees the building, while Cecilia goes into the Arts Club bathroom. In a stall, she hears a woman enter and go into the adjacent one. It is Deidre. She is weeping, while repeating, "Clubbed by the arts. Clubbed by the arts . . ."

This makes Cecilia think again of what Herr M did to her, and then of her Aunt Rose and how my mother's actions and words clubbed *her,* and that for Deidre *she,* Cecilia, has become Rose. It is then she starts weeping as silently as possible, not just for herself, but for Deidre, too.

Being completely overtaken by her upset, Deidre does not hear anyone in the next stall. However, when a couple of minutes later two women walk in, effervescently praising how well the other looks, she quiets, wipes her eyes with her fingers—smearing her mascara further. She then grabs her lipstick from her purse and, with her hand shaking, attempts to reapply it. Not caring that this probably makes her look even more disheveled, she opens the stall door, turns her face away from the women, and runs from their over-animated chatter.

Cecilia by then has pressed herself into a corner between the inside of the door and a wall and stands there immobile for several minutes—well after the women have left. What makes her finally move out of the stall is a female voice calling her name—a waitress from the club. She had forgotten to sign for the lunch. As she writes her name, she thinks about how much the afternoon has truly cost.

NIJINSKY'S DOG

Nijinsky danced his last dance, "World War I,"
in January of 1919. He then suffered an
irreparable breakdown.

Nijinsky's dog, if he had one, died last August.

She was a beautiful animal
with all that was rational
beaten out of her strong
cleanly chiseled head.
We'd circle each other,
lonely, in the heat
of the late summer nights,
both of us waiting for you—
for some crumb of attention.
When I didn't finish the dinner
you'd sometimes offer,
you'd slip it into her bowl
and she'd spring toward you,
more starved for love than food.
I'd watch her from my chair,
passing the time until you'd turn yourself
toward me—remember (O please)
I was there. Out on the ledge

she'd sit, elegant and damaged—
her scars buried in her dense gnarled
fur. Since I've come up here I twist

my hair so hard it snaps
and now I have a bald spot
that my barrettes can barely cover. You

almost seemed to cry
when you told me that she died.
But as I came closer I saw
your eyes completely
dry. You left her
on that hot August roof—
the tar blistering
her dog feet. She couldn't stand
to touch the surface
so she sat and sat
on that asphalt edge,
her mind on fire with memory
of how you once took care
with her, gave her a yard
to play in, rolled with her
in cool green grass.
She'd dream of that
and want it back, before
the war that destroyed her world:
your wife's shrieks *take the goddamn
dog if you leave*

me. And the dog
in her dog mind thought and thought
it was all her fault.
I wish I'd been there
when she took her leap
into the too blue, parched
air, over the anchored

oak tree and the naive lilies
reaching toward the idle sky,
to see her resolve—the pause,
then the quick

amazing move—the elevation, the gift
of rising, her thick mane ablaze
against the dazed noonday sun.
How she broke
free in that *grand jeté*,
sailing in holy
madness past her dog life,
her soul bounding out
of her sad dog eyes
while her ragged body hit
a barren patch of earth.

c. slaughter

AFTER THE MISERABLE lunch with Deidre, Cecilia
returned even more so to thinking about the disas-
trous dinner with Herr M and the all-encompassing
consequences of it—of the damage it had done to
her, both internally and externally—her broken spirit
and the wretched gossip. The debris—the scum—
from it something she feels she can never clean up.

He forbade her to publish the poems. Said he would ruin
her career. He said people would know it was *his* futon in
one of the poems—its urine smell, the urine of his child.
She had shown three new ones to a friend and her so-
called friend had shown them to him. He was particularly

paranoid because he was fighting for joint custody of his two year old daughter and in a pit-bull rage he snarled predatorily at her over the phone that the poems—*these poems*—if read by his wife's lawyer or worse, the judge, would cause irreparable damage to his chances. As if a lawyer or judge would read a poem and, even if they *did*, care. *Poems* as evidence? Not in this country. Never. She sent them out anyway and they did get published. Even though she could not seem to take good care with her body, she felt she *could* with her art—or at least try.

In addition, the poems seemed the only way to relieve her humiliation over what had happened. Yet the deadness she felt—a sick bulb twisting into itself, lost in its path of which way was up and out—seemed to be expanding faster than the speed of her writing. This is not to say she did not want to master the art of forgiveness for both him and for herself, but she could not. She read as many self-help book sas she could tolerate—some with religious overtones—and several on the practice of Zen, but none of what she read on forbearance, self-acceptance, and grace could reach the chaos going on so deep inside her. She even taped little sayings on the rim of the radiator cover next to her writing chair, but all they did was fall to the floor when the heat was turned on.

How she wanted to tell Celie right after it happened. But it was a bad time in her life, too. Emotional. She had just come out of the hospital and was trying to get back to normal. Back to her job at the fancy dress shop. She called her absence an "exhaustion." The doctors recorded it as a "breakdown."

Everyone was told when visiting her there to speak of nothing serious—only things "as light as air," as one too-perky nurse had put it—so as soon as she was in the car with Celie, driving her home—six days after it happened—Celie wanted to know all the important things she had missed these past couple of months. Cecilia took a breath and sputtered out "Herr" and stopped. When Celie said, "What?" she said, "I meant to say weather—that the weather has been just awful." Then she smiled and continued, "You picked a good time to be inside."

She drove her to her modest apartment and then went to the pharmacy with a fistful of prescriptions, returning to the fragile Celie with a bag filled with vials of pills. At that moment Celie most definitely was not the right person to tell.

How she wanted to tell her mother. But every time she tried it was clear her mother did not want to hear any detail—let alone the whole of it. Her mother, too, had become fragile. Physical. She did persist for a couple of weeks. One day when she mentioned Herr M, her mother just called him a "rascal," took her hand and said, "Cecilia, I *too* have had a few rascals in my life." She could not tell if her mother was being ironic, sarcastic, or her memory had momentarily gone into hiding from her body's sickness.

Once, she even brought up Diaghilev—Nijinsky's mentor—so that she could then segue into Herr M. She told her mother how he took the young Nijinsky from poverty straight to the Ballets Russes. How he tormented him, forced him into unwanted sexual acts. How he threw him out when Nijinsky finally asserted himself and how this contributed to Nijinsky's eventual collapse—that after he danced his dance, *World War I*, which he had choreographed so as to capture all the cruelties of war, he suffered an irreparable breakdown.

No matter that she was dying, Aunt Lettie's response was sharp and fast, "Art *choreograph* a war, *capture* a war— a *real* war with *all its cruelties? Never!*" No, her mother did not want to listen to any of this. So they went on to speak only about Nijinsky's genius. His use of straight lines and angles as opposed to the serpentine and spiral. How he allowed only essential steps into his dance and how this made every move more powerful.

Then her mother would return to her story of her own mother going to see Nijinksy dance. Aunt Lettie described in detail Nijinsky's costume as the Faun, just like she had to the relatives, when Cecilia in her room had struggled to hear her mother's words. Outwardly, Cecilia was enthusiastic with the repetition, because she saw how much this brought her mother an authentic happiness— that this pleasure, gleaned from the long lost past, lit her up and anchored her. Inwardly, after it happened, Cecilia felt completely untethered and lost.

She could not tell her father. Since his retirement he only liked to concern himself with the smallest of things. Cross-word puzzles, the sports section of the newspaper—never the front page. He especially liked to read about golf—the *putt, putt, putt* into that tiny hole. As for his wife, all he wanted was to take her out of the hospital and put her in hospice. "Yes, close the door on *this* room," her mother would say to Cecilia, pointing to herself. Cecilia found those the saddest words she ever heard her mother say about her father.

It was clear her father certainly did not need or want more grief—or problems—especially from her. They had never spoken about anything important. To him she was pretty much irrelevant, as if her birth was created only by—and for—her mother. Her relationship with him was always formal—lacking any depth of emotion—so, at best, all she would get from Samuel Slaughter was some amount of fluster, like when he heard her read her poetry.

She could not bring herself to tell Michael. She did not know what he would do—how he would react. He seemed exactly the wrong person to tell, that his response would only add to her own rattled confusion, her shame, her—at the time—amorphous rage.

So she told no one—at least for a long while—what had happened that night. How, afterward, she could not catch her breath. It was a Sunday—the beginning of the second week of January. That Monday he called to apologize. How he kept saying *sorry, sorry* over the phone as he had done the night before—after it happened— and repeating his excuse, "I just got carried away," and his warning, "You cannot tell anyone. Do you understand this? You do understand this? Do you not?"

It seemed to her she must have had a seizure—her legs and arms started moving uncontrollably, she started gagging and she was having trouble breathing when he was almost finished with her. She remembers her naked body shivering on the bare, hardwood floor, almost quaking, and hearing the same *sorry, sorry* litany and the same excuse and warning.

He then sat down naked next to her and said, "Can I make you some tea? *Some tea? Some tea?*" As if begging. Finally, she agreed to *some tea*. Much more for him than for her—as if by drinking it, *that* meant forgiveness.

Monday she went to the doctor, because of her breath. She

still could not catch it and she had a poetry reading in two weeks. She needed her breath and her composure back. Dr. Astrich questioned her about the bruises that were beginning to swell on her inner thighs, her breasts, and the upper areas of her inner arms. He asked, "Did someone hit you, knock you down, pin you to the ground—beat you?" However, because he was becoming increasingly nervous, he made a joke of it and added, "Have you taken up boxing?" She quietly replied, "No, I fell." She thought, "Like Eve. Naive *Eve*, naive *me*, both of us fallen to earth."

She kept repeating to him, "I've lost my breath and you have to help me find it. I need to get it back." It did sound odd, the way she put it, but he knew she was a poet and he liked how she expressed herself so he just smiled and did not question her further. Just told her if her breathing was still giving her trouble in a week to come back for an X-ray, which she did. It was walking pneumonia, for which he gave her a prescription for an antibiotic, saying, "This will cure it quickly." She would, in fact, walk with it—a lodestone on her chest—for six months.

Then, "Nijinsky's Dog"—a poem he had never seen—a poem she knew would enrage him even more, was published a little over a year later. The poem existed as *a kind of telling*—a metaphor—an inaccurate, yet good enough record of how she felt afterward.

Her only witness to what had happened had died. *The dog*. His dog. When he left his wife, he took the dog and moved into an attic apartment with her. She remembers going up the winding outside flight of stairs of that house and seeing all the lovely furniture inside, the gleaming crystal fixtures through the large, sparkling panes of glass trimmed with swags of creamy silk. She thought how much she would like to be going there. It was so unlike the narrowing space where she was heading—a place the owner had rented out and seemed to care nothing about— its two small windows bare and filthy. When he greeted her at the door with the dog, the first thing she noticed about her were her large, sad eyes. Then, her fur—so matted and knotted, so uncared for.

She jumped off his roof in late August of that year. He told everyone she had fallen. "Like *Eve*? Like *me*?" Over and over, she thought this. She listened to others talk about it with both outrage and relish. "He *left her* on that hot August roof to teach a class!" She wanted to scream at them, "She just couldn't stand it. *Couldn't stand any of it, anymore.* Just couldn't. So she jumped." "A *grand jeté*, sailing in holy madness," is how she wrote it. "A suicide," is what she thought.

Right after she took off her coat he handed her something wrapped in bright colored tissue paper—robin's-egg blue—and with delight said, "A gift!" When she unwrapped it she found a bracelet. She was surprised— completely caught off guard—and flattered and she could feel the blood rush to her face. All she could think to say was a strong, but flustered, "Thank you."

"Silver and obsidian," he replied with great pride. "I bought it for you. It reminded me so much of your heightened, compelling intensity."

She put the bracelet down on his desk, then carefully folded the crisp tissue and placed it inside her purse. She wanted so much to appear organized and calm. In fact, she was all excitement inside. Then, she picked the bracelet up and touched the rounded blade edges of the stones and thought of the burning lava from which they had been born and the lustrous, thick, octagonal silver nuggets that linked the irregular chunks of deep blue obsidian—a rare color for this stone. She loved how the clasp was made of round silver magnets and how easily they met, snapped together, and held tight. She put it on her left wrist.

He was polite and spoke slowly of how pleased he was to see her and complimented her not on her face or body, but rather on the delicate necklace that hung over the turtleneck of her sweater—a plain silver chain from which a tiny, turquoise enameled starfish dangled—and how well it blended with her new bracelet. He had a good eye for detail.

On his worn couch he lead the conversation. First he asked about her mother. There was always a great concern in both his facial expressions and his voice when he spoke of her mother. When she lowered her head and said, "Not good, not good at all," he shook his and replied, "Too bad, too bad." It was clear she did not want to talk about her mother's illness anymore—she was just too close to death—and he immediately picked up on this, changing the subject to that of the intellect, for which she was relieved.

He talked about how important the role of the poet-critic was in the analysis of contemporary poetry, *not* just that of the academic, whom he felt sometimes drained all moisture from the topic. This, too, was unexpected—given that he was an academic and a critic, but not a poet.

He asked her what she thought of several poets and listened intently to her opinions. When she finished, he suggested she consider writing an essay about what she had just said. That he would be *pleased* to read it. And beyond all this, he continued, smiling, "Maybe we could collaborate on a series of such essays for a book." She had never thought of herself as a poet-critic, but she very much liked the idea of it, the possibilities of it—another positive invention of herself. At that moment she felt so focused on, and included unlike all her childhood exclusions, especially the insults directed at her from my parents— sometimes subtle, sometimes not—how they always gave her the role of the Wicked Son at the Passover Seder and their labeling of her to the others as the "dandelion."

She loved the way he shared his mind with her and she loved her new bracelet. Toward the end of their conversation—right before dinner—he talked about a book he was writing on film noir—why these films continued to be popular. How he believed they still spoke to contemporary audiences about trust-relationships—"To see things in the dark as they truly are," was how he put it. He then added, "Perhaps after dinner we'll watch the movie I am writing about right now—*The Postman Always Rings Twice*—so you can tell me what you think." She felt so safe with all this talk until she mentioned, "These movies always seem to inevitably involve the betrayal of the most unsuspecting."

He erupted into a laugh that seemed sinister, making her feel terribly uncomfortable, and then he glared at her—his eyes suddenly so absolutely empty. At that indelible moment she was not sure *she* was seeing things as they truly were. Instinctively, she looked the bracelet, and it occurred to her that it *was* an out-of-the-ordinary gesture for their relationship as it existed in the present and she became nervous. She thought of a starfish out of its element, flopping on the dry sand, fighting for its life, and she held tight to the charm on her necklace. He saw this and suggested they eat.

He had made a chicken dish. It did not smell quite right, because it was not fully cooked. She could see blood spots on the meat, and as she delicately tried to separate it from the bone—the cooked parts from the raw—with the dog quietly sitting next to her, it happened. The dog was as startled as she when he sprang from his chair and yanked her from hers. His hands were already on her breasts. Then she felt the dog's paws at her waist. She could feel the dog shudder. "Is the dog trying to protect me or is the dog wanting me to protect her?" she wondered in a thought-panic. At that moment the dog seemed half-human, half-animal and she, Cecilia, *seemed half-animal, half-human.* Her mind was whirling as she wondered, "Are we one and the same being?" She even thought of Nijinsky as the Faun and his becoming *half-animal, half-human*—her associations all a dervish dance.

He screamed at the dog and she ran under the table—hid there. Cecilia saw the dog under it as he pulled her to the futon. And yes, she *could* smell the urine from when his daughter had napped there earlier.

The more she cried for him to stop, the more he ripped at her clothes. Her hair went flying all over her face, her now bare skin, her breasts, while the dog stayed huddled, almost frozen in her own mountain of fur, except for the chewing, *that* unrelenting chewing, *her* unrelenting chewing on herself, her eyes crazed from the chaos. She and the dog stared at each other after it was over as Cecilia cowered on the soiled, hardwood floor. Now, the dog is dead—dead in the unrelenting heat of that August. The tarred roof burning her dog feet.

Driving herself home that night so badly bruised and mind-broken all she could think to do was to make up lines for a poem. A poem to distract her, to help her get home. Doing this did keep the headlights from the cars coming toward her and the taillights from the cars speeding past her from completely smearing into each other, as she kept wiping away the tears that would not stop arriving. Over and over the lines repeating in her head:

> He bought me
> a bracelet
> of silver and obsidian
> and after he broke the bread,
> devoured it
> he could not stop
>
> saying
> "Sorry, Sorry"
> over and over again
> "Sorry, Sorry"
> circling like a vulture
> over me over
> a bracelet of silver and obsidian.

After the "dog poem" was published he called at least twice a week, his number popping up on her Caller ID, but he only spoke the first time, saying, "Now I *am* going ruin your career. I have the power." After that he would just bash the phone down, as if to make sure she would hear the crash—to frighten her further, which it did. Still does, although the calls stopped a couple of months ago.

So she sits in her chair, worrying as to what he might do next and now also with her own, fully shaped, knife-sharp rage, thinking about all of it, thinking he was the last person inside her, which makes her sick—makes her feel polluted and that she will go to her death with this fact.

Everywhere she goes she imagines, "Someone is going to come along and throw me to the ground, drag me deeper into that dark forest where the archdemons await—Lucifer, Mammon, Asmodeus, Satan, Beelzebub, Leviathan. The German."

She checks her body for marks every day, as if he had left something in her which she can never get rid of, something that will rise up. Some stain that eventually will make itself visible—that the cells in the deep layers of her body are mutating into some hideous blossom. *Which they are.* The heart's melanoma—a fury spreading with its pronged-in, black, ragged edges and its forever festering red center.

She keeps all men, except Michael—who spends much of his time with her as if they were the closest brother and sister—at a friendly, but measured distance. When she does go out it is usually with someone she knows well, mostly a relative, or to a place she regards as "safe"—like the dress shop. If she does go somewhere alone, she disguises herself with layers of clothes, plus scarves or hats—tucking her distinctive hair inside them. She stays at home a lot in her chair writing such lines as "in my corner shrinking from any vibration that could allow the delicate poised snow to be shaken to avalanche." Then, she signs her name, "Cecilia Slaughter—still poet," and thinks, "Funny, those words—their double meaning."

She thinks about her mother, gone, the dog, gone, even her father with a quick, clean heart attack six months after her mother's death—"Each with their leap, or fall, it doesn't matter, out of here." She remembers how well over a year ago she buried her mother's diary—with the stem of the bald flower pressed between its pages—next to the bracelet of silver and obsidian and how they now lie beside each other with their separate, wild, silent screams.

And she *does* wonder if Cecily has written a play using what she has heard, however much it might be in error. Half of her now cowers in the corner of her own room, thinking about this and the further trouble it could cause, while the other half continuously lifts off this planet into that hot noonday sun—her mind ablaze—into the clear, blister of *that* August air.

Then, in her chair, she contemplates: "Perhaps it's time. Time to tell someone. Time to tell *everyone*. Time to tell at least *some* of it. To find out how the telling feels so as to possibly save myself from my own considered leap into the atmosphere."

THE LOVERS

Each night before sleep, while in
their bedtime clothes, he takes her
eyebrow brush with the tiny comb
on one side and he parts her
hair, rubbing the dark blue
plastic teeth over the crown of her
bowed head. First, he uncovers
the bald spot, tells her it's not
so bad, so big, and then
he tries—how he tries—
to hide it with the long strands,
and always in the gentlest of voices he says
now, no one can notice. For years

this is the only way they've come together,
at midnight, with the one stooped lamp on—
or sometimes a flashlight—so he can see more
clearly and describe for her the stubs
(*thick or thin?* she whispers) that are pushing through
her center. She loves the pull and scratch
he creates on her tender excited
skin. It eases her mind, erases
thought. Though these ecstasies are not

what he imagined some twenty years ago,
with her tongue deep in his mouth—
his in hers—in each other everywhere, in
the car, on the couch, even in bed.

They made love according to the manual,
moved in ways understandable,
unlike now, their shadows
on the shade—two bent bodies
barely touching, strangely loving.

c. slaughter

EACH TIME BEFORE Michael leaves, he combs Cecilia's hair. She sits in front of the computer and surfs the internet for life's lighter side, which usually means going to several online celebrity gossip sites. Often she will mention some of what she is reading, if it is inconsequential enough.

All the while Michael stands behind her, combing her long hair and he can feel her whole body calm as he untangles the knots she has made in it during the day. He likes to think it is at these moments that he is unsnarling her entire life, not just smoothing out her hair under the dim lamplight.

Sometimes Cecilia will look for a small, five-star hotel anywhere in the world—she travels well on the computer—and talk about the two of them maybe going there. "*Someday?*" she questions herself out loud. Michael's excitement for the moment is authentic as he puts down the comb, grabs a small pad of paper on her desk, and writes down the name of the one she has clicked on to, although he knows they will never go. He has come to realize Cecilia will never again wander too far from here. Her writing room is an anchor to this world—as Michael has convinced himself he is, especially when he combs her hair.

When she is finally relaxed, Cecilia asks him to check the bald spot atop her head. Sometimes she even asks him to draw it. To make a tracing of it. She has many of these tracings, which she keeps in her desk drawer. He makes the best approximation of it that he can—trying to be as exact as possible—but his talent for drawing is minimal. He counts the number of hairs trying to sprout from the spot and adds them to the picture, because he knows she will then ask, "How many?" as she will about its size. "A quarter, a nickel, a dime?" Then, with a hint of humor, she will add, "Valium—five milligrams?" Her voice is sweet and childlike and this makes it harder for him to show his frustration upon her request to do this. He knows she wants the spot to be smaller than the last time he drew it, but it has taken him years to understand that she does not want it to entirely disappear. It has become too much a part of her. She calls it "my flawless flaw," continuing, "I look at it with awe"—laughs, then puts this line, or a version of it, into a poem.

Sometimes, resting here, inside my casket locked in my vault and my old thoughts, I long not just for Wyatt's quick, strong, forceful hands, but also ones like Michael's—so gentle. But I also wonder if I—or any of my cousins for that matter—were raised to appreciate such masculine kindness, at least for any length of time.

Cecilia has taken Michael into a world he did not know existed and he has gone agreeably. She has taken him with no force. It does not matter that they are divorced. He came back after only a few months under the pretext that she probably needed her checkbook balanced—which she did—and to make sure there was enough food in the cupboards and refrigerator—which there was not.

Some nights he lies next to her and reads from the

biographies of the Russian poets—Akhmatova, Mandelstam, Tsvetayeva, and Pasternak, and as she is about to fall to sleep she will quietly sigh and say some variation of "How could they stand such oppression and still be so brilliant, Michael? Do you think perhaps they were made more so, because their words were the only things they had to hold on to—like others do their jewels?" He likes it when she says his name.

I know she believes she would not have been able to survive what they had to endure—the censorship, their unending exiles. I cannot decide. Growing up and especially after my death, I had seen Cecilia jump many hurdles, but, then again, I had seen her tumble down into a pit within her mind, filled with demons calling to her. "Mandelstam jumped out of a window in exile, and survived," she says to Michael. "But Tsvetayeva hanged herself." She repeats this in a tone that teeters between sadness and marvel.

Cecilia does not seem interested in what the Americans did to themselves—Plath, Sexton, Berryman, Lowell. It is a large outward force, an outward oppression—history's dictators trying to suffocate words, that absorbs her attention. Of course, I know so much of this comes from Aunt Lettie's history.

In the months after the divorce, Michael tried dating other women. They were easier to find than he imagined. Once the divorce was made known, many women, in fact, found him first. He would take each to a nice restaurant, but never one he went to with Cecilia. The oddest thing he found happening on these dates was how many of these women told him that they were, or aspired to be, a poet. Also, most of them arrived dressed in black—some trying to look like young, hip students, others like pseudo-Goths, most just going for an expensive, exotic look. Yet, no matter how they presented themselves, all of them at some point in the conversation would tell him how much they *loved* Cecilia's poetry. Then, annoyingly to him, they usually followed it with a "but" which meant *they*, of course, were different. Different in style, in content—whatever—forever the implication being if they were just discovered they could come to be regarded as well as she—if not better. It was at this point Michael would start to tune out, especially when they attached how healthy they were, implying, sometimes subtly, sometimes not, that Cecilia was not.

Some would tell him how much they exercised. A few even asked—still at dinner—would he like to feel their biceps? Their triceps? He, of course, would accommodate them, however odd it looked in a public place. He found it amusing and also discovered that any kind of physical mention about themselves was always a prelude to what they would inevitably offer later in the evening.

He did have sex with a few, but always made sure he was protected. It was not so much for him, but for *her*. Even at those moments he would think of Cecilia—her obsession with germs. And he would smile and the women would think he was smiling at them. Each time he would put on a condom he would think of how she always stretched the sleeve of her sweater over her hand when she touched a doorknob or used the joint—never the tip—of her finger when pushing the button on an elevator.

One day they had a terrible fight in public when he forgot and actually pushed an elevator button full force with his naked thumb. He did have to admit the best thing about these new women was that on the way up to their apartments they did not care what he touched. Yet even this, somehow, made him remember Cecilia too much in the positive, for the thought would suddenly charge into his mind that these women might be completely unclean—perhaps even pigs. He would laugh to himself when thinking this and want to tell Cecilia about what she had done to him—how much she had invaded his thought patterns. He knows this would have made her laugh and she would have replied, "I'm not that powerful," which she would mean.

Everything Cecilia says, she means. Everything she says she is going to do, she does. This is one of my most abiding memories of her when we were children and why what she did to Deidre at that lunch truly bothers her and has helped send her whole being into a further spin away from the person she thought she knew to be herself.

For the most part she lives her life in too straightforward—too literal—a way. Certainly a mistake when it came to Herr M. It is only in her writing that she values double meanings, metaphors, and hidden texts, or when she speaks about "poetic justice" and the too many ironies within the Slaughter family.

The women Michael dated talked a lot about what they were going to do and then added a *when* or an *if only.* So no matter how toned their bodies, how full their refrigerators, how they actually could cook, how they so obviously took care to balance their checkbooks, the more Michael gravitated back to Cecilia in her chair—her hair loosened, her head bent over her long, yellow pads of paper heaped onto her lap, her room filled with books from the library, so as to keep each detail she used totally accurate, her only exercise sitting on the floor checking and rechecking facts, then getting up and returning to her chair. He loved how filled with care she was with her words.

Cecilia never asked if Michael had sex with other women—if he touched them. He wanted her to, so he could tell her "Yes," and that the more he did, the more he came to hate it—and them. How they seemed cardboard cutouts of her. Then, he would have told her how much he loved her. How the weights she placed on her mind— its lifts and stretches—were so much better than the hardened muscles of the women with whom he had slept. But she never asked.

Within four months of the divorce Michael had given up all the other women and returned to Cecilia. Some people told him he had lost his mind—I would not have gone to this extreme, but I was filled with hard worry for him. Some offered him the names of their therapists, their friends' therapists. They reminded him of how difficult Cecilia was to live with—of her mood swings, her deep depressions, the isolation she insisted on when she was writing, of how her mother's sorrowful history had infected her.

On their second date she had warned him of her complicated sadness. That her mother was an Auschwitz survivor. That her father was more obsessed with his sister than any other woman and had no interest in his own wife's story. "How sick is all that?" she would say more than once with a twinkle in her eye, and it was then he knew he was caught by this woman who could find whimsy in the middle of just about any twisted story. Her ability to see things from every side—her mind a Rubik's Cube of grief and polished delight—hooked him.

They keep separate places, but most nights he is at her apartment. It does not matter to her when he shows up. If the door to her writing room is closed, he quietly turns the

TV on in the den, lies down on the couch, and often finds himself asleep there until morning. Sometimes Cecilia is just going to bed when he passes her in the hall in the early morning. He will ask what time she wants to get up, then go with her into her bedroom, set her alarm, and rush home to change his clothes for work. Even at these times, he is happier having slept on their old sofa than next to any of the preened, pared-down women.

Nothing is preplanned, but some days, late in the afternoon, he will call and ask if she would like to go out for dinner, or perhaps for him to just bring over two large vanilla shakes topped with hot fudge. Lately she opts for the latter. When he arrives, if the door to her writing room is open, he knows he can ask if she would like to watch TV. They go to Turner Classics first, to see if they are showing an old, romantic movie. One of Michael's favorite times is watching Cecilia watching a movie—curled into the corner of the sofa, milkshake in hand. There, she looks so safe. It is at that moment he thinks, "This is good, no one can hurt her." This thought of his—this hope—makes me sad for them both.

He knows people have hurt her—he knows this directly from his years living with her and most recently both from her cousin, Celie, and from Cecilia herself. Celie called him late last week absolutely frantic about a man Cecilia calls Herr M. "You know, Michael," Celie said with great agitation, "the name she has dropped into some of her most recent poems. When Cecilia said it out loud to me, she said it quickly so it sounded like 'harem.' It's clear she now includes herself as an addition to the collection of women he's damaged."

She told him that he must not tell Cecilia anything

that she had just told him or what she was about to tell him. Michael sighed heavily and said, "I know all about Herr M. Cecilia told me too, and I'm going to take care of it," which made Celie even more upset and momentarily puzzled him.

"No, Michael," she said, "I want to—I have to take care of it. I *have* to do it!"

"Do what?" he replied.

"I-have-a-plan," she said in a strange, halting way.

To which he quickly answered, "You're not equipped."

He did not mean to hurt Celie, but he truly could not imagine she was capable of all that much. He thought, "She spends all her time in that dress shop selling clothes and besides that—and everyone knows this—she'd not so long ago broke apart and is still trying to glue herself back. Her life has been difficult, but unlike Cecilia, she really has no passionate outlet for dealing with what she's lived through." Not that Michael wanted to get psycho-analytical. He did not. He had paid too many bills to those jerks sitting staring at Cecilia—his mind still angered by the thought that the only impression they had made was their heavy butts indenting their pricey leather chairs.

After Cecilia told Michael about what had happened with Herr M—after he swore first to just listen, not react, and to *never* do anything about it—he went directly to the police. Of course, he used Herr M's real name, but because of his extreme upset, he found himself initially calling him Herr M, to which they responded with a resounding *"What?"* However, it did not matter, for when he regained his composure and told them his real name, they replied in unison that the person they needed was Cecilia. They needed her to fill out the report and questioned him as to

Why now? for what had happened that January night was well over a year and a half ago. All this so close to the same time she insisted on the divorce, the same time she refused to let him near her, covering her body with layers upon layers of fabric even when she was at home.

When Cecilia finally told Michael of the attack, he did stay composed—as composed as he could in front of her. There was too much terror in her eyes—although not in her voice, for she spoke in a rote, matter-of-fact way. It was her eyes that broke his heart, gave her away, and he could not even bring himself to say something like, "So all the crazier-than-crazy behavior of yours *then* was because of *him* ruining *your* life—and *mine. Our future.*"

She said she had just told Celie and was now sorry for doing so because she could tell Celie was much more upset than she revealed—her reaction far too controlled. Then, as an afterthought, she looked at him and cried, "Michael, can't you see how *everything* I do is wrong? *Everything.* Rose and Emil were right. I am just a weed!" He started toward her, but she put out her hand as if to say "stop" and said, "Please, oh please, Michael, don't get too upset. You promised."

So he stood there just listening, not asking the questions now spiking his mind—and lying about what he was going to do, more so than he had ever done with any woman, which felt odd because she was the only one he had ever loved. He *had* to do something more than just go to the police. Even before he went, he knew they could be of no help if Cecilia would not talk with them, and it was clear to him she would not. It had taken her twenty months to tell him and Celie and that was as far as she would go for any straightforward, public kind of healing.

He stood there thinking about how he had to be clever. She stared at him, then said his name as if to snap him out of the strange look he had on his face, and when he realized this, he asked if she would like him to comb her hair, which by now had become terribly snarled from her twirling of it as they talked.

His hands were shaking as he picked up the comb. He wanted to hit someone with it. Anyone, but not Cecilia. She took her place in the computer chair. However, this time was different, for she clicked on the internet for the latest news—and what came next surprised him. Not like what she had just told him about Herr M, but in a different way. In the past when they would watch the news on TV, Michael was not allowed to comment. He would see her taking it all in—the bombings, the killings, the buildings collapsing, the mangled bodies being lifted out of the rubble—but she refused to talk about it. All during the marriage they lived by her rules and this was one of them. If they saw the news together, he could not react. He had to be silent. Both Michael and I knew this had to do with what had happened to Aunt Lettie. Cecilia has read so much about the Holocaust, but will not discuss it in any kind of depth.

But this time was different. Suddenly she turned to Michael and spoke about the headlines, about what was going on in the world. At the time I wondered if her telling Celie and Michael about Herr M had begun to free her. I thought of sludge. A bottle corked with sludge finally popped open and underneath was clear water.

Her comments poured from her fully formed, and Michael stepped several steps away from her to just listen as she then began to recite a poem with an anguish equal to what he, at that moment, was holding inside of him.

She closed her eyes and as the tears slipped from her lids, past her lashes and down her face, she spoke.

> Where the Tigris and Euphrates meet
> is the Tree cemented in concrete.
> The fruit all picked and eaten.
> Where the Tigris and Euphrates meet
> the holy road once filled with date palms
> and wild geraniums wandering every bush
> is smothered with bombed out bridges
> and scorched tanks and peddlers
> with their fractured stands
> that hold the spoiled apple and the orange.
> Where the Tigris and Euphrates meet
> the dried mother womb sleeps,
> buried under slabs of tongues and rubble talk—
> the wetlands drained, the marsh a small weep,
> the garden above starved for its life.
> Where the Tigris and Euphrates meet
> all that's left is the knowledge warned of.

When she finished, Michael completely lost his composure and raged, "That snake. I am going to kill him." Because, even though the poem addresses battles far away, and even though she suddenly spoke to him about the news, he knew the poem arose from what the low, filthy Herr M had done to her and how deeply poisoned she was by it.

Cecilia responded with a panic-scream, "No. No, Michael! You promised to stay calm!" Pulling himself together as best he could, he watched his bare feet move over the eggshell-colored carpet toward her and focused on how clean everything was in the small room where they were at this moment—how untouched—and he kissed her head at the Seventh Chakra spot.

It was then he realized how much he was becoming like Cecilia, how insulated the space was where they now lived—how unlike his life in the years before he met her, before the vertigo that was her mind spiraled into his. He used to be a guy who watched baseball—a lot—had a favorite team and each time they won his day was complete, and each time they lost, his day felt ruined for at least an hour or two afterward. He played poker every Tuesday night and never came away with less than fifty dollars more in his pocket. Now, he knows more than any other accountant about the Russian poets under Stalin. About Mandelstam throwing himself out a window and how his wife Nadezhda recorded it, recorded *all* of it.

A week after her telling him about what happened, Michael is again combing Cecilia's hair and cannot stop thinking about the poem she recited; about killing Herr M; about Nadezhda Mandelstam unendingly writing down everything. That at least she *did* something.

This night he will stay over, and Cecilia, after working for hours, will come to bed and lay her body next to him. He will wake up and read to her and she will curl tight against him, resting her head on his stomach—her being so fetal against his, her long hair tossed over his body like a luxurious blanket.

He now knows that all his life—the life that is left to him—they will spend in this position, or the one with him standing over her smoothing her hair, or on the sofa with her tucked into a corner of it slowly sipping a rich milkshake and with him doing the same just a small space away.

They are watching an old-fashioned, romantic movie in black and white—here there is no blatant sex. The picture is crisp and clean and clear. He will not let her slip into the depths of hell like in some Greek myth. "Whatever it takes," he thinks, "I will do it." He has convinced himself of this.

MANIA

Sometimes I talk too much
at a shrill pitch and the bitch
part of me carries off
my conversation in directions
I'd never travel with more peaceful
lips. But when my brain swells
and pushes on the small bones
on my face, what spills out
seems so rich. I think
everyone loves me so much.
Until, alone with the bloated
moon, I hear the rattle
of my voice and its twist—
the gnarled path it takes running
after any catch, grabbing
first place in a race
it does not want to enter,
accepting the trophy
with a curtsy practiced
for royalty. Hater of both halves
of myself—raving
slave, desperate dictator.

c. slaughter

WHEN CECILIA FINALLY told Celie in a back room at the
shop exactly what the critic Herr M had done to her,
Celie was shocked and sickened. But she stayed calm, or

at least as calm as she could, hopefully hiding her increasing distress. It was in near the end of her hospital stay that Cecilia told her with such excitement in her voice of his invitation. Celie did not remind Cecilia how she had said to her at the time, "Maybe it isn't such a good idea to go to his apartment alone for dinner." Celie tells herself, "Yes, that now would only add to her grief. Anyway, I was probably too vague in my warning by just saying too quietly, 'Perhaps he isn't such a nice man,' given the fact that she had just explained to me that he was going through an unending divorce—his fourth. I should have been clearer—more adamant—so in a way this *is* all my fault."

Also, there were things about Herr M that Celie could have told her that she had learned of more recently—that she knew of at the moment of Cecilia telling her about the attack—which would have been unbearable for Cecilia to hear, and this only enlarged Celie's extreme upset.

After Cecilia left, she ran into the bathroom and took a double dose of her medication. She stayed in there for about fifteen minutes and then reentered the sales area of the shop. It looked like a carnival—the clothes, the women, all the colors that filled the huge room seemed to be moving too quickly. She wondered if she might have swallowed too many pills in her distress. She felt both her mind and body were being taken on a merry-go-round, which was spinning too fast—its loud, discordant music blasting into her ears. All she could hope was that too fast would not mean out-of-control. She tried to pace herself the rest of the day—she spoke and walked slowly and was extra polite to everyone as if that would stop the flailing of her throbbing brain. It felt like a rabid bat was trapped inside her skull, crashing itself against her too-thin walls of bone, and that her head was about to crack open from the pain.

Some months ago a client of Celie's had revealed to her she had a niece who was getting her MFA in poetry at the university and she had been in a class Herr M taught. Of course she used his real name, just as Cecilia had when she told Celie of his invitation for that dinner. According to Celie's client, she believed her niece had little or no sexual experience when she met him, but then he began an affair with her. With great anguish, she said to Celie, "How could a professor at such a prestigious place get away with something like this? I thought *those* days were long gone." She repeated this over and over, while Celie, trying to distract her, showed her the latest sweaters that had just arrived for the fall.

Celie hated hearing any horrible story. However, in the shop when her clients vented their problems to her, as they frequently did, she had perfected the art of compassionate nodding. But this made her feel so used—that once again she had become the dumping ground for other people's issues, had become the Sin-Eater for her customers.

Her client went on to say, "My niece is very shy, not attractive, and stutters when she speaks. Clearly this so-called *great* man—this great intellectual—treated her as a receptacle until his divorce was final, for when that happened, he abandoned her and moved in with someone else—*three weeks* later. Now, my niece is too depressed to return to school, and I'm worried she might be suicidal."

She then asked for Celie's advice. "*Me?*" Celie thought, rather startled, "Celie Slaughter, never married, who's never had a lover! Though men like Herr M make a good argument for celibacy—a life of just fantasy, no matter how lonely."

Then, Celie considered, "Maybe she asked me because she had heard about my own instabilities." She did not know if she should worry that this was still being discussed or that she should take it as a compliment, because she was now considered "recovered," now seen as "very together." She had heard some of the whispers. Ultimately, she decided it just did not matter. At least she had learned some small thing from her therapist—"People talk. You can't stop them."

Today, however, she knows too many awful things about this one man and she is finding this too much of a coincidence—as if she were *meant to know, meant to do something.*

Cecilia said she had told no one else, and Celie believes this to be true. Yet, when she saw her poem "Nijinsky's Dog" in the *American Poetry Review,* Celie was perplexed and frightened. At first, she thought it was just Cecilia's heightened imagination at work, but as she kept rereading it, its subtext, its imagery, and metaphors, began to scare her. She now understands more clearly how much autobiography was there.

Celie cannot get Herr M's thug fists, the heft of his body on Cecilia, out of her mind. Cecilia shook when she described how each time after he got her, he told her to "Turn! Turn! Turn Over!" "Celie," she said, holding on to both of her arms as if they were lifelines, "I thought it meant that finally he was going to get off of me, let me up. Let me go. But it wasn't true—it just wasn't true. I couldn't catch my breath."

Then Celie remembered the winter before last, just a few weeks before Aunt Lettie's death, how heavy Cecilia's breathing was when she drove her home from the hospital, which Cecilia attributed to a mild case of bronchitis. "Nothing serious," she reassured her. Celie later learned it was walking pneumonia, and it took until the summer for her lungs to become clear of the infection.

Now Celie believes Cecilia will never be totally uninfected by what has happened—that she will not be able to get up completely. She thinks, "Some things can never be gotten up from fully—at best they land on our backs, like rocks we forever carry with us."

Celie has always loved Cecilia's poetry. Its melancholy. Its unexpectedness. The way her words make her face, and almost accept, her own emotions. They do, for sure, make her feel less alone. She loves the places Cecilia carries her both literally and figuratively. Sometimes she has to look up what Cecilia's referring to, but then she learns even more and feels smarter. Cecilia's language gives her sadness a shape. Always has. At least for the moment she is reading it, she can contain her own feelings within Cecilia's lines.

Yet, now she does not know what to do with the rage that is spiraling inside her—a rage as large as any she has ever known—because of this man. A man she has never met, but now has heard about in two awful, anxiety-filled situations, each horrible in its own way—however, similar. Now that she knows the facts—the truth—not just the rumors and the guessings as to what really happened to Cecilia, she wants to hurt him, hurt him badly, which sounds preposterous, she knows, because she is the furthest person from powerful. And she has read enough literature, both sacred and profane, to know that dealing with the Devil is always big trouble.

That evening, she wondered what he looked like, so she searched for him on the internet. She got many pictures and studied them for almost thirty minutes. He had a full head of thick, wavy, black hair, his sideburns beginning to gray. His nose was straight and close to perfect. She thought he would look more like a goat, but he did not—although he did have a thick, black goatee, also flecked with gray, which made him look devil-like. "Perhaps to cover a weak chin," she thought. His lips were full, giving the impression they could be a supple place for words to pass through. However, in several picture a few of his teeth were jagged, almost to the point of looking broken. "Maybe as a result of all the lives from which he'd taken a too-hard bite," she said out loud to no one.

With all this studying of him, it became clear to her that his real power was in his dark eyes—a softness to his stare, coupled with an odd sexiness, as if he were saying, "I can show you a good time and will never, ever hurt you." Celie felt drawn to them even through the computer screen. "That's what the Devil—or a psychopath—can do to you," she said out loud again, when she forced herself to finally click off all images of him. But, even then, she could still see his face staring at her and it kept her up most of the night, along with his words to Cecilia. *Turn. Turn. Turn Over.*

She tossed in bed for hours looking for a cool spot, and trying to figure out what to do next. "What do I, Celie Slaughter, do? A woman who always stands on the sidelines of life, smiling with designer clothes in her hands, helping other women dress well, so they can go to parties with men who might *rape* them"—a new thought she cannot wash from her mind.

"What does a woman do who just works in a dress shop and watches TV or reads books, a woman like *this*, who knows too much that can't be told—what does *she* do?" All night that question hooked her mind and dragged it into every fevered, scary crevice of herself—triggering her earliest, most frightening memories of her grandmother grabbing at her, as if Eva were about to crush her small body—sometimes even leaving bruises on her that took a week or two to disappear—and comparing this to what Herr M had done to Cecilia. She could not stop making this connection. She felt like she was on fire—that her bed was covered with slowly burning charcoals.

When the sun started its rise, she fell into a half-sleep—a slimy, cold sweat covering her, making her feel like she was not totally human, but part reptile. It was not the first time she had felt this way. After the breakdown, while in the hospital, the division became even more pronounced—like she was split down the middle with a "crazed, coiled thing" inhabiting half of her, the other being just a chasm of fears.

In her early morning hallucinations, she kept hearing the girl with the stutter desperately trying to articulate something, but only able to make choking sounds, and kept seeing Cecilia, her eyes too wide, her pupils too dilated, unsuccessfully trying to cover black and blue marks all over her naked body.

She awoke from this stupor with a leap—almost did not know where she was—when her alarm went off. She had to get up and go to the shop and paste a grin on her plain face. It was while she was getting dressed that she gave herself permission to open her mind as wide as it had ever been, and then *the idea* burst in—*the idea* to buy a gun. She allowed herself to understand why sometimes people more than fantasize about wanting to kill someone—someone other than themselves.

On her lunch break, she searched the suburban *Yellow Pages* for gun shops. There were none nearby. She remembered years ago there being one not far from here. She was a teenager and considered suicide a possibility—a way out from not being good enough. Not good enough to be a Slaughter—not smart enough, not pretty enough, not *Aunt Rose* enough. Always carrying around the awful feeling that someday—and soon—she would embarrass herself so badly that the only solution would be to die immediately after that moment happened. Also, there was her unending terror of Death, created in her grandmother's apartment—created by her grandmother herself—and as she got older it seemed one way to conquer Death was to take control. To stop fearing when Death would get her she would take charge—take charge of *it*. That was when, at thirteen, she searched for an address of a gun shop and found one within five miles of her house.

The only one she told about this was Cecilia. It was at a time when it was clear to her that Cecilia did not feel good about her own self. She had seen the deep red marks on her arms and the small scabs on her thighs. The *obvious* pickings at herself.

They would sun themselves in Celie's backyard, the record player in the family room swooning out Johnny Mathis's voice—"A Certain Smile," "Chances Are," "The Twelfth of Never"—into the summer air and talk about finding their "one true love." One day the phone rang in the kitchen. Her mother answered it and then came out to say, "A neighbor woman is complaining about the noise. She's trying to study for a test to get a certificate to teach Braille to the blind and the music is interfering with this." That is how Aunt Esther so blankly put it in her tired voice. Then she turned from the doorway to the yard, went into the house and turned the music off.

Celie rolled onto her stomach and whispered to Cecilia, "I'm a bad person." She said it as if she were half-kidding, but Cecilia, all too seriously and sadly replied, "So am I." It was then they really started to talk and she found out how much she and Cecilia did have in common—not just that their fathers were brothers—but the awful ways they felt about themselves.

She told her about the gun shop nearby and Cecilia all too quickly said, "Oh, Yes! Please Celie, give me the address." Then, suddenly and surprisingly, they both burst out laughing. But today, searching for such a place, Celie is far from laughing. She has to *do something*. She has to *do this*.

The awful things we humans do to each other flooded Celie's mind, overwhelming her. She thought about the Holocaust, the Inquisitions, the Cossack massacres, the Crusades—the world's griefs. Some days she cannot turn on the news, just retreats into a Marx Brothers movie—or, better yet, a silent one. Nothing can interrupt, no voice bursting in with the news of some breaking terribleness or a tape running across the top of the screen, updating her on the most recent catastrophe.

She still remembers the stories about how her mother kept writing to the American Red Cross about her grand-mother's family. She thinks of her grandmother and the terrible irony—how fifteen years ago on her last day she crossed the street when she saw Adele coming toward her. How she turned from her—in a way killing off her eldest daughter—and Celie wonders if in that single act, in those few steps, a pure, horrific grief rose up in her grandmother, killing *her*.

She thinks about how we have to be careful whom we kill off. But then she realizes Herr M does not fall into any category she has ever known and that nothing she can do to him will kill her, that in hurting him she will only feel better.

On her break she closes her eyes, but can still see the people on television walking with placards taped across their hearts with pictures on them, and underneath their desperate words in bold type, Have You Seen Him? Have You Seen Her? Sometimes she is really glad she has no one, no one to lose—Cecilia being the one exception and she cannot bear that someone has hurt her. She wants to tape a sign across her own heart that says

> Herr M Is A Rapist.
> Please Help Me
> Do Something About This.

At the end of day she sits in the back room of the shop—just a giant version of the coat closet in her grandmother's apartment—crowded with clothes that hang there lifeless, and she thinks about *all* the empty people who will fill them and beyond that all the bad things they will do while so finely dressed—all the rules they will break. And, of course, she thinks of Adele and the Yom Kippur Night Dance.

She thinks of Adam. She thinks of Eve. Of God watching them in their innocent nakedness—how in the beginning they did not need clothes, did not have anything to cover up. How alone He must have felt with their betrayal. *His Rage. What He Knew.* She thinks how utterly alone she is with *what she knows.*

Then suddenly, she takes a deep breath and feels omnipotent—she becomes Jehovah, the Messiah, the Savior—the Holy One. She wonders if this is the manic, base part in her rising up again, and she does not care. All she knows is that she has to do something and do it quickly— Herr M *has* to be punished. *Has* to be stopped. And it is then her head finally clears and she gets up and leaves the shop.

IF I SET
UP THE CHAIRS

When the people come in to pray
they'll need somewhere to sit.
I'll be the one to help them stay
while they make some sense of it.

And when they are done
and go home fully blessed,
I'll be the one
to clean up what's messed.

Will that be equal enough
to what they do,
if I do that stuff
will it satisfy You?

c. slaughter

CELIE WAS WEARING OUT again, not just from what she had just learned about Herr M, but from all the giving, all the pleasing, all the hurting. This should not have been a surprise to anyone who knew her history—Celine included. So when Celie asked Celine to accompany her to a gun shop, Celine should have taken it more seriously. Instead, she quipped, "Celie, are you *that* tired of trying to make everyone happy that now you're just going to start shooting all of us?" Celie paused, took a breath, and just said, "It's for protection."

Maybe you have to be dead (be that distant a witness to all the unending irrational havoc we cause ourselves and each other) to truly understand what an awful idea it was for Celine to agree to go with Celie that day. Here, beneath the ground, I can watch the people above just going along—passing time—not giving others' requests or behaviors too much thought. Or maybe in this particular instance, and more likely, Celine is just too self-absorbed and had it been anyone else who knew Celie well, the response would have been an emphatic "No." Anyone else would have questioned her in very precise ways as to what she planned to do with such an item. It was certainly not a secret that Celie could self-destruct.

Clearly an extra layer of fatty tissue surrounds Celine's brain, resulting in a huge gelatinous involvement with herself, blocking any thought of how dangerous an excursion this could become for Celie. Cecilia never would have allowed it and would have made sure Celie got better help. And if she had known the gun purchase was on her behalf—because of what she had finally told Celie about Herr M—she would have been horrified. Even Cecily, with all her contorted thoughts, would have known that a gun in Celie's hands would serve no one any good purpose.

Cecilia would be at her mother's grave the day Celie would go to the gun shop and that was the very reason Celie had chosen it. On October 4, the anniversary of Aunt Lettie's birthday, Cecilia devotes the whole day to traveling here to lie next to her mother. It is one of the frequent times during the year that she is determined to be at the cemetery. The first thing she does when she arrives is to curl over her grave. This autumn, her hair will blend into the russet color maple leaves that still warm us. For now, these visits are the only time that Aunt Lettie's agitated sleep lifts and she calms—in "eternity time" her rest will soon become peaceful.

After about twenty minutes Cecilia slowly gets up and speaks to each of us as she carefully positions white lilies next to our inscriptions. Then she carefully traces the embossed letters that make up each of our names with her fingertips, as if she is caressing us.

Celie knew that on this day Cecilia would not check in with her until late at night and since she was the only one who called her daily, there would be no one else who would worry if she could not be immediately found. Some, including Celie's brothers and their wives, would go for months without getting in touch with her. She had taken a sick day from the dress shop to go to the gun shop, so no one there would bother her.

All Celine could think of after Celie invited her was that she had never been to a gun shop, and it intrigued her because she would have to pick something extra special to wear, something *different* from that which she normally wore, and she was excited to see how she would appear in the mirror in a new and possibly spectacular look.

What she ultimately chose were black blue jeans, a black belt with highly polished silver studs, and a black spandex three quarter sleeve T-shirt with a cowl neck that could be pulled to one side to expose a shoulder—all from Victoria's Secret. She told the woman taking her order to send the clothes overnight, which added forty percent to the cost. But she needed to know quickly if the look worked. And anyway, she convinced herself, she rarely did catalogs and was amazed by how little each item cost.

After she ripped open the delivery and put everything on, she looked at herself in her huge, ceiling-to-floor-length mirror and said, "Cool. Yes, very cool," out loud and thought, "unlike the visibly unhappy Cecily, who always dressed in dark clothes, I don't look Goth. More teenager, trim and quite slim, actually thin"—except for her hiked-up breasts, which she raised her hands to cup— held in place by a firm, thickly padded, pointed-tip bra. "Yes, young," she said to her reflection. She then ran to the local upscale shoe store and bought some black Frye cowboy boots with beautifully sculpted wooden heels.

The fact was, her face looked prunelike and her behind sagged and seemed disproportionately wide and flat, like badly poured pancake batter. However, not studying herself too closely from the back—too taken by her frontal image—she did not realize this as she happily picked up her black Gucci purse and put it next to the outfit. Dissatisfied with that choice, she ultimately chose the uninitialed, less ostentatious, more expensive Bottega.

Five days later, on the gun shop trip day, Celie put on baggy khakis and a rumpled gray cotton pullover. She never gave her clothes any thought when away from the shop, and as she dressed she realized how very much she had begun to detest all clothes—how much she enjoyed being alone in her apartment completely naked and how this was becoming more and more of a habit because of the pleasure it brought her. She also did not seem to care if anyone could see her this way through her windows. Increasingly, she liked the freedom of wearing just her skin, for its lack of pretence.

She had come to hate the way her customers fussed over what they wore—how they tried to cover up bad feelings

about themselves and masquerade as someone else—
someone who had great confidence. And since the clothes
could never give them a strong, permanent identity, rather
quickly they would return for another something—most
likely a more expensive item, thinking the higher the price,
the higher their feeling of self-worth.

Of course, being the top saleswoman at the shop,
she kept such thoughts to herself. She knew Cecilia
would have laughed and agreed with her—that keep-
ing these thoughts to herself on the "sad purchases for a
faux confidence" *was* smart. However, Celie also believed
that unlike herself, Cecilia's own nakedness frightened
her and that these past many months she had noticed
that Cecilia used more and more layers of clothes to cover
herself. Cecilia's description of Herr M's attack on her
naked being, how she "shivered, then shook, then finally
fully quaked into a seizure near the end," now never left
Celie's mind.

Celie knew she was not attractive, but she also felt she
had wonderfully smooth skin and she loved to cover it
with thick Kukui Nut Coconut moisturizer, and then lie
on her bed, curve her head onto her arms and smell the
soft richness of herself—the pleasure of her own silkiness.
She believed her skin's perfection was because it had never
been passionately touched. She never saw its sad pallor.

The day Cecilia bowed her head and slowly, somberly,
and fragilely detailed what had happened to her with Herr
M, Celie went home and took two showers, put extra
lotion on her skin, and curled into the purity of her virgin
nakedness, draping herself in her one great indulgence—
an expensive, pure white satin comforter—and appreci-
ated her unmarked self a little more.

When Celine arrived, Celie handed her a meticulously drawn map with directions on how to get to the gun shop. Celine was driving her white Mercedes two-seat convertible that Aaron had given her several years ago for her fortieth birthday. "To cheer you up for all the years that really didn't show *at all*," was what he said to her, with a nervous laugh.

In truth, the years had not been kind to Celine and she fully looked her age, plus ten. Too much sun. It was an addiction for her, as were the men. As Cecilia had put it to Celie, "Celine is always in need of a tan and a man." It was true that when she walked into a room, people looked. That flash of shoulder length, overly-bleached blond hair and the startlingly bright colors she wore were always good for a double take.

On her way to pick up Celie, Celine fantasized about the rough, muscled men who would be at the shop and how their heads would turn when she entered; which in fact they did, but again not for her imagined reasons, but rather for her high-pitched giggle coupled with a naiveté, which could have been interpreted as stupidity, and for the too-loud questions that she asked. "Why do you need a permit? I thought this was a *free* country?" she said in a sassy voice, as she batted her lacquered eyelashes at the hardened man with his work-worn wrinkles and tough skin who stood behind the counter. He took his guns quite seriously and looked like he would not mind shooting her after her barrage of childlike questions and flirtatious mannerisms.

Finally, he took out a shotgun and said, "Perhaps you'd prefer this?" Then he snapped its pump, which made a loud noise, and pointed it at her. Everyone there suddenly stopped what they were doing to look at what was going on. Celine acted unfazed, telling the man in her best Mae West impersonation, "I can handle *anything* I'm a *worldly* woman." This made him smile in a way that puzzled Celine, but she chose at the moment to see it as a compliment—which it was not. He had known women like her from his private detective days and found all of them pathetic clichés—deflated balloon creatures, whose authentic feelings had been sucked out of them or never truly existed, and all they did was play at strong. He remembered how much trouble they could cause the people who got too close to them—their demands, and the sometimes frightening, dangerous lengths they would go to get attention.

He also knew that the instant when he pointed the shotgun at her would come back to haunt her. She would wonder why he had done this to her and she would worry that it was possible he did not like her—or worse, that he wanted to hurt her for some unknown reason. He knew insecurity and paranoia ran high in such women.

He was right, for when Celine slipped into bed that night and pressed herself against Aaron's exhausted, flabby body and shut her eyes, she saw the barrel of the shotgun pointing at her and the sinister looking narrow tunnel of its darkness froze her. She neither slept nor moved until sunrise, just lay there in a cold sweat that rose from deep within her—a place of terror and pain she sealed the door to years ago with the death of her baby sister and the image of her father shaking Celeste to *wake up.*

Celie came prepared. She made sure she had a pen and paper in her purse and took notes while she listened to the man behind the counter. She studied the application form and worried about the question, "In the past 5 years, have you been a patient in any medical facility or part of any medical facility used primarily for the care or treatment of persons for mental illness?" After a pause of almost a minute, she decided that sometimes you just need to lie and proceeded to put a large X in the *no* box.

She also decided that however interesting the pump action of the Remington 820 shotgun was—the one that had been pointed at Celine—she preferred the Colt semiautomatic pistol. It looked just like the one Uncle Abraham—Cecily's father—had from World War II, which Cecily had shown to her, Celine, and Cecilia. Celie also thought the handgun could be carried so easily in her purse, unlike the other, which looked like it would need at least a violin case.

She learned from the man behind the counter that the shotgun was more successful in scaring a person and, if need be, more accurate for hitting the target. "The shotgun shells—their spray—would be better for someone inexperienced, better than a single bullet." But to her the pistol seemed a more private purchase. "The shotgun," she told him, "seems too glamorous," which made the man with the reptilian skin grin at her. She was more than happy to take the slip of paper he offered with the addresses of firearm ranges where she could practice once her application had cleared, which she had convinced herself it would.

After she completed it, the shop's photographer—a strong, pretty, young woman—positioned Celie in front of a screen to take her picture. When both the man and the photographer questioned her as to exactly why she wanted a gun—Had there been some trouble where she lived? Was someone bothering her?—she quickly answered, "For protection. I live alone." She had practiced these words in front of her medicine cabinet mirror for days. But still, when she had to say them for real, her voice cracked, which embarrassed her, and she blushed. The effect this had on the man and the young woman was to focus even more on helping her. They would remember her seriousness, her politeness, her vulnerability.

Celie, however, did not notice this, so intense she had become on learning more and more about guns, for with this knowledge came the growing, exciting reality that the plan to kill Herr M was truly in motion. She could *do* this. She had thought of sending letters to the university about him, telling the administration about the terrible things he had done, and one to his live-in girlfriend, a woman who had escaped from Castro's Cuba as a small child and was now teaching at the university. She had more degrees than any three people and kept winning awards with large sums of money attached for her writings on nonviolence—an irony not lost on Celie. But in the end the letter idea did not seem powerful enough. It did not settle her, could not clip off even a corner of her upset.

Now that she had figured out what she really needed to do, she felt she was on a religious mission—her own crusade—her Christian purpose, as she began to call it to herself, although she still considered herself a Jew. Through the years religion had become a mixed-up thing to her, like so many of her thoughts, just a jumble of ideas.

But with this purpose there came a sacredness. To kill an evil man seemed a good thing and certainly equal to what any Slaughter had accomplished. Suddenly, to Celie, being the most beautiful, the most talented, the most popular, the smartest, the richest, all the mosts she had grown up with, seemed so small and superficial against her own assignment.

She was no longer just doing this because of what Herr M had done to Cecilia, but also because of what he had done to her—Celie—which she knew was odd. Herr M was rapidly becoming a symbol for everyone who had hurt *her*—a trigger for her escalating emotions caused by all the people who had pushed at her for more and then for *more* again and added to this, all the people who had pushed at her mother, Aunt Esther.

While being positioned for the photograph—her mission becoming so real—she remembered a poem Cecilia had written especially for her when she was almost ten and Cecilia twelve and she smiled, which she really would rather not have done in a photograph for such a purchase.

She and Cecilia had never wanted to go to the family-mandated Friday night services at their new, fancy suburban temple, so they tried to figure out different ways—alternative ways—they might please God. One Friday night at the Shabbat service, Cecilia handed Celie a folded piece of paper during the silent prayer. Celie read it and burst into uncontrollable laughter. Both she and Cecilia were quickly ushered out of the sanctuary and later paid heavily with solemn and harsh lectures from their parents, both rabbis (junior and senior), and the cantor and as punishment made to go to even more Shabbat services—the summer ones, from which until this time they had been exempt.

As Celie stood there staring back at the small camera she said, quite inadvertently, out loud, "If I Set up the Chairs." The young woman photographer said, "What?" To which Celie replied, startled by how the words had just fallen out of her mouth, "Oh, nothing. I was just thinking of something—something I have to do." She then took a deep breath, her face gleaming, and silently repeated the poem to the lens of the camera, as if it were the eye of God.

> When the people come in to pray
> they'll need somewhere to sit.
> I'll be the one to help them stay
> while they make some sense of it.
>
> And when they are done
> and go home fully blessed,
> I'll be the one
> to clean up what's messed.
>
> Will that be equal enough
> to what they do,
> if I do this stuff
> will it satisfy You?

For Celie, repeating Cecilia's lines, which had been handed to her in the temple so many years ago, to the camera, it seemed as if the eye of God truly had winked at her, although it was just the shutter on the lens. Of course she knew this, but she also believed it was *more* too. Cecilia had taught her about metaphor—how one kind of object or idea could be used in place of another to suggest a likeness between them. Plus, Cecily was always talking about subtext—the importance of it in the plays she wrote. How under the dialogue were all the unspoken motives and beliefs of the characters—the truth as to what was *really* intended.

Consequently, for Celie standing there having herself photographed for the gun application became a much

larger thing and she calmed more than she ever had with
any of the medications given to her by any doctor. When
the strong, young woman told her she was finished and
everything would now be processed, Celie bowed her head
as she had done many times in temple as a child, when the
rabbi removed the Torah from the ark, and the law of God,
with all its commandments, was about to be read. For the
first time she felt aglow and anchored and religious.

When Celie arrives beneath the ground she will have to
learn how to slowly rid herself of her angers by listening
to the music here, especially the clear, pure bells. Eventually I will take her to visit Lao Tzu and she will come to
understand his words:

> Weapons are the tools of violence and all decent
> men detest them.

She will come to appreciate this because Celie is a good person and always will be, no matter what she thinks or does.
     However, when Celine arrives, she will likely stay locked
in her above-the-ground mind-set and not be interested in
what is possible to learn from our unending journey. She
will probably gravitate to the large circle of narcissists who
pock the underground and stay forever fascinated with
themselves—fastened to their vanities—never to spiral up
and out of the mirror of their own stories.

Celine's preoccupation with herself definitely peaked that
day in the gun shop, where she continued busying herself staring at all the different knives in the large display
case by the entrance to the shop—their various elongated,
curved shapes. She thought of all the men she had known

and the various elongated, curved shapes of their private parts. How Lew had once traced the curves of her body with the sharp edge of a small steak knife—over her fully plucked, shaved, waxed, naked skin—and how much it had aroused her. When he had called the next day to ask her if she were "still marked," this had stimulated her even more as she took off her robe, carried the phone to her mirror, described to him what she saw, and touched herself with great excitement.

She also stared at the handcuffs, with which she was quite familiar. Lew liked to use them on her. This excited her too. She thought about how they would giggle over buying more "equipment." It made them feel devilish, like their particular affair was more special than anyone's—*ever*.

She looked at the various kinds of ropes in another case and remembered how Morris kept asking if he could "watch"—watch her with another woman—and how she finally gave in to his request—a birthday present to him, of sorts. That day Morris arrived with some rope and he bound her wrists so she was helpless. Then the woman did all kinds of things to her. The only thing Morris told Celine to do was to suck the woman's breasts. She thought it best not to admit to Morris how much she had enjoyed it, how much it had aroused her. Afterward, however, she worried a lot about what her father, Emmanuel, would have thought of her participation in this, given his issues with such behavior. Then, she pushed this idea out of her head because of the fact that he was dead.

She is fairly quiet about such goings-on that Morris continues to increasingly insist upon and especially about how much she looks forward to each excursion, just pretends she is doing him an enormous favor for which he greatly rewards her with another eighteen-carat object.

With all these items surrounding her, Celine smiled as she wondered whether any of her cousins were capable of such adventures and concluded they were not, no matter how violent and strange the language sometimes was in Cecilia's poems or how reckless—in a mannered way—Cecily tried to make herself look. And, of course, thinking about Celie in *any* area of experimentation was hopeless.

"Poor, frightened, nervous Celie," she thought as she looked over at her cousin. But as she stared at her, Celine was stunned. For the first time she could remember, Celie looked rather lovely and calm—almost euphoric. It made Celine even happier that she had so willingly agreed to go on this adventure. That among these weapons and items for bondage, both of them had found some pleasure. And being Celine, she saw no problem in any of this.

SMALL GREEN

I do not go away, but the Grounds are ample—
almost travel—.

Emily Dickinson

She's tried Jungian, Freudian, Transactional
Analyses, even Rolfing, the instructor's knuckles
kneading her skin, fingers pushing up
her nose, fists down
her throat, his dog barking
next to him. She'll tell you the issues

have lodged themselves in her connective tissue
or confide in you about the therapist
who lies in his Naugahyde recliner,
the rips in it camouflaged with masking
tape to keep the stuffing from popping,
and the day he reached deep inside
himself, pulled out his own
caked-on secret, showed it
to her, and how she fled—
because she knew for him there was no cure—
to a braless humanist who played Hindu
music and had her pound
a battered paisley pillow and yell
about her mother and father.
Acquainted with every pamphleteer, she's anchored

herself to a small green chair and watches
neighbors pack their cars for summer travel,
longs to go anywhere, always prepares a bag
twice—once for luck, once to be ready—
and when she doesn't leave, she runs out
to buy the latest self-help book and slowly returns
each folded item to its own familiar shelf.

c. slaughter

CECILY KNEW THAT her call to Deidre would surprise and
perplex her. But she also knew that Deidre would be confused and upset—actually furious and humiliated—after
her lunch with Cecilia and Celine.

Celine had promised to immediately report to Cecily
what had happened at the lunch and she kept to that
promise. Cecily knows that Celine carries around a certain amount of guilt—at least as much as Celine is
capable of—from the rumor her father started about her so
many years ago, and that Celine's given her far too much
information about her escapades with men (and women).
Celine clearly talks to Cecily in a much more explicit way
than to anyone else in the family, maybe because Cecily's
considered on the fringes of the cousin clique—pretty
much always has been. My parents certainly pushed Cecily
aside after Manny's statement about her and how it spread
throughout the community. They could not tolerate *any*
gossip that worked against them or the family, which they
pretty much considered one and the same.

Celine always prefaces what she says to Cecily with a
nervous giggle and these words, "Cecily, promise me you'll
not put this in a play." "*Of course*," Cecily always replies.
But Celine does worry a bit that Cecily has too much

information about her and this does make her a little anxious, which works well for Cecily, for it allows her to ask favors of Celine and get information about the family she otherwise would not have.

Cecily was right. When she called Deidre as soon as she arrived home, Deidre seemed disoriented not only by what she had just experienced, but also by Cecily's invitation to take her to lunch in a few weeks. She did not want Deidre to feel she was crowding in on her, so giving her some time between lunches seemed a good tactic. At first Deidre said, "No, I don't think so. I'm tired. Really tired." Cecily responded, "I understand," in her most empathetic voice and then enthusiastically said, "We'll have a good time! I promise. You'll see. Anyway, it's not right now." Deidre hesitated, then agreed with a wishy-washy, exhausted, "Okay—I guess."

Like Deidre, Cecily was fed up with the suburban writing groups she had attended and felt far more talented than those women and the occasional retired man who would wander in and within the year die or just disappear. They would gossip too much about successful writers, rather than focus on the language that brought these people their honors. Also, they were sticky friendly to each other—until one got published. Sure, they were outwardly excited for the person, but, no matter how minor the magazine from which the acceptance arrived, when the happy writer left the room, their tongues would turn to swords, which they drove into the work of the temporarily high-spirited, absent one.

Cecily *knew* she deserved better than these women who would just as soon pass their time bragging about their children's accomplishments or, better yet, their husbands' promotions, or in their worst moments, the best sales going on at the high-end shopping mall. They continuously flattered each other's work as long as the playing field was level—the unspoken code was that no one could stand on any stepstool of success, no matter how low it was to the ground.

There was one woman who started to achieve some outside recognition, which she knew to keep to herself. Then she suddenly left the group. Ultimately, she moved away. When she disappeared, they mocked her work a lot, especially after her writing started to appear frequently in high level literary magazines. Such was this atmosphere. Interestingly, however, they all adored Cecilia. She was their backyard star. Cecilia sightings were always discussed. This made Cecily nauseous, but she kept her feelings to herself, pretending how much she, too, adored her cousin. She had to admit they did treat her quite well because she was related to Cecilia, although this, also, made her sick. Right before she left—at the last session she attended—Deidre showed up as the new person. Cecily could tell from the look in her eyes that Deidre really did not want to be there either.

Cecily had recently quit her therapist, Dr. Mann, who in truth was a stupid man. He incessantly bragged about himself, taking up at least ten collective minutes during a session to tell about his comings and goings or some psychiatric paper he or some other therapist had delivered at a conference. The one paper that sticks in my mind the most was about Sylvia Plath and that most likely she had PMS and if she had only gotten an early diagnosis, she could have been saved. I hated how he spoke so authoritatively about this talented, dead woman's innards.

It seemed to me a worse intrusion than being alive and discussed in such a way. Clearly I identified too much with the possibility of this. It was as if someone were barging into my life, *my story*—reimagining the facts of it with me too far away, completely unable to explain or fight back. My total frustration over this proved, once again, I still had more work to do on myself in the art of letting go of what anyone *says* or *does* above the ground.

Sometimes Dr. Mann would describe some recent trip he had taken with his wife to what he thought was "a really fancy place"—while Cecily would be thinking, "Yes, on my nickel." Or he would attempt to critique some highbrow art movie he had just seen, straining to be the quintessential intellectual. He even kept out a blurry newspaper clipping of himself with four other aging, bald men—all therapists, at a meeting of little consequence—for months on the coffee table in front of where his patients sat, so no one could miss it. It was distracting and Cecily, like I am sure anyone who saw it, felt obliged to say, "Oh my, what is this? Is that you?" When this not-so-subliminal script was presented to Cecily, it prompted a ten-minute discussion on the circumstances of the photograph, during which he became too animated, causing his face to swell and become garishly bright, so that he looked like a red balloon blown up to the very brink of orgasmic explosion.

Cecily felt that Deidre was definitely a better person with whom to speak and someone who could be of far greater use to her than he. Anyway, he already did not approve of so much of her behavior, nor would he have of what she now had in mind. Actually, he would have been appalled. Anyone would have been. Here his appraisal would have been focused and accurate.

She picked the same place—the Arts Club—as Cecilia had chosen. She wanted Deidre to remember how badly she had been treated. It was a large part of her plan. Cecily was already there when she arrived. Deidre looked more worn out than Cecily had remembered. Cecily stood up as she came over and shook her hand and said, "How happy I am that we're finally, officially meeting. That awful writers' group really didn't count." They both nodded their heads in agreement. Cecily gave her the enthusiastic focus she knew she had not received from Cecilia, or for that matter Celine, for Celine, as she reported it, had been instructed by Celie "to just talk about myself a lot."

Initially, Cecily kept the conversation at a light, airy level—nothing rushed or pushy in her speech—and that did eventually help put Deidre at ease, for her discomfort at being there was obvious. She spoke too softly and not very much, and just took delicate sips of her soup, leaving half of it.

Having a hearty appetite, almost a lust for the food, Cecily ordered the shrimp with pasta. It must have been contagious because Deidre ordered it too, and began to eat with a gusto she did not have at the beginning of their meal. Cecily watched, astonished, as Deidre started to impale the large shrimp with her fork and swallow them whole. She did this with the pasta too, stabbing at it and chewing it with large jaw movements. She had become all accelerated motion.

Finally, when they were almost finished with their entrees, Cecily sighed and stared at her. Then she said one word: "Cecilia."

"Yes?" Deidre replied, as neutrally as she knew how to do. It was only then her pace slowed.

"You *know* her." Cecily said this not as a question, but as a statement.

"Yes, yes I do. Somewhat. Just a bit." Deidre replied with great hesitancy and some amount of sticky melancholy and then she asked, "Is she as beautiful as your Aunt Rose?"

Cecily tried to control how frustrated and infuriated she was by this question and just said as evenly as she could, "I'm not here to talk about Rose." So sickened was she by everyone's *Rose sickness*—her own included.

"What do you think of *Cecilia*—what do you think of her?" Cecily insisted.

"Think-of-her?" she answered.

She said this haltingly, sounding like a Rogerian therapist who just repeats the patient's words back in the form of a question. But it was clear Cecily would have none of this and for the first time Deidre felt a slice of Cecily's well-known impatience and large forcefulness—which she intended.

"Do you *like* her poetry?" She *wanted* her voice to sound borderline accusatory.

"Well, yes," she said. "In truth, I really do. Do you?"

Cecily gave a huge sigh. It was almost as if a puff of smoke came out of her mouth at that moment. She did feel dragon-like. She replied, "It's okay. A little self-serving, wouldn't you say? But okay." Then she paused and leaned forward and said, "Have you read 'Small Green'? It appeared in *Poetry*."

"Yes," she replied. "It's sad. I especially liked the Emily Dickinson epigraph."

"Well, she didn't *write* the epigraph," Cecily snapped. "Do you know she never goes anywhere, except to the dress shop, an occasional lunch, and to give a few local readings? Mostly, she just sits in her apartment, in that tiny writing room of hers. Except, of course *for*— "

Cecily then stopped and looked at Deidre as if Deidre

were supposed to finish the sentence, which she did not, would not, could not. Cecily had now moved into high gear.

"Except for what?" Deidre finally, carefully, with her best innocent voice, replied. Cecily could see a stringy residue of shrimp caught between her teeth and that made Deidre's seem all the more vulnerable.

"Except for what?" Cecily said too loud. "*Except for what?*" she continued. "Don't you *know* about the critic?"

Cecily then took Deidre's hand, patted it and said, "Don't be shy." Deidre looked at her palm and then wiped it on her slacks. She did not want Cecily to see this, but she did. Cecily knew she was becoming successful in making her feel uncomfortable. Her look demanded a response.

It was then Deidre remembered the question—the question about the critic. She restated it—"Did I know about the critic?" It was clear to Cecily that Deidre did not quite know what she wanted to say, but finally replied, "I remember the poem 'The Interior of the Sun.'" Then, suddenly not being able to control herself, she blurted out, "*Did he hit her? Did she let him? Is he the one* in *that poem? Is he the Herr M in the poem? Is he?*" The questions were not really for Cecily—for Cecily to answer—it was as if she were asking the air, which seemed to grow too thick for her, for she coughed and could not clear her throat for several seconds.

Cecily laughed a too-loud laugh. Definitely what Deidre said had pleased her.

Cecily waved her hands and said, "*Hit* her? He *raped* her."

"*Raped* her?" She said in a voice she could barely find. Then added, "Well, I'd heard that rumor, but—"

"Yes," Cecily glowed. "It's true," she continued with great relish. "It's just been unequivocally established."

She then looked around the dining room a little self-consciously to see if anyone else had heard her, but they were pretty much alone except for a well-dressed couple at the far end of the room. They seemed so dignified from this distance. She thought, "They must be talking about something artistic." She wanted to be invited into their conversation. She was certain if she were surrounded by such people she would not have to be here trying to plot something with this silly woman. She would be recognized for her talent and not need to deal with the Deidres of this world. She staunchly believed, "If given the chance, I could rise above everyone, *literarily* and literally, especially my family."

"Poor Cecilia—" Deidre started to say, when Cecily interrupted her.

"Poor Cecilia, you say! I heard about the lunch! What did she *give* you? Tell me. What did you come away with?"

These words, "What did you come away with?" almost seemed to make Deidre cry and Cecily saw her look over at a table, where she guessed it all had happened—or rather, where nothing did. As Cecily followed Deidre's eyes she could tell Deidre felt she knew her every thought, her every feeling, and Deidre's face looked scorched. She turned toward Cecily and spoke with an equal dose of forced strength and growing upset, her body starting to lean downward, becoming ungracefully slumped toward the table.

"He actually *raped* her?"

"Yes. And she deserved it."

"No one deserves *that*," Deidre quietly replied, trying to pull herself together.

Cecily smirked, then put her now completely sweat-filled hand on Deidre's, and asked her in a slowly paced, yet piercing way, "Do-you-hate-her?"

Again, sounding like a Rogerian therapist, but now dazed, she said, "Hate her?"

"Yes, hate her."

"No," she answered, unconvincingly.

"Well, you *had* to have hated her after that lunch."

Deidre then woke up to the obvious question and asked, "How did you *know* about the lunch? You called almost to the minute I arrived home that day."

"I *have* my ways," Cecily said with great authority and a certain amount of pride.

"Yes, I did hate her after the lunch, but I don't anymore," she said halfheartedly. Now looking quite scattered, she quoted a line from Cecilia's poem, the one Cecily had mentioned earlier, as if just muttering to herself:

> Acquainted with every pamphleteer, she's anchored
> herself to a small green chair . . .

Then she said she had to leave. That she was feeling sick. However, as sick as she was, when she looked at Cecily it was clear to her she still did not know what it was that Cecily wanted from her and she meekly asked, "Why did you invite me here?" When this question was met with just Cecily's intended silence, Deidre's fingers nervously pinched the still crisp, white tablecloth. Finally, she gulped out, "Yes, remembering the lunch does make me hate her."

"Good!" Cecily said, patting her same hand, and adding, "Perhaps now we can begin." She then laughed and said, "Wasn't that the last line in *Portnoy's Complaint*? Wasn't that what the therapist said to Portnoy?" However, Deidre's anxiety had completely taken over and she could not focus on anything literary.

"Begin what?" she blurted out.

"I want you to help me."

"Help you *what?*"

"*Hurt her,* of course," Cecily whispered. "You know you want to. And remember," she continued, "I *can* help you. I do have some amount of clout in the poetry world."

Deidre looked like she was going to vomit. She took Cecily's hand off hers, stood up, and said "I think I ate a bad shrimp. I'm going to be sick. You'll have to excuse me." She then ran out of the room. Cecily heard her in the hallway cursing, "Damn artist's stairs."

Cecily smiled, thinking, "Mies van der Rohe wouldn't have been pleased." But, reconsidering, and knowing a little about his huge ego, she thought, "He probably wouldn't have given a damn, maybe even laughed." Then she saw Deidre race toward the elevator and disappear.

Cecily wasn't bothered by this at all. She had set in motion what she had intended—Deidre would not forget their conversation. She was sure of this. Cecily knew she would see her again, and she knew Deidre could be of great help to her with her plans, which she was just beginning to assemble—and, hopefully, to construct even better now that the rumors about the rape had proven to be true. It was clear Deidre did hate Cecilia—hate that Cecilia had promised her something and had given her nothing. It was also clear Deidre was ambitious and that they had this in common. Cecily thought, "She's just weak, but I am strong, so in a way we'll make a good team." Her guess was that Deidre would try to run from the Slaughter family, try to make it without Cecilia, without her. But she knew Deidre would return to her, that her flight was only temporary.

MENS REA

I

Without intoxication or insanity
I put on the rubber glove,
ideal for one time use—
lightweight, tough, disposable, cheap.
It fits either hand—
right or left, good or bad—how easily
it becomes my second skin.
I write with it on—how well
it holds my pen. No one
can read my covered palm—
the past, present, future of
who I am, unknown.
My voice cannot be traced
to the outdoor phone
nor my prints found on the dime-
store paper. My fingers sweat
against the balloony latex.
I'm tempted to take it off,
blow it up—burst open
the situation
that keeps me so hidden.

II

The worm has a simple brain—
just a pair of ganglia,

while the advanced reptile's
is large and complex.
I did not remember this.
The pink jellylike ball
inside my skull lost
a considerable amount of blood
when you constricted my body,
hissed into me
causing irreparable damage—
although the EEG and the MRI
could not produce the image
of why I wanted to die.
Demented is what I keep
calling myself, forever
confusing your rage for desire
for me, for *Eve,* alive
in the garden with all that overripe
passion—the rotten spots
in the vegetation now so visible
with my glasses on—I see
the snake always waiting
for some soft and starving woman.

III

This autumn the leaf-like
bundles of nerve
cells in my cerebellum
brittle and I have
lost my balance. Purposely,
Knowingly, Negligently,
Recklessly, I write
you this poem, send copies

to your family and friends.
The hard thick bones
of my head that protected
me from the blows
of this world have thinned.
I know evil in advance
and this time do not plead
ignorance. I claim no
extra chromosome or excess
of dopamine or serotonin.
I intend
for something bad to happen.

c. slaughter

A YEAR BEFORE Uncle Emmanuel's colon cancer killed him, he joined an all-female aerobics class. Since he did not have the energy to make his yearly trip to Las Vegas, it was his final effort to watch breasts bob up and down and beyond this to give quick, too-tight hugs to women, who at first found him innocent enough. In the beginning, the women were delighted to have such a lively old man in the class, working so hard to stay fit. They thought him cute and sweet. However, after a few weeks passed, each felt a growing discomfort at the way he fixated on their bodies. How he used the inner parts of his flabby arms to press into the sides of their chests. How his hands would casually touch their exposed flesh—a shoulder or an upper arm, while in over-animated conversations with them—and how he would then wipe their sweat ever-so-nonchalantly around the rim of his lips. Rather quickly they all noticed this. But the day they secretly agreed to gather to talk about his

behavior with their instructor after class—about not wanting this stout, elfin man with his thick grin in their class
anymore—he collapsed during a "spread your legs, arms
above your head, clap, flex, jump—ten times," exercise
and was carried away in an ambulance, never to return.

From then on Manny Slaughter was relegated to a bed
where he lay flattened both physically and spiritually, while
the morphine drip seeped into him. As he grew thin, then
thinner, becoming a sliver of his lusty, round self, his bodily
functions forever messier, no narcotic was able to fully
alleviate his pain. Consequently, he swore and screamed
his way into death, so ultimately all that remained of him
for those who had dedicatedly surrounded his bed were
the piercing echoes of those last, vile words they heard
from his increasingly large mouth, which seemed to overtake his otherwise shrinking face, and the awful names he
repetitively called each of them, as if everything that was
happening to him was their fault. He clearly wanted to
encapsulate them with such language and to take them
with him into his hell.

When my mother found out her brother had joined such
a class, she laughed and laughed. "How cute he is. Always
the imp," she would say to her other brothers and Samuel
and Benjamin would agree, secretly wishing they had his
chutzpah at the late dates in their own dull lives. They were
mesmerized by the possibilities of the class and could not
control their own fantasies of all those women—"all *ten* of
them"—in their skimpy, bright spandex, stretching, bending, prancing, perhaps even galloping to rhythmic music.
"The thought of it!"—they would whisper to Abraham,
who remained the quietest on the subject. For beyond the
others Abraham understood the possible implications of

Manny's behavior, how it would not take the women long to catch on to his brother's perversities, and the possibility that they would file complaints against him. He thought about how it was becoming a different world, where women stood up for themselves, would not allow certain lines to be crossed and had many more outside safeguards. And then he could not help but think of his own daughter and the pain his brother had caused her.

When Manny Slaughter arrived here and realized what was possible, the first thing he did was to try to find the path to all of history's great whores. He searched his small mind, then he asked directions to where he could find Anne Boleyn and her sister—"what's her name," as he put it. Even with his limited knowledge, one of his great idols was Henry VIII for all his voracious appetites. For a while he even sought out Anna Karenina—not realizing she was not a real person. With this, I found him far more humorous than I ever did in life—and more stupid. He had remembered Garbo playing her and pictured himself as Vronsky at the time. "Love 'em and leave 'em," he would grunt to his brothers as if he were the biggest shot of the four—which, in this area, he was. Of course, he had no interest in finding Garbo herself or any other woman rumored in life to have had even a hint of lesbian inclinations. Even in death Uncle Emmanuel is obsessed with homoerotic gossip.

Finally, when he found Tolstoy and bothered him as to where Anna might be, Tolstoy was so startled by this awful little man's intrusion on his peace and his bizarre question, that he shrieked at him about both *his* and *Anna's* immorality. He then called Manny "the biggest moron in all of history" for thinking she was more than just a mere character in a book and growled that he was "almost certainly too hopeless for any kind of Christian redemption," which bewildered Manny's mind even more than the morphine drip. He wanted to shout back at Tolstoy that the Star of David was on his casket, but he did not, feeling for the first time that he was up against an overwhelming force of a man whom he could never come close to managing or manipulating. So he fled.

Cecily never forgot how Uncle Emmanuel would press his chest into hers and cup his hands, seemingly by accident, around the sides of her disproportionately large breasts. After it happened more than once, she realized that this was no misstep—it was all a measured act of feigned innocence, and she viewed it as an evil, too-obvious trick. Consequently, she would distance herself from him at family gatherings by going to the farthest point in the room from where he stood. However, he always sought her out with open arms—and hands.

She envied the flat-chested models in the high fashion magazines, who did not even need a bra, let alone one that was a 38DD. She resented how when her breasts began to grow, almost uncontrollably, at the late age of seventeen, the phone suddenly began to ring all of the time with boys calling, forever calling, wanting to know if she were "free," in both meanings of the word. But Cecily had already pulled into herself and built a thick, crustacean shell made out of a wrath way before Uncle Emmanuel's hand stratagem. What he had done to her earlier was far worse.

The fight between Cecily's father and his brother when she was thirteen started because Abraham worried that Manny had been making arrangements with shady characters to get the lowest prices for the carpets they sold at their store and what was being delivered was stolen merchandise. When he nervously and carefully told Manny of his concern, it inflamed the latter to the point of calling Abraham all kinds of names, including *schmuck, schlemiel,* and *shlub,* ultimately landing on the cruelest thing he could think of doing to get back at Abraham, which was to target the thirteen-year-old Cecily with a name that twisted her mind into a Gordian knot. Her disorientation from this was something from which she would never get loose.

Of course, Manny never said the word directly to Abraham. He was far more clever and told of his worry about Cecily—"her possible inclinations"—to the mothers of his daughter Celine's friends, who were Cecily's friends, too.

Initially, Cecily noticed that none of her friends were returning her calls and were quick to walk away from her at school. When she told her mother of this and of her confusion as to why this was happening, Aunt Lillian had no choice but to tell her about the calls she had received from concerned mothers in the neighborhood, and then mother and daughter just stood there shaking in their too-bright yellow, 1960s kitchen inside their mid-sized, tract row house—a place where sameness and conventionality were revered and not to be disturbed. However, Aunt Lillian carried a rage from what Manny had done to her daughter straight into the grave. She idealized the lives of her sisters-in-law's daughters and silently hated them— especially Cecilia for her gifts of beauty and talent, thereby making it impossible that this would not seep into Cecily. So it was better than good for Aunt Lillian when Cecily began plotting something to get back at Cecilia. Underneath the ground, inside the underbelly of herself, Aunt Lillian has stayed stuck.

When Cecily first heard the word and learned of the concept of same sex relationships, she was just getting used to the regular facts of life, which ironically she had learned from Celine way before Aunt Lillian had gotten up the courage to explain such things. Uncle Abraham in his reserve, temerity, and exhaustion wanted no part in this, nor was he capable of outwardly dealing with what his brother had set in motion concerning his daughter. The terror within himself that he brought back from the war was too deeply imbedded in both his mind and body, making it impossible for him to directly challenge another person.

Cecily's own fantasies had been of the popular, athletic boys who never spoke to her in those seemingly unending years of her body's flat fallowness. Interestingly, at least to Cecily, when she began to rapidly bloom, almost uncontrollably during an especially hot summer in the season of her seventeenth year, the boys did not seem to care at all about the rumors. In fact, with "that body" it only made her more attractive in mysteriously wild ways, which most boys at the time could only imagine. Only a few had seen pictures of such encounters in the magazines that their fathers thought they had carefully hidden. Cecily, however, by then had emotionally shut down, so all the attention she began to receive from boys—no matter how popular—had come to mean little to her. Her silent disorientation from the words Uncle Emmanuel had carefully planted grew into a brittle fury—an anger carefully and slowly turned outward in canny, clandestine ways which would continue to thicken and harden throughout her years. Ironically, it would be she who would come to most resemble Manny Slaughter in her ability to wound others.

When Cecily heard the most recent talk, which confirmed that Cecilia was in fact raped and how others were raging over it, she could not stop thinking about how to best use this. Cecilia herself was talking more and more about it, but only to very specific people, one of them being Michael, who Cecily learned had come back to live with Cecilia—to protect her—and was planning some kind of revenge against Herr M. Cecily hates the way Michael is always there for Cecilia, even in divorce—*how no one ever really abandons Cecilia.*

She thinks about how *no one protects her.* Even at thirteen, how *no one* rescued her from the gossip, from the only path at the time she knew to take—that self-imposed isolation which felt like it was coming more from the outside in, which in truth it was. *No one* set the record straight, *no one* grabbed Manny Slaughter by the throat and tried to choke him, or had even the impulse to cut off his viperous tongue—not her hesitant mother, not her frightened father. Cecily thinks about this a lot. And now with Michael coming to Cecilia's rescue and planning God-knows-what for Cecilia's honor and her sanity, Cecily finds herself almost out of control with fantasies as to how to hurt Cecilia.

In her barren apartment, where the only sign of some life is a tall, half-sick ficus tree next to an extra-long couch that has never come close to being filled with visitors, she sits and ruminates about calling Herr M (whose real name, as everyone knows by now, is Ivan Durmand)—all the time hating Cecilia's nickname for him and yet also becoming too attached to it, which she finds annoying within herself. She looks him up in the phone book both at the university and at his home and when she discovers it twice under "I. Durmand" it makes her both smile and feel a little fearful. "I. Durmand, I. Durmand, such an easy pun," she says out loud as a quick, adrenaline rush branches inside her body.

She wonders if he would agree to meet with her and thinks perhaps he might, if he believes she has information that would be of benefit to him. She even fantasizes about him becoming attracted to her with the same uncontrollable lust it is rumored he had—perhaps still has—for Cecilia.

Everything Cecilia has or had, Cecily wants and wants more of—as if she is smart enough to pick out the good from the bad, distinguish it and handle it. Her hubris and her envy are that great even though *having it all* over-stimulates her. She feels as though she might explode either way—if she gets nothing or gets too much.

In her play Cecily clearly sides much more with the "critic" than the "poet," as if the poet deserved whatever happened to her that wintry night. The stage directions are to make the lights go "ice white" with a long pause of cold silence, like something one would find in a Russian novel. She thinks of Boris Pasternak. She really likes this effect, is quite proud of it. The only sound and image on the dimly lit stage at this moment would be that of the wind forcing a branch to scratch at the critic's window—made to look like a witch's claw also trying to grab at the poet. However, she is not quite sure what she has written will be a good enough defense of the critic, for it is hard to defend a man against even a highly manipulative woman, if something intensely brutal happens.

She is also worried Herr M will not agree to meet with her now that he is living with a woman with a pristine reputation. The gossip is that this makes him feel reborn and unsoiled—cleansed—although his legacy of damage to women is long, and to think of himself in this way would make anyone with any knowledge of him wince, or at least smirk. Cecily knows this.

At night alone in her bed she fantasizes about killing Herr M, then having the police arrive only to find Cecilia standing over him with a gun in her hand. She dreams of this a lot, but upon waking, she can never figure out how, in reality, she would be able to pull this off and this causes her great frustration. Yet of all my cousins—actually, all the people I know who still walk on the earth's fractured shell—it is Cecily who is the most capable of such an act.

Cecily also imagines variations of how this might happen. In one, it is Michael who kills Herr M and Cecilia completely breaks apart upon hearing what he has done for her. Cecily then writes a book—creative nonfiction—about Cecilia and beyond this, about the entire Slaughter family and she becomes even more famous than she could have been as a playwright, because creative nonfiction is becoming the hot new thing. She sees herself composed and well-dressed and on television.

Cecily will never come to understand Lao Tzu's words:

> There is no greater sin than desire,
> No greater curse than discontent,
> No greater misfortune than wanting something for
>   oneself,
> Therefore he who knows that enough is enough will
>   have enough.

I know when Cecilia recently searched out his sayings to calm her shaky self down and found

Too much success is not an advantage,
Do not tinkle like jade
Or clatter like chimes

she sighed and nodded. She feels she is living proof that a fairly high profile in the low world where much of American poetry resides, is definitely not worth it.

Now, in most of Cecily's waking hours, she plots out ways to accomplish Herr M's death, forever focusing on how to trace it back to Cecilia. She remembers her father's gun—the one another World War II private picked up in the chaos from the boiled mud ground where her father was dragged away. How the man secretly brought it to her mother along with Abraham's dog tags and Lillian made a shrine of them and prayed there on her knees to bring her Abraham back. The rabbis at the temple, of course, knew none of this, a mezuzah on the door being the only acceptable amulet deserving such reverence.

Cecily only learned about the gun's existence and the shrine her mother made, after her father died and Aunt Lillian brought a box down from a high shelf in the closet and wept over it. Abraham had survived the gruesome battle of Tarawa in the Pacific. All the adults in the family knew of this and had talked in an agitated and excited fashion about it to anyone who would listen. But when they learned he had ended up on one of the Japanese "hell ships," as they were called, which were attacked by the Americans because no Red Cross flag was flown, they were speechless. "Friendly fire" was the term the Slaughters were told and they grew sick and silent on the subject to outsiders at my parents' instructions.

When Abraham was finally rescued—one of the few—and returned home mute on everything he had been through, the only grief Aunt Lillian ever heard from him was years later when he would lock himself in the bathroom and weep the chant, "*My own brother, my very own brother, attacking my only child with friendly fire. Friendly fire.*" Aunt Lillian would listen to this over and over, getting as close as she quietly could to Abraham's locked door, her arms folded, rocking herself back and forth, silently repeating her husband's words.

The effect of what Manny had done reignited Abraham's fragile, fevered self and this event gnawed at him for the rest of his years, and although he was the youngest, he became the second child of Idyth and Cecil to pass away. Manny preceded him by two years—a very small justice. Though for Abraham—unlike Manny—he was more ready for his journey to this place and found the passage far less painful, even a relief, for it proved to be a permanent escape from Manny. Here, he has successfully cleansed his mind of this brother.

A "prisoner of war" were the words Cecily overheard, as she got older. "And yes, it took *all* of us to paste him back together," the adults would tell their friends with more than a touch of arrogance—my parents being the worst offenders. Although at the time Cecily did not know everything, she found what they said condescending. "Why didn't they see him as brave?" she would think. "A man who tried—forever tried—to keep going. A man who, given all he'd been through, still had enough faith in people and their goodwill to have a child, no matter how vicious the world."

By the time Cecily learned of her father being on a hell ship, he had died. Unfortunately, when Cecilia, after Uncle Abraham's death, also found this out, she, too, made the comparison between friendly fire from his country to that of his own brother's known awful behavior toward him, saying to Cecily, "The pain of this has to be excruciating." Even though she said this with great mournfulness, all it did to Cecily was to increase her furor toward Cecilia. If I had not been dead, it would have been the first, and the only, time I would have covered Cecilia's mouth with my hand to stop her words.

Now, while Cecily waits to hear from the theaters about her play, this storm toward Cecilia builds, always with the nagging feeling that it shows—which could make her even more unappealing a person to take on—and, alone on her couch, she worries out loud, while waiting for the phone to ring, "Perhaps they have just forgotten about me, or *they know*—know that the play is about Cecilia and *no one* wants to hurt Cecilia—Cecilia with her large eyes, pale skin, and long, thick hair. Snow White Cecilia, whom no one would hurt and get away with it. Except Herr M." And for Cecily this is only a gift for it raises all kinds of possibilities both in her creative life and in the reality she has been forced to live in since that day so many years ago when Uncle Emmanuel *raped her*—however metaphorically—at thirteen and she did not know what to do or to whom to run. Unlike now, where her imaginings of the possibilities of what to do and where to go are becoming endless and almost unmanageable.

When even Deidre, after their lunch, is unresponsive to her calls, her rage and loneliness overwhelm her. She calls her (she vows) *one last time*. Finally, Deidre decides to pick up the phone when she sees Cecily's number and listens, listens carefully to Cecily's latest plan.

PARANOIA

She dreams of an angry animal awaiting her
arrival on an abandoned island
and tries to figure it out
with her paperback Freud.
Sometimes she thinks
the answer lies
in a different source.
Sometimes she's convinced
the accumulated clues add up
to almost nothing.
But mostly she just feels
prey to all the evils

she can imagine,
focuses on every furious
story, remembers each misleading
offering perfect with the promise
of everlasting happiness—
the once upon a time

she was caught
in another person's
spell. Someone gave her token
love which she took
for real,
and it terrifies her
to know
how much she wants to kill.

c. slaughter

WHEN CECILY FINALLY called Herr M, it might as well have been me—a dead person. She nervously announced that she was Cecily Slaughter and would very much like to talk to him, stridently asking, "Can we meet? *Of course,* any place of your choosing." At first, he was confused and could not place her. After a long pause an image of her clicked into his mind—she was the swollen, distorted version of Cecilia. "Yes," he thought, "Cecilia Slaughter," and immediately he felt his heart beating faster.

Both his rage and passion at the thought of Cecilia rose up and renewed itself at high pitch. Of course, he did not want his voice to show any of this, reveal even a hint of emotion, so mostly he stayed quiet and covered the mouthpiece of the phone when his breathing became too obvious. The last thing he wanted was to discuss—or quarrel over—with this intrusive woman was Cecilia. Most certainly he did not want to show how the mere mention of Cecilia's name could affect him—cut to the depth of his body's passion.

Cecilia had arrived with Cecily at a crowded poetry reading at the university a little over two years ago. He had yet to be introduced to Cecilia, but he had noticed both women—one so gorgeous and the other a cartoon caricature of the other. He should have stopped himself then—his smoldering urgency to know this woman.

Weeks later they began to meet for coffee, where they spoke of literature in general and her own work in particular. However, he always prefaced their conversation by first asking about her mother, which pleased her because he was such a good listener. She had told him about Aunt Lettie's illness at their first encounter, it being foremost on her mind and telling him what was happening with her mother did temporarily alleviate a little of the anguish she was feeling. She liked his concern.

The last time they met—before his invitation to *that* dinner—he went a bit off topic and talked about *pleasure.* Cecilia sat across from him—her violet eyes so wide open, her whole being seeming *so wide open*, at least to Herr M—and quietly listened as he said, "I think two adults who are attracted to each other should further realize their relationship through *pleasure.* That the times they spend together should not be just verbal, but also physically *pleasurable.*"

Cecilia just smiled her stunning smile, as if mesmerized by him, then suddenly awoke from her trance, looked at her watch and realized she was late for an appointment. She jumped up, shook his hand and said, "Thank you. I love your giving me and my poetry so much attention. See you soon, I hope!" He thought she *got it.* "Who wouldn't have?" was his strong feeling. Especially when, a few days later, he called her and said, "I'd like to cook you a dinner. Something special." She did not miss a beat with her exuberant, "Yes, I'd like that!"

She appeared at his door aglow in impossibly soft, clinging winter clothes. I *do* understand the desire to be a semi-seductress, but, in this case, it was a huge mistake. When she took off her coat, her pants and sweater clung to her from winter static—he remembered its crackling noise and the sparks that encircled her. It made him feel that her whole being was electrified. They both laughed at this and he thought it a good start . . .

He could not suppress his impulse to want to mess her up, starting with taking his thumb and pressing it over her perfectly formed lips to erase the too-bright color on

them, which hid their own natural radiance. Her nipples
had hardened from the cold and they stood out, even
against the sweater she wore, which felt like that of a kit-
ten's fur when he touched her arm, and that, too, added
to his building arousal as he welcomed her further into
his place. It was then he presented her with the bracelet
of silver and obsidian. He thought it the perfect moment.
He proudly told a colleague, "I think the gift will be a nice
touch," and then he laughed.

Hours later, even after she was naked and shivering and
crying on the floor, he could not take his eyes off her—her
thin frame, her oversized breasts, their areolas the palest
pink. Even now, long after the *incident*—which is what he
calls it—where he does admit he "lost it for a few minutes"
and for which he apologized more than once, he can still
get excited by this image of her.
     "Anyway, what did she expect?" he thinks. "Coming
to my place alone, so carefully put together, nothing
ragged about her. Clearly coming up to my place dressed
to entice." He knows he saw her interest in him from
the beginning—in her eyes, her smile, her not-so-subtle
coquettishness.

Now, this woman—he guesses her sister (cousin?), given
her last name—has called him, charging in on him, into his
new life, thinking that he will just jump like some puppet
and agree to meet her. That she can, with her strange, deep,
determined, masculine voice and peculiar request, pull his
strings and make him hash over things about Cecilia he
clearly wants to leave in history. "*No way,*" he thinks.
     He told Cecily as carefully as he could, "No, I'm not really
interested in speaking about the past. Reformulating it." But
she continued to push, telling him she had "information,"

as if she believed he was some stupid fish that she could bait and hook and drag him into God-knows-what. He had had enough of these kinds of women. These types. Their manipulations. He had moved on.

Cecily was shaken by his turning her down and tried her hardest to keep him on the phone. She babbled on and, of course, the quieter he became the more she tried to fill the silence with fast-paced talk. Something about a play she had written about a poet and a critic. "Would you like to read it? Would you?" she repeated, and then too nervously laughed. He did not like her manner—her clumsy attempt at being coy, the sheer desperation she thought she kept so well hidden, and her heavy, nasal Midwestern twang. Also, her voice had an unappealing huskiness, unlike with some women where sexiness comes through such low tones. To him, she was the flip side of sultry, with no awareness of how ridiculous she sounded and how inept she was as she pleaded her case.

It became clear—almost from the start—that he was dealing with yet another Slaughter woman filled with deep disturbances that he no longer wanted anything to do with. He could sense her own anger toward Cecilia, which she clearly thought she contained so well, expanding inside her. When he hung up the phone he prayed to a higher power that he would never hear the Slaughter name again.

Yet afterward he sat down in his chair and could not stop himself from returning to his times with Cecilia. The tease of her. Her impeccable presentation of perfection and his giving in to his increasing impulse to undo it. He had never felt anything like that before, nor did he want to again. He knew he more than frightened her. He knew what he did was wrong and that he had terrified both her *and* himself.

Then, he hit the flat, wooden arm of his chair with his fist and thought, with great anger, "I am *not* the Nazi she has created in her latest poems, just as she is *not* her mother with her own devastating history." It was obvious to him that Cecilia tended to continuously create situations, consciously or unconsciously, which attempted to provoke scenarios that paralleled those of her mother.

More and more as time has passed, he feels *he* is the victim given all the poems she has written since then, which, no matter how much they are disguised, are clearly about him. He continues to believe the paranoia of her reaction afterward was too dramatic, too theatrical. She *wanted* something to happen. He also knows this is a hard sell and some will never be convinced of this.

The color of her porcelain breasts tipped with the virgin shade of a young girl's untouched nipples and how he wanted to suck them, suck them to a woman's lifeblood is something he can never forget. It lays there in the back of his brain like a large animal, sometimes dormant, sometimes not. As does how he could not let her up, once he had her.

However, he feels he is inhabiting a different space now, and can only hope she is too; but he worries that the unrelenting obsessiveness in her poetry spills over into her real life (or vice versa) and the fantasies she has created from what happened will continue to cause him trouble.

He thinks, "She could have been considered a major talent if she had been able to rein in her words, thoughts, and actions to just the page, but she will never be able to do this and it will ultimately destroy her not only professionally, but personally. It would have been best if she had written just a couple of gorgeous, angry books and died young, like Plath."

The first thing that flashed through his mind when he saw her at that packed reading was whether the color of the hair on her head—autumn leaves at their thick, blazing peak—matched the thatch between her legs. How urgent his impulse was to undress her. How quick he was to ask someone, "Who is that woman?" Easily, he found a colleague who knew of her and her poetry.

Of course, all those coffee-shop conversations they had were for him just a prelude to having her—having her underneath him, nude, his body an enormous weight holding her down and possessing her. He was sure she could tell this by the way he stared at her during their get-togethers—and especially by what he had said at that proper, public conversation, about *pleasure*. How she ultimately handled it all has become a completely different matter.

He will never stop believing that Cecilia, unconsciously, was readying herself for what happened—as if her whole life, her whole history was preparing for it. He was just the man who hooked into the scenario—a brute force uncontrollably charging into her, a character in the personal history play of her own creation. A play like the one that absurd woman Cecily referred to and with which she had tried to impress him in that nerve-wracking conversation.

He remembers that she said she knew the perfect way to get back at Cecilia. She mumbled this at the end—as if by then she was no longer talking to him, only to herself and the chorus of craziness that was her mind. Her voice had become a swirl of agitated disappointment after he turned down all her suggested possibilities of an in-person encounter. His final words to her were a polite, firm, measured, "No, I just do not want to revisit this subject."

Now, he worries, "Am I the critic in her damn play and if so, how have I been characterized? What has *this* one done to me?" Then he thinks, "Female artists. *Fuck them.* Yes, at your own risk," allowing himself to laugh out loud at his own bad joke. He is a little less concerned when he remembers how disagreeable her voice became when she mentioned Cecilia. Her growing rage toward Cecilia, which she could not conceal—that strange muttering at the end of the conversation about getting back at her—makes him feel that he is not the target of her wrath, that she actually wanted him to actively collude with her in some plot against Cecilia. Or entice him in some way to be part of one of her own imagination.

He then thanks the fates that Arletta is not like *those* women. She is rational, poised, and self-contained—never losing her composure. A brilliant scholar, a natural public speaker, a commentator on society's ills and how to correct them. They live an anchored, balanced life and he has become more centered. He keeps all extreme fantasies to himself and so far, in the months they have been together, this has worked well enough.

Unavoidably, the call reignited many thoughts for him about Cecilia—of her long hair and the way it fell over her breasts. He does still enjoy the memory of the hopes he once carried about the range of possibilities of their nakedness together. He thinks, "Perhaps if I were a poet, by now I would have written a hundred sonnets about Cecilia's breasts. As a critic, it's different. I reproach her temperament, her suppressed tempestuousness, the temptress she is and keeps not so deeply hidden inside herself—which only redoubles her appeal—and most especially her inability to take any responsibility for what happened."

This self-awareness, felt with such certitude, puffs him

up and makes him feel omnipotent as he speculates, "Some might say I damaged her soul, but that January evening when I opened that door what I found was a woman dressed in carefully chosen shades of burnt scarlet and wine-colored soft fabrics, already damaged and subtly *asking for it*. She was all subtext. My agenda was more direct." For him, with Cecilia it was *always* about power and sex— still is.

However, to anyone who mentions the "dog poem," or the dog, he will adamantly reply, "I *loved* her. I took good care with her. *That day*—that awful August day—a neighbor passing by told me he saw her—saw her fixate on a beautiful red bird, perhaps a cardinal. The bird flew too close to her and she leapt at it as though she thought she could capture it." He then continues, "Isn't that what behavior is sometimes about—unbridled, irrational acts to attempt to capture that which we cannot?"

I think about this last question a lot as I have tried, however unsuccessfully, even after all this time and some amount of gained wisdom, to free myself from my yearning for Wyatt—still so fiercely gripped.

THE CROSSES I

On my way to the Holy Land
I passed effigies of knights
spread out on their tombs,
their legs a display of precise twists
to exhibit how many crusades they fought.
On my way, I couldn't find

the promised dry path through the sea,
though I looked and looked.
Two boats sunk, but I was saved—

the good child who believes
what is told to me. On my way

I saw a man crucified on an X-
shaped cross, his immobile legs
on winged display. Another, hung
head down with feet stretched up—
the martyred, at once awkward
and lovely. I saw a man

in a loin cloth, his side was pierced,
his legs were crossed.
I stared, then forced myself

to look away. *The good child who does*
what is taught to me—

to find the fragment of wood
within the gold and jeweled
reliquary—ruby for blood,
beryl for rebirth, pearl for purity.

The good child who tries to do
what is asked of me—
when I arrived, I dug through layers

of dirt to discover
the container disappeared, the land emptied.
I couldn't go home
with nothing to share.

The good child buries herself there.

c. slaughter

SHE DID NOT KNOW if he would be home as she began
the long drive to his house. She did not even call to see if he
would pick up the phone so she could just hang up and then
be somewhat confident of finding him there when she would
arrive over an hour later. Of course, it was possible that just
Arletta would be there and she worried about that—about
what she would do then. She did not wish her any particular
harm, at least nothing she could focus on at the moment no
matter what her ambivalence was about Arletta's character—
for all she cared she could live out her life winning prizes for
her books on kindness, loving your neighbor, and the glories
of her *new* homeland, which in fact was not that new since
she had pretty much grown up here.

Her topics, however clichéd, made people hopeful and
she did believe Arletta was at least somewhat sincere—as

well as quite clever and driven by a mega-ambition. Yet, she did wonder if when these ingredients were mixed together they could produce a truly good person. She certainly was not a blatantly evil one like him, just a manic overachiever who plotted out the course of her life methodically and, so far, enormously successfully.

Others took notice of this, too. (As did I, given my own issues—both above and below the ground—with the all too blatant success-grabbers and attention-mongers.) Many were quite aware of how well Arletta aligned herself within the university and used the shoulders of new, important acquaintances to stand on and how this always seemed to lead to someone who stood taller and consequently to another large cash fellowship to improve her life—buy nice clothes, a house—and further her career. Whether eventually there will be a growing backlash from all of her good luck and, if there is, she will be strong enough to ride it out or canny enough to diffuse it, is yet to be decided, but I am guessing the answer will be yes. For now, the one thing that is for sure is that everywhere Arletta goes, she strategically positions herself in the most advantageous ways to take those successful, higher leaps which, given my best instincts coupled with my lessons with Lao Tzu, I find intensely unappealing.

She thought of Arletta a lot as she set out on her journey and imagined what she *knew* had to be the truth—that in her childhood Arletta had someone—her mother? her father? both?—who truly believed in her and told her she was wonderful and that whatever she chose to do with her life she would be successful. That she was unstoppable. She could make all of her dreams come true.

The more she thought of these words and made of them a litany in her mind, "wonderful, successful, unstoppable," the more she craved to return to her own childhood and start over, find for herself such a figure to help her—as if a child could actually do this.

These past months, especially, she had found herself if not falling, at least stumbling over the smallest of hurdles, and worse than this, becoming mind-clumsy. The more she tried to do everything right—to coordinate her walk with her talk, the more she strived for gracefulness, the more she fell short and it was clear that this was becoming obvious to others. However much she attempted to cover up her awkwardness and panic when she was with people—especially if there were more than one person to deal with—increasingly, she was becoming outwardly brittle. If there had ever been any suppleness to her actions, it had dried and the false confidence she publicly exhibited to compensate for this only added to the escalating pressure of a final break inside of her. She knew this.

As did I.

"Right now," she thought, "Arletta is definitely the It Girl of the academic circus and with this it is inevitable she will begin to have her own cabal—however small—of enemies hovering nearby, hoping she'll misstep—perhaps even break her neck or at least slip on some unnoticed black ice, which would force her to wobble off for at least a while." To her mind this had already happened, with Arletta's relationship with Ivan Durmand, a man fading in attractiveness—his face sagging a bit, his waistline thickening, his thought processes most likely slowing—yet still maintaining enough charisma and connections. She could only think Arletta must have her own insecurities about her ability to move forward alone and the all-too-familiar

need of females for male help with advancement. Or perhaps, Arletta was just a realist, knowing that this path was
still, unfortunately, the most propitious and rather than
rail against it, to just use it.

To her it was obvious, too, that Arletta knew how to
keep her story of where she had come from—her struggle
up from the restrictive, heavy Cuban mud—strong. She
had seen how she glowed on stage—almost ignited—
when she gave the details of her early life. She behaved as if
she had never told any of it before—like a brilliant actress
does reciting her lines, becoming the character she plays
each night, even though she has played the part a hundred
times before and it, quite likely, has grown somewhat stale
inside her. "Maybe Arletta's deftness with this should also
make one wonder further about her true self, or selves."
She added this to her basket of Arletta thoughts.

She believed Arletta shut herself down when it came
to any rumors concerning Ivan Durmand, put metaphori-
cal blinders on and earplugs in if someone directly approached to confront her about him or even alluded to
any talk about the damage he had done.

She once, quite by accident, found herself in a room
with her and it was clear from the high alert look on
Arletta's face, she wished she were not there. She could tell
Arletta had made a connection with her last name when
they were introduced for she took a step back from her and
more than this, averted her eyes from hers and arched her
spine too straight. Even Celine, who was with her, noticed
this, which made her believe Arletta's actions were filled with
even more discomfort than she had realized at the moment,
given Celine's absence of sensitivity to nuance about anyone
other than herself. Celine had said of the encounter, "That
woman seemed *almost* afraid of you. How could *anyone* be

afraid of you? You *are* strange it's true, but to *fear* you? *Right?* No one should fear you?"

She just grabbed Celine's hand in a cousinly fashion.

She continued to think about Arletta while she was stuck in the impossible city traffic. Beads of sweat were forming on her forehead and the palms of her hands felt fevered. Her mind was becoming a cold, wet rag, heavy with too many thoughts. Even with the heat in the car on full blast, she could not get warm enough. It was below zero outside and that was without factoring in the wind chill. She imagined when she stepped outside the beads of sweat would turn to frost and her face would glitter like on a clear night when all the stars are out and can be so clearly seen. Thinking this gave her some peace—that more than ever, she would at that moment merge with the outer atmosphere. She would no longer be alone with the snarled, closed-off upset inside of her. Finally, she would be in sync, conjoined with something infinitely larger than herself. This image of her face twinkling like the stars made her feel religious in a Zen-like way and brought her a momentary calm.

Her thoughts wandered even more as she looked at the barren trees—the funereal lace of their branches on both sides of the highway. Their stripped, over-extended, broken patterns were more consistent with the way she felt inside. Then, she imagined the carefully mapped, clear-sighted plan Arletta had for herself—that soon she would leave Ivan Durmand and make a move to someone higher on her totem pole of ambition, and how she, with this trip, would cut her own notch into the wood of it and make this easier for her. She would free Arletta, just as her parents had freed themselves and her when they arrived in Miami with great secrecy and she learned to grow up shrewd enough to say to people with great earnestness in this country what she thought they wanted to hear, maybe to the point of actually believing it herself—her voice at once vulnerable and articulate. *She* had lost that touch, if she truly ever had it.

She envied her, hated her, and wanted to help her escape, because it was important to her that *some* female feel that free. In the Slaughter family it seemed no woman got out alive—deadened or dead was their destiny. "Except for Aunt Rose," she thought, "who lives forever, with her feeding tube and crew of attendees, always demanding and receiving more than any ten persons' shares of attention."

Her anger and impatience with everyone had definitely grown weighted and ungainly. For months now whenever she went outside she had a terrible aversion to all strangers—strangers walking too fast, too slow, strangers driving what seemed too close to her. Strangers in stores not waiting their turns, talking too loudly on their cell phones about the mundane matters of their lives—the unending details of their comings and goings from here to there, as if every move they made was crucial to their world, to the *entire* world—while pushing too near her body, the foulness of their breath polluting her insides further.

Added to this were the salespersons' talk—talking down to her with the detestable "Honey" or "Dear," not just giving her what she asked for, always trying to sell her something *more*, taking advantage of her all-too-obvious vulnerability which made her seem that she could easily be intruded upon and convinced to purchase anything they pitched—as if they could make her believe that a change in eye shadow, a new fragrance with a hyper-seductive name, or the cheery color of some lipstick could stabilize her. "If only," she would think as each one chattered on. It was hard enough these days for her to just enter a store—any store—and ask for what she needed.

Everywhere she went it seemed everyone used too many words, making her mind even more a clutter. It was as if no one could appreciate the precision of efficient discourse so as to lessen the outside noise—their tongues all thickened thumbs, thumping out more sound, drumming out more nonsense of self-importance and condescension. There seemed a competition out there with so many people trying to trounce each other in the narcissistic territory of the "I," using her current most hated word—busy. "Yes," she emphatically thought, "more and more, people seemed to be going for the Olympic gold in busy."

Yet, now that she realized she was about halfway there—on her path to straighten out what had been done, done to her in her twisted life story—in this jammed traffic, she felt only compassion for the people around her. She listened calmly as they pressed on their horns and studied their impatient, angry faces—all the animated energy they used as they poured more redundant, trivial talk into the receivers of their phones, and she looked at each one with a sincere patience.

She felt both a pity and an empathy for their lone-liness—as if everyone were trying to cover the jagged potholes of their lives with the thin pages of a newspaper, trying to run over the news, the truly sad stories imprinted on the fragile sheets and on themselves. Silently she thought, as she watched them, "Someday, one by one, each of you will tear or burst from all the dam-age done from the rock-hard edges of your life you so ceaselessly try to ignore." But, at least on this ride she did not have the almost uncontrollable urge to roll down the car window and shout this message out to them. She wanted to tell them quietly, "The pliability and softness of the cushions all of us use to comfort ourselves can only be temporary. The multiplying hungers for distractions can only give us the feeling of safe passage to a point. Eventually all diversions lead to the same isolated destination." The truth was, even on this mission that felt so right, she was still her old, glum self.

However, with the gun quietly resting in her purse, the voices that sometimes would scream at her saying, "Everything you do is wrong. You're not good enough. Not pretty enough. Not smart enough. *Nothing* enough," had silenced. She had bound herself to the Old Testament version of revenge. At least by her interpretation. She thought, "It's being practiced every day if you just listened to the news—in the world, in *this* city, in backyards, inside homes." She became the God of Israel, the Ineffable One. She became Yahweh, the name observant Jews never say out loud and with this thought she said His name out loud. *Yahweh. Yahweh. Yahweh.* And it made her feel giddy and wildly happy.

As I watched her, I could only hope some other thoughts would rise up in her to calm her, to stop her.

She ruminated on how easy it was to buy a gun—fill out an application—hedge a bit on the truth of how balanced you were—have your picture taken, and wait for it all to be processed. Just a couple of months—if that. Then come back and make a purchase. Or better yet, use an old one.

One that looks like a harmless relic, but is not. One with a family history.

She deeply felt Arletta's vision of the world was unrealistic—so simple-minded and wondered why people lined up to buy tickets to her lectures. To her it was as if when they entered the Great Hall to hear her, each picked up a blindfold to the world—all the complexities of history, all the misery caused by humans.

Arletta would tell her audience how lucky they were to be living in this country and how easily the problems here could be solved. She would do this with seemingly great respect for their intelligence, making references to the Greeks and Romans, to their history and mythology, paralleling these to the present—to current events, movies, music—and what they could learn from the long, lost past—its lessons, its mistakes, and all its glories. She did this without being pedantic—without arrogance—pronouncing that anything wrong now could be fixed through generosity of spirit, good deeds, and friendship. Her speech pattern was the perfect balance of angelic and evangelistic.

She went to listen to her three times. Since she had an insatiable craving to know everything about Ivan Durmand, to examine him from every possible angle—piece by piece, particle by particle in as microscopic fashion as possible—she also had the need to know more about the woman with whom he was living. Even though she sat hunched in a far corner with a scarf covering her head and dark glasses on so no one would notice her, she could still see that on stage Arletta looked as composed as Queen Katherine of Aragon and she remembered thinking even that elegant, aristocratic woman had lived with a monster. Yet when she thought of the comparison of Henry VIII to Ivan Durmand, she smiled at the stretch of this and how it was far too much a compliment to the latter and his very limited polluted puddle of power.

Each time she saw her, Arletta was dressed in a dark, trim, perfectly fitting designer pants suit with a striking necklace of Spanish stones, as if to remind everyone of her lineage—her adventurous and powerful heritage. Of course, she never spoke of its violent history—the tortures, the awful, senseless carnage, which, in fairness, could be the history of any country and always in the name of some god. No, Arletta would not ever go into that.

The necklace she remembered most was quite large and made of saffron colored carnelian. It had geometric squares and ended with a large, highly polished tear drop which fell at the perfect place on her skin so as to delicately, purposely, cover any hint of cleavage. Yet, the suggestion of sensuality was clearly intended and definitely effected. The color of the stones intricately entwined in the shine of thick, pink gold wire only added to the glow of her smooth, naturally sun-kissed tan skin. She thought of Celine and how that *was* the color she always strived for, only to end up with some variation of orange on herself from the many brands of cream she purchased during the winter months.

She imagined every woman in the audience wanting to ask her where she had bought such a necklace—and all the others she was known to wear. She certainly wanted to—however superficial the impulse. To her the brilliance of this self-decoration with its subliminal effects were far more fascinating than anything Arletta wrote or said. She just could not react the way the others did.

Today, before she left home, she put on a necklace she found at the shop. Supposedly it is authentic—the center drop of it being a circular coin sliced in half, recovered from the El Cazador shipwreck. It had a tag on it with its history. The vessel had disappeared into the winter sea in another January—1794 to be exact—and the treasure it was carrying discovered only recently—1993—by a fishing vessel named *Mistake*. She smiled at that when she first read it.

She wondered who wore the other half of this small, full moon disk. If it had brought them bad thoughts or good luck. She wondered, too, if Arletta would admire her necklace with the coin at the center of which was a Spanish inspired cross, embellished by four black onyx tips separated by four curved rows of four clear-colored cabochon gemstones. Her urge to buy it gave her the small hope that perhaps in wearing it she might become stronger—more like Arletta. That she could be empowered by such a necklace—however ridiculous that thought seemed, and was not.

Certainly Arletta's words gave her audiences hope—a vision of Eden before the apple, gave their minds a rest like a meditation or a sermon and that for some moments after they reentered the world they felt smarter, and everything seemed brighter now that they were filled with the belief that easy solutions were possible. At least until they got into their cars and had to deal with the incessant messages left for them by disgruntled relatives or coworkers. Or from having none at all—nothing received from the ones whose voices they truly needed to hear, so as to give them a little affirmation, a boost of positive attention to get through to the next day—a little polish for their spirit. Soon enough, the drivers next to them would begin impinging on their space and the dirty looks, obscene gestures, or the games of chicken with steel vehicles would begin and the words—always the words—when they turned on the news from the disembodied air would start spitting on them again with the events of the day so much larger than their own lives. Nothing picayune here—rage raining and reigning everywhere. Maybe then they would wonder about the validity of Arletta's vision or perhaps just be grateful for the distraction of it. Most likely by this time they would have forgotten much of what she had said—it being too sallow in its shallowness to last even the drive home—and be left with just a small halo effect of its optimistic pleasantness.

She is a bad driver. She never knows what to do when the merging cars take their aggressive places on the highway. She always feels that this leaves her with no space. That she is being crowded out. That the road she is trying to take for herself is being intruded upon by someone far more confident. Someone stronger, someone bolder. She has tried so hard to hold on to a path in this world of being—of being a Slaughter, of knowing she was unacceptable from the beginning for being a daughter. Always with the realization of not being—not being the everlasting Rose. Of never being able to outwardly perfectly comply or inwardly deal with the rules and expectations set for her way before her birth, no matter how hard she initially had tried. Yet, as she kept touching the leather of her bag and feeling the shape of the gun, with her target closer—now just miles from here—all this seemed of no consequence. She felt what she was doing was not random; what she was doing was filled with great purpose; what she was doing had many dimensions; what she was doing was multifaceted and hard like a diamond.

It was then I became truly frightened.

She touched the sweat that now completely covered her face. It had become fluid, like a second foundation and that, too, felt perfect. Now she imagined, when the air hit her exposed skin as she stepped out of the car—so close to her goal—she would look less like the sprinkled stars in the night sky, but more unified, like a cold, hard jewel. That finally, she would resemble a gem of great value.

Suddenly, in the middle of these dot thoughts, which she knew, if she drew the lines all connected to her maze-puzzled life, she realized she was on *his* street and she started checking the numbers of the houses, which was difficult because it was now almost past the twilight hour in the city-filthy, dark hole of midwinter and the homes were closer together than she expected, some almost disappearing into the next with no light shining on their addresses. She was surprised by the narrowness of each house, but tried not to make of this a metaphor—let it intrude or multiply. She had to keep her mind locked into the reality of what she intended and not leap around in the possibilities of language.

When she finally saw a number near enough, she found a parking spot—one where the city had plowed the snow high, so she fit in easily. The car and her frostbitten thoughts were now imbedded in a concrete igloo of ice. She turned off the car's lights and the ignition and paused, took some deep breaths to try to steady what felt like a not-unfamiliar arrhythmia of her heart. Then, she slipped the gun into her coat pocket, stuffed her purse under the passenger side of the seat and stared at the thick rubber soles on her boots, hoping they would keep her from slipping, keep her anchored to the ground when she got out of the car and edged along the newly fallen snow which deceptively covered layer upon layer of built-up ice.

Her plan was to find the house—the house he and Arletta bought together—by walking toward it, her head down so she would look weather-beaten like everyone else just wanting to get home at the end of a hard workday. She would go up the steps or the concrete walk to the front door—whichever it was—and ring the bell. If everything worked as she imagined, Herr M would open it, stare at her, and before he could slam it in her face she would take the gun—now resting so snugly in the deep of her pocket—point it at him, while looking straight at him so he could see *her, see* who was doing this to him. See *her* and that would be the last image he would *ever see. See her. Her shooting. Her shooting him.*

As she walked, all her thoughts were about death. About the soul and its being released from the mind-body and how she longed for this—for some perspective on what we do to ourselves and to each other and the poem "The Soul's Aerial View of the Burial" started racing around in her mind, and she said it in the smallest whisper, like a prayer to the air—its frozen emptiness the perfect audience—

> Everything is black or white—
> the mourners' heavy wool coats
> wander over the crisp snow,
> their arms holding on to whoever's left—
> while I wait for them to seal
> the perfect rectangular hole
> so I can go—to where

I do not know.
But for now I muse above the bony
trees, about how fragile
the dance is that they do,
and how I don't remember
ever having such an unfettered view.

And in saying it, she hoped that when this was over, she, too, would see everything clearer and be freer. But she was not sure, for now she was beginning to feel lightheaded.

It was at this point a little hope rose up in me that she would turn around and go home . . . but she did not.

When she found the house, it was even narrower than the others, turn of the century old and three stories high. It was not made of brick as she had imagined, but rather a faded yellow clapboard from which the paint was peeling, perhaps with some of the strips turning to rot. The children's story of the three little pigs jumped into her mind and she said out loud, "Not even of brick." At that moment she felt like the wolf, quite capable of blowing this house in, which was, after all, her intention.

Then she thought, "This doesn't look like the kind of house that Arletta would stay in for long. This doesn't seem like a place Arletta would *ever* live. Surely her exit will be sooner than later." She idealized Arletta's future once again and pictured her gracefully dancing away into warm, spring air to a larger, grander house with lots of lawn and flowers blooming everywhere. In her mind Arletta's story always, inevitably, led to a happy Hollywood ending.

She was unsteady, her gait definitely off, as she slowly headed up the shoveled, cracked, concrete path which ended with five overly large steps of wood. Only one light was on, in an upper front left-side room on the attic-like top floor. She imagined him there with its sloped ceilings—that were soon to fall in on him—ensconced with his books, perhaps grading papers or preparing tomorrow's lecture—which now would never happen—or listening to some classical music or smooth jazz, feeling so safe and warm.

Perhaps he was reading Nietzche's *The Genealogy of Morals*, going over his favorite part on how the world is intrinsically filled with cruelty and violence, given the instincts inherent in humans, and how it is up to a higher thinking man to develop his own code of morality, not be led or convinced by clichéd beliefs—"let us be aware of the tentacles of such contradictory notions as 'pure reason,' 'absolute knowledge,' 'absolute intelligence.'" He had read her those words early in their relationship and she thought him an expansive thinker and a passionate scholar. Now she believes he used this treatise as an excuse for any and all of his behavior, his voice becoming so theatrical as he continued, "What a mad, unhappy animal is man! What strange notions occur to him; what perversities . . . what bestialities of idea burst from him, the moment he is prevented ever so little from being a beast of action?" How these lines have stayed memorable in her mind, like an indelible stain. She guesses one could say she had been forewarned.

She wondered how Arletta's philosophy could possibly fit with such beliefs and whether or not they argued a lot about this from their not ivory but wooden tower. However before she could get entirely lost in this quagmire of thought, the rising and dying noise of someone trying and retrying to start the frozen motor of a car shocked her out of her wobbly, over-intellectualizing and returned her to the imminent impermanency of Herr M's own situation and this made her smile and helped steady her some. As did a Life-Saver she unrolled from her other pocket with her ungloved hand and placed on her tongue. At this moment, the bitter, sugary taste of the lemon one helped unify her senses. Her eyes began to focus better.

She saw that the front porch was darkish gray. The depressing color seemed contradictory—it should have been lighter, as in a welcoming. As it was, the entrance to the house looked like a cave. The floorboards creaked as she stepped on them and there was a matching wood swing held up by rusty chains. She imagined that when it was new it had been painted white and had brought great delight to those who had swung on it. Children. Parents. Lovers. She walked around it as quietly as she could and had the urge to sit on it to rest so as to further help balance herself, though it looked like it would make loud, squeaking sounds or worse, that if any weight were placed on it, it might fall from the low, warped wood ceiling from which it hung.

It was then she thought of a title for a poem: "The Rapist's Porch Swing," quite aware of its multiple meanings and with this, that night two years ago quickly came back to her with too much memory: her initial bewilderment when he leaped up from his chair and pressed his open mouth onto hers; how the force of this act, coupled with the bristly hairs of his goatee made it feel as if a mask were pressing against her face; how empty this opening to his body felt— like a rough dark pit into which he was trying to swallow her; how he then quickly yanked her to the futon; how he

pushed her down on it; how he would not let her up; how
he kept saying, "Turn. Turn. Turn Over," with her idioti-
cally thinking if she did so, he would let her up and how he
did not. How that was just the beginning of his pushing—
his pushing himself into her any which way it pleased him.

The feelings of that terror, the physical pain, and the
seizure that overtook her when he was nearly done all returned as she stared at the porch swing—its bench becoming his penis and her arms the rusted chains—yes, these
past two years, the rusted chains just trying to hold herself
up by writing—writing about what had happened that
night, so she would not go crashing to the floor, completely broken and useless. Then, the image changed—
consolidated itself—and she became both the chains and
the bench in all their wreckage, an object on the brink
of becoming a complete heap of junk. Something to be
tossed to the curb or thrown into an alley, then picked up
by a foul smelling truck, and carried off to the dump.

For well over a year, most of it in silence, except for her
pen, she had tried to keep her grip, but the chains had
become too worn and were about to snap from the ceiling
of herself and no God-hope could hold it up. The rhythms
she created in her writing room could no longer swing
her high enough to reconcile what had occurred in that
dungeon apartment.

How she went filled with the anticipation of having the
attention of such an *important, attractive man*. How she
went with a rise in her step and a girlish flirtation, which
she was now sure had emanated from her face and body
and from her velvet slacks and soft angora sweater that she
had carefully chosen for the occasion. Everything about
her that evening was so soft.

"Yes, a soft target," she thought and with this, once again, the full grief-rage welled up inside her, like a river overrunning its banks, for her own unbearable naiveté, for her own vast stupidity, for the wasteland that night had made into her future, and she started shaking.

The lemon Life-Saver had already dissolved on her tongue and she reached down into her pocket for another. When she saw it was green, this brought a smirk to her face, because of how green she had been as she had so cautiously climbed those outside, slippery steel steps to the place he inhabited that evening in January—the month which holds the hope of new beginnings and positive resolutions, but, like any other, can explode into unimaginable endings.

She thought of Michael to even herself further.

And with this, I prayed that the power of Michael in her mind would make her turn back. But it did not.

She thought about the phone message she had left him saying that if she were not home, she would be back soon and to bring milkshakes topped with hot fudge, adding, if possible, to please rent the movie *Wuthering Heights*. She imagined his familiar sigh at this suggestion and him saying to himself with tired amusement, "Again!" She did all of this so he would not think anything was out of the ordinary with her not being there when he arrived. That she was just out, running a common errand. That she was okay. In her mind she was always worried that Michael would show up *here*—show up to kill him. And with this thought she looked around.

It was important to her that he have at least a little more time thinking that everything was getting better. That she was improving. She tried to give him that impression and could tell he was beginning to feel optimistic about this from his words the other evening when he said, "Perhaps we could eventually put all of this behind us and build a new future." She stayed quiet, giving him an enigmatic smile and a slight positive nod, which he was used to and to which he lightly responded, "So what exactly are you *really* thinking?" She only continued to smile. Something he also found familiar.

It had been a mistake to tell him anything about what had happened. She saw this as soon as she had begun opening up to him. Of course, once she started, he would not let her stop. Afterward, she had tried her best to reassure him, saying that being able to talk to him had been cathartic. But she had heard what he said all too clearly and had seen the way his face and neck had reddened as she spoke and how afterward he stood too still for too long a time, his skin looking as if it were about to burn off.

She did not want this gentle man to take on any more of her problems than he already had. She did not want him to be the one to take action. She wanted to free him. To free him of her. She wanted him to be finally free of her so he would be able to release himself into life again.

She closed her eyes and pictured him putting the large shakes in the refrigerator, placing the movie on the kitchen table, taking off his warm, black overcoat, black leather gloves, and unwrapping his long Burberry scarf from his neck. She had bought it for him as a gift and he wore it religiously. How he would then put a glove into each pocket and neatly wrap the scarf around a hanger, place the coat on it and fit it carefully into the hall closet. He then would quietly check to see if perhaps she had arrived early—if the door to her writing room was closed. Since it would not be, he would sit down on the couch and turn on the TV—watch something he knew would not interest her, and how he would be pleased to have some time to himself for his own indulgence, and this calmed her.

She also thought about some of the titles of the poems she had written these past two years and the poems themselves—her small, frightened, yet daring little poems, her little selves—her pathetic, struggling, little persons— "Melancholia," "Claustrophobia," "Paranoia," "Schizophrenia," and on and on. How they had taken over her mind, populated her life and yoked her in, centered her some—kept her from becoming a splatter a little longer and she thought about what anyone might make of them after this night, after the act that was about to happen.

By now, her mouth curved into a large grin. Touching it with her ungloved hand, it felt stuck there and she wondered if she looked like a madwoman at this moment—*if she looked like the terror-stricken image she had of Grandmother Slaughter; if she looked like the Insane Idyth Slaughter.* If, in fact, her own history had finally imploded within her—not just from Grandmother Idyth, but from the not-so sealed pit of reptiles her mother carried with her from Auschwitz, which forever crawled inside her mother and had slowly entered her the more she found out another detail of her mother's story. Then, she stared at her smooth, high, black boots, and it was the first time she realized how much they looked like the ones the Nazis wore when they goose-stepped their way along so many pavements toward their vision.

She thought about the story of Celie's grandmother Eva, sitting with her daughter, Esther, as Esther wrote to the American Red Cross looking for Eva's parents, brothers, and sister long after the crematoria had taken them from her, with her not knowing for years that they had gone to ash, and she stared again at the sight of her now horrifying boots. She thought of Celie and how she was born into Eva's hysteria after she found out what had happened to her family and the shrieks of all of Eva's fears into the baby Celie's ears and how they had infected Celie. At this moment all journeys that ended in disaster seemed to crash into each other and into her.

She thought about the critics. She could almost see the high-powered ones lined up in front of her like a firing squad, and of their possible commentaries about the body of work she had created. If she would be added to their short list of great, yet crazy female poets and if they would come to write volumes about her, too, or if she would only keep the lesser ones busy, writing with a gossipy tabloid fascination about her and her ever so miniscule mini-moment in literary history, and this only hardened her grin and created a new rush of wired energy within her at the temporality, nonsense, and vanity of all of it.

It was then I prayed as hard as I could for her to stop, as if I could reach her, even though I knew I could not.

She lifted her gloved hand to ring the bell, the same hand that would reach into the deep pocket where the gun lay quiet. Her only fear at the moment was that the bell would be broken or would be too soft and that he would not hear her. "*Hear me. Here me,*" she thought. Another chant from childhood and a line from a poem whose title at the moment she could not remember. She absolutely washed from her mind the possibility that Arletta would be there. It *had* to be he who opened the door. She said out loud, "*It had to be.*" As if by saying this, she could will it.

The bell had a too-loud buzz. She thought of a buzzard—a bird waiting for its prey. Circling. Then she heard someone coming down the many stairs, and she wondered if he had a new dog and if the new dog would accompany him. And if the dog would be female and if she would be beautiful, yet look beaten—if her fur would be unwashed and glued together from her constant gnawing on herself, and his neglect. But there were no animal sounds. Just those of someone heavy-footed. Then she heard *him*. She heard him say in an annoyed way, "Who's there?" She stayed silent and, being the buzzard, she rang the bell again. And again, he said, "Who's there?" Only louder.

Suddenly, the first floor lights flicked on. She leaned over and peeked through the dirty dining room window, incongruously trimmed with clean, white lace curtains, and she saw him coming down the stairs. He *was* alone. And in seeing this the adrenaline in her body reached a euphoric surge she had only sometimes experienced when writing a poem—the words arriving almost too rapidly with an overwhelmingly ecstatic, yet excruciating excitement building inside her in trying to catch all of them—as if all language at those spectacular moments was being funneled into an opening at the top of her head from a place high above—a golden place of great, unbounded splendor.

Angrier, he yelled, "Who's there? Damn it! Who's there?" Hearing his irritation, she rang the bell again and then again, because she never felt more the master—more the master of herself and of him. And this feeling made her giddier—made her glide higher. She *liked* being the tormentor. She *liked* finally being in charge. Then he opened the door, and there he was looking tired and sloppy. And she took the gun out of her pocket and shot him.

CLEAN

Still, against the heavy wind,
the spoon of cherry wood

no longer moves
the liquid in the pot.

Locked in the lamplight sweat
of the eternal night winter,

the disturbed quiet is quite safe—
suffocates the closed room.

Looking out, all that can be
seen is a knothole in the oak tree.

Gone is the fig, the oyster, the mango,
the red candle—its wick.

Gone is the bean, the blackberry, the carrot,
the parsnip, the horn of the rhinoceros.

The cupboard is both
emptied and latched.

The man in his blister heat
will not come back.

The kitchen is so clean,
everything's in its nook.

c. slaughter

AFTER CECILIA KILLED Herr M, she got back in her car and drove past his old attic apartment where the rape had occurred, slowed the car to a stop for a few seconds, stared at the top floor, then made her way east, down to the lake and turned the gun on herself.

She had wanted to fill the deep pockets of her coat with heavy stones, like Virginia Woolf had done, and then walk into the water and sink down into it. However, because it had been the coldest December in forty years and such weather continued, creating a frigid January, the lake looked like it was made of concrete—secure enough that anyone might be tempted to skate on it and this made her worry that all that would happen if she walked across it was that it would just crack a bit—if that. Added to this was the chance someone might see her, for a full moon now lit the night sky, disturbing the darkness, and if someone saw her they might for the moment feel heroic, stop their car, leap out, and try to save her.

She did consider the small chance that she might be able to find a weak spot in the ice and could stomp on it with her boots and force a split. Then, she would be able to slip herself down into the frigid water and quietly drown. She liked the image of herself doing this. It seemed graceful. But with the gun still in her pocket and her energy maniacally high, without much hesitation about fifteen minutes after the death of Herr M, she decided to put the revolver in her mouth.

The police found two notes in one of her coat pockets— the same pocket that held the broken roll of Life Savers. One was folded over and on the outside read in a flowing, delicate, clearly feminine script, *Michael*. On the upper inside fold were the words of Kuo-an-shek-yu:

> I have returned to the root
> and the effort is over

On the lower half were the words:

> I leave you
> My love—
> All that I own
> My poems
> Your freedom
>
>   c.

The second note was really just a scrap of paper with some fragments of lines from William Wilfred Campbell's poem, *The Winter Lakes:*

> Never a bud of spring, never a laugh of summer . . .
> But only the silence and white,
> The shores that grow chiller and dumber . . .
> Hushed from outward strife . . .

In the other pocket the police found a bracelet of silver and obsidian placed inside carefully folded blue tissue. They asked everyone in the family about its significance. No one knew.

Cecilia did not understand, nor could I have expected her to, that given what she had just done, her hardest journey had now just begun. She had wanted so much a correction to ease the awful carbuncle of memory she carried with her about Herr M and also about her mother and Karl. She wanted to become more like Anne Frank writing and hiding in *that* attic from those trying to destroy her and her family, all the time believing in the goodness of people. But Cecilia could not come to believe in such goodness. Because she had been raised a female Slaughter, she was too filled with a devastating emptiness and anger.

Although she will not sleep in the forever growing potter's field of the fitful, psychopathic evildoers with their ceaseless night terrors, she will be on a path of unrest unlike any other she had known in the life she just left.

She and Herr M will meet again and again in different ways—different forms of perversions based on sex and power—and torment each other over poetic license and its price. Eventually, if she has the strength to turn her back to him, her path will lead to a place of knowledge, forgiveness, and peace.

Herr M, on the other hand, will wander for all time looking unendingly for the perfect conquest. He will do this initially with great determination and zeal, then with an unbearable exhaustion, yet he will not be able to stop. A Sisyphus, of sorts.

He will continue to tell anyone here who will listen *his* side of the story. His emotions will be most stirred when he speaks of the dog. About how he did nothing wrong with her. How much he cared for her. Cecilia will always take a distant second place in any feelings he has of regret, repeating only, "I *did* apologize."

The police notified Celie first because they found her name and number in Cecilia's wallet on a card as to whom to contact in case of emergency. Upon hearing the news, quite expectedly, she broke apart, and at Cecilia's funeral she collapsed, for she saw that Adele, indeed, had died and recently, for there was just a wooden grave marker—no plaque yet. However, with better medication and new doctors she recovered within the year.

Joshua and Jeremy and their wives, having fled the country after the murder (this being easy to do since neither union had produced any children and adoption out of the question) to escape the reporters, the gossip, and to find some kind of peace of mind on a tour of Japanese temples, actually learned some things about generosity of spirit. For the first time they truly became Celie's brothers, and they finally *saw* her and they helped her.

Here, I cannot but think of Emerson's words: "Every earnest glance we give to the realities around us, with intent to learn, proceeds from a holy impulse, and is really songs of praise." And I praise them for this.

When she got better, they gave her money to open up her own shop—*The Finest Linens to Dream On.* Joyce and Jocelyn frequent it often as do their friends and, of course, all of Celie's former clients.

Eventually, Celie's heart did dance—some.

As one might have easily guessed, Michael was inconsolable and filled with self-recriminations about how impotent he had been in not acting promptly—in doing *nothing*. He grew physically ill, as sometimes the anguished, stunned, and lovesick do. Soon he will die and find mindpeace—never to seek out Cecilia again. The good of heart do eventually come to a state of blessedness.

Everything here is rather balanced, religious, and just. Einstein spoke of *a spiritual force at work in the universe* and although he did not obsess on it, just went on with his work, he was right.

Once again, Cecily revised her play, about the poet and the critic, now adding how the poet kills the critic and then herself. She sends it to every theater company she can think of, but unknown to her, no one wants any part of it. Never will.

She believes it is her finest work. Maybe it is, but I, too, refuse to read it. Clearly her determination to beat out Cecilia in terms of success did not stop with Cecilia's death. Instead it grew larger, into a singular obsession as cold as ice determined not to melt.

She even considers killing herself, thinking, "Maybe then I will become famous—after all, didn't Cecilia become even more so in death?" She thinks and rethinks this possibility as she will when she appears here in an old age and forever waits for fame to arrive.

Deidre wrote a couple of poetry books that were published by a small press—unknown to most. At her insistence, her husband threw a lavish party on the occasion of each publication. At both of the festivities she sat at a large, expensive, intricately carved oak table with long-stemmed yellow roses in a vase next to her—sent to her from herself. Her husband reluctantly hired violinists for quiet background music as she signed the cover page of each book for all her invited friends and relatives. She used a gold trimmed Mont Blanc pen. The hors d'oeuvres served were so delicious everyone commented that there would be no need for dinner.

Clearly Deidre could not find an independent self-path—the one she sought for about a month after the lunch with Cecily. Within a couple of weeks she was already stumbling on it.

After her first book was accepted, a feeling of entitlement and hunger for more attention grew within her like a tumor with an intractable appetite. It has made her spirit bone-thin and continuously famished.

Now, she always dresses in black, never hesitating to tell anyone who will listen, "It's in memory of Cecilia Slaughter." Most just roll their eyes when they hear this, silently thinking to themselves, "Oh, please." After the two published books nothing more will happen for her of a literary nature and she, too, will also begin to wonder if she needs to die so as to become famous.

Sometimes she meets with Cecily at a fancy downtown hotel bar to discuss the merits of artistic suicide and the various possibilities as to how to do it—*which tools* as Anne Sexton had put it. The two do, in fact, role play, maybe even believe, they are Sexton and Plath competing over the preferred method for a self-inflicted death and like them, they drink too much when they discuss the topic. The waiters watch—ignorant of the literary history the two are trying to recreate—finding them ridiculous, but fun for middle-aged women. They look forward to their return and serving them. They are big tippers.

Deidre, in death, will try to join the Plath-Sexton group—Lowell and Berryman will be there. Needless to say, they will ignore her.

Celine, now left with just too much family pain and loss, has added more men (and women) to her life and more flashy designer clothes to her closet, as well as more of the finest jewelry she can get Aaron and the others to buy her. She has the embalmed look—the stretched pallor—of a too-often-face-lifted bag woman, layered in lots of money. She pays and pays to get what she wants, like her father, and as with him, nothing is ever enough—or ever will be.

The most interesting thought Celine ever had was when she was six and wondered if her baby sister had been accidentally dropped into the wrong family—which she was. Celeste was reborn into another family and renamed *Ida* after her new mother's mother. Ida, or *Idy*, as most people call her, goes through her life with a sometimes cacophonous sound in her head that she cannot place, but with which she has learned to live.

I *know* the dead cannot influence what happens to the living, but sometimes I cannot help but reflect on the irony of this and wonder—who would not?—if Grandmother Idyth finally took possession of one small thing— the dead baby Celeste, making sure she was given safe passage to another life and a variation of *her* name. I muse on this, then let it go.

I do not know of the inner workings of everything. I may never. Nor am I sure anyone completely does or should—even Lao Tzu. With this he would agree. Here, it is more about acceptance of what is and what you do thereafter.

As for myself, I have grown tired of the intricacies, intimacies—the interminable detailings—of stories, even my own. I have quit my memory's mind-search for Wyatt. Suddenly, it became easy, like deciding to uncage a rare bird—free its beauty from my stare—and watch it fly away.

I have little need for things to work out differently than they do. Now, I just look at a situation, see it as it is, without wishing it were otherwise. I am finding that peace that the desperate living and the restless dead long for. Some others here are finding it, too. Who they are or will be, I dwell on less.

However, even here, people do surprise you. Who would have guessed that Great Aunt Eva would suddenly turn toward Adele, *see her* as her little girl with the dazzling, golden blond curls, her bright young face and dark eyes all sparkle and reach out to her small and lovely and hopeful child.

Eventually my mother passed from her above-the-ground existence and was lowered into the space next to me. I was pleased by the simplicity of her casket—its lack of adornment, its dull finish. I thought it would be ornate, like the one they placed me in, except more so. When I saw it, I was encouraged. Yet, when I turned toward her, she turned away and this is how she has stayed.

I am surprised that I have so little to say about this—a result of the place of peaceful indifference that I am finally able to more fully embrace.

Soon all above-the-ground life intrusions—all fightings, all frettings, all lovings, all hatings, all collectings of material possessions—no matter how luxurious—all gossip, all wrong-spirited hopes, and all convoluted talk will evaporate.

All that will be left, all that will be salvaged, as testimony to the existence of the Slaughter family will be the fragile—and yes—temporal legacy of a few poems.

While they still exist, I hope you will choose to read them.

As I rest.

ceci slaughter

WIDDERSHINS III

Eventually the scars become glitter
on the skin—small stars. The damage
caused by what or who, a journey
into a hidden solar system—nightmares (spectral horses galloping
through a galaxy of terror). My bed
is placed toward the door under
a crossbeam in the ceiling, crosswise
over the floorboards, in the direction corpses
are carried out—feet first.
The rays of the moon fall across
its sheets—always messed.
Each morning they invite all
spirits to come in and rest.

I would like to sleep now—dream less,

but someone has hung a blackbird's
right wing on the closet hook
and no matter how I try not
to look at it—I look.

c. slaughter

ACKNOWLEDGMENTS
(in order of appearance)

Grateful acknowledgment is made to the generous editors of the publications in which the following poems and chapters, or versions of them, appeared:

POEMS

"The Bells XI" is reprinted from *The Note She Left* by Susan Hahn. Reprinted with permission of author. Published by Northwestern University Press, 2008. This poem was first published in *The Kenyon Review*.

"The Crosses V" is reprinted from *The Note She Left* by Susan Hahn. Reprinted with permission of author. Published by Northwestern University Press, 2008. This poem was first published in *New England Review*.

"Widdershins I" is reprinted from *The Note She Left* by Susan Hahn. Reprinted with permission of author. Published by Northwestern University Press, 2008. This poem was first published in *Boulevard*.

"Flowers" is reprinted from *Harriet Rubin's Mother's Wooden Hand* by Susan Hahn. Reprinted with permission of author. Published by the University of Chicago Press, 1991. This poem was first published in *Poetry*.

"Widdershins II" was originally published as "Widdershins IV" and is reprinted from *The Note She Left* by Susan Hahn. Reprinted with permission of author. Published by Northwestern University Press, 2008. This poem was first published in *Boulevard*.

"Trichotillomania" is reprinted from *Harriet Rubin's Mother's Wooden Hand* by Susan Hahn. Reprinted with permission of author. Published by the University of Chicago Press, 1991. This poem was first published in *Shenandoah*.

"No Sad Songs Sung Here" was originally published as "Pity Song in Solo Voice Without Accompaniment" and is reprinted from *Self/Pity* by Susan Hahn. Reprinted with permission of author. Published by Northwestern University Press, 2005. This poem was first published in *New England Review*.

"The Interior Of The Sun" was originally published as "The Interior Of The Sun II" and is reprinted from *Mother In Summer* by Susan Hahn. Reprinted with permission of author. Published by Northwestern University Press, 2002. This poem was first published in *The North American Review*.

"The Devil's Legs" is reprinted from *Confession* by Susan Hahn. Reprinted with permission of author. Published by the University of Chicago Press, 1997. This poem was first published in *Poetry East*.

"Yom Kippur Night Dance" was first published in *Fifth Wednesday Journal*.

"The Sin-Eater Of The Family" was originally published as "Widdershins VI" and is reprinted from *The Note She Left* by Susan Hahn. Reprinted with permission of author. Published by Northwestern University Press, 2008. This poem was first published in *Boulevard*.

"Confession" is reprinted from *Confession* by Susan Hahn. Reprinted with permission of author. Published by the University of Chicago Press, 1997. This poem was first published in *Boulevard*.

"Nijinsky's Dog" is reprinted from *Confession* by Susan

Hahn. Reprinted with permission of author. Published by the University of Chicago Press, 1997. This poem was first published in *The American Poetry Review*.

"The Lovers" is reprinted from *Confession* by Susan Hahn. Reprinted with permission of author. Published by the University of Chicago Press, 1997. This poem was first published in *Poetry*.

"Knowledge," which appears in the chapter, "The Lovers," is reprinted from *The Note She Left* by Susan Hahn. Reprinted with permission of author. Published by Northwestern University Press, 2008. This poem was first published in *The Kenyon Review*.

"Mania" is reprinted from *Incontinence* by Susan Hahn. Reprinted with permission of author. Published by the University of Chicago Press, 1993. This poem was first published in *Prairie Schooner*.

"Small Green" is reprinted from *Harriet Rubin's Mother's Wooden Hand* by Susan Hahn. Reprinted with permission of author. Published by the University of Chicago Press, 1991. This poem was first published in *Poetry*.

"Mens Rea" is reprinted from *Confession* by Susan Hahn. Reprinted with permission of author. Published by the University of Chicago Press, 1997. This poem was first published in *American Voice*.

"Paranoia" is reprinted from *Harriet Rubin's Mother's Wooden Hand* by Susan Hahn. Reprinted with permission of author. Published by the University of Chicago Press, 1991.

"The Crosses" was originally published as "The Crosses II" and is reprinted from *The Note She Left* by Susan Hahn. Reprinted with permission of author. Published by Northwestern University Press, 2008. This poem was first published in *New England Review*.

"The Soul's Aerial View Of The Burial" is reprinted from *Incontinence* by Susan Hahn. Reprinted with permission of author. Published by the University of Chicago Press, 1993.

"Clean" is reprinted from *The Note She Left* by Susan Hahn. Reprinted with permission of author. Published by Northwestern University Press, 2008. This poem was first published in the *Atlantic Monthly*.

"Widdershins III" was originally published as "Widdershins XII" and is reprinted from *The Note She Left* by Susan Hahn. Reprinted with permission of author. Published by Northwestern University Press, 2008. This poem was first published in *Boulevard*.

CHAPTERS

"Trichotillomania," *Michigan Quarterly Review*, Vol. XLV, Number 3, Summer 2006.

"No Sad Songs Sung Here," *Michigan Quarterly Review*, Vol. XLVII, Number 1, Winter 2008.

"The Devil's Legs," *Boulevard*, Vol. 26, Numbers 1 & 2, Fall 2010.

"Yom Kippur Night Dance," *The Kenyon Review*, Vol. XXVII, Number 3, Summer 2005.

"Confession," *Boulevard*, Vol. 23, Numbers 2 & 3, Spring 2008.

"The Lovers," *The Kenyon Review*, Vol. XXX, Number 1, Winter 2008.

"If I Set up the Chairs," *Fifth Wednesday Journal*, Issue 7, Fall 2010.

During a fellowship from the John Simon Guggenheim Memorial Foundation, I had the time to write my first prose, which turned out to be a version of the chapter "Yom Kippur Night Dance," setting in motion this book's journey. I am unendingly grateful to the Foundation for the myriad of gifts that productive year of writing brought me.

ALSO BY SUSAN HAHN

POETRY

Harriet Rubin's Mother's Wooden Hand

Incontinence

Melancholia, et cetera

Confession

Holiday

Mother in Summer

Self/Pity

The Scarlet Ibis

The Note She Left

PLAYS

Golf

The Scarlet Ibis